MW01603055

Acclaim for
Asa and the Holstein Queen

"What a fun read! History feels much closer when we learn it through our family and community. In this entertaining and educational story, Lynne Gough welcomes us into her family, giving her ancestors a chance to walk and talk again. This should be a great introduction to genealogy that will inspire budding researchers!"

Candice Buchanan, M.A., C.G., Greene Connections Archivist, PA

"Through this winsomely illustrated story, I took a journey I won't soon forget. I listened to the fireside stories of war and Indian raids, I watched the harshly beautiful western landscape change from the seat of a California bound covered wagon, and I learned much about this rich golden state that I call home. I fell in love with the Holstein Queen, Tilly Alcartra, and gained a deep respect for the author's exceptional great-grandfather, Asa W. Morris, who recognized and lovingly developed his cow's amazing potential. Supported by sound genealogical and historical research, the tales of the Morris family faithfully bring our shared American history to life. This creative work is a true inspiration for family historians, both young and old."

Lisa Henderson, Vice President, Davis Genealogy Club, Yolo County, CA

"Because I was a member of the 4-H Club many years ago and showed Holstein calves at local fairs, this story had wonderful resonance for me! It also connected me with a company of gold rush pioneers who courageously travelled across the country, mined for gold, then had the flexibility to abandon their quest in order to create their own golden history through farming in California. The story is embellished by photos and lovely illustrations. It is certain to be enjoyed by tweens, teens, and adults."

Mary Davies BScN, MScN., Ontario, Canada

"A family epic as wide and wonderful as our country. Beautifully told and illustrated, it will enthrall readers of all ages. I love this book as much as I loved *Little House on the Prairie* when I was growing up."

Mary Beth Pastorius, Architectural Historian, Greene County, PA

"In this significant historical novel, Lynne Gough unfolds the story of her family in the context of the national experience. She accomplishes this expertly, writing with an assurance and straightforwardness that will appeal to adolescent readers, as well as many others. The centerpiece is her great-grandfather, Asa W. Morris, born and raised in Southwestern PA, who finds his fortune on the other side of the country in Yolo County, CA. By looking at generations before and after Asa, Gough is able to encompass nearly two centuries of American history reflected in the experiences of real people. The subtitle of the book 'An American Story' is most appropriate to the family's quest.

At its heart, this is the tale of a farm family, its connection to the land, its dedication to a kind of hard work that carries certain dangers and more than hints of mortality, and its commitment to livestock. It is no coincidence that the co-star is Tilly Alcartra, a champion Holstein dairy cow."
                                                David Cressey, President
                         Cornerstone Genealogical Society, Waynesburg, PA

"Lynne Gough has written a remarkable work of historical fiction about her American pioneer family, based on original sources. In this fascinating tale of determined optimism, the Morris pioneers prevailed over daunting set-backs through the genius of seizing opportunity. This debut novel transports us to a time when family bonds transcended personal limitations to deliver a champion: Tilly Alcartra, the Holstein Queen."
            Kimberly Richter, B.A., Educator and Curriculum Development
                          Winship/Robbins School District, Robbins, CA

"I found *Asa and the Holstein Queen* quite charming as it led me through some of the momentous events in American history, personalized through eyes of the author's family. One of its greatest strengths is that it illustrates that special grit, inventiveness, and resiliency that has allowed Americans to survive and eventually thrive. It is inspiring for readers of all levels. And, as a fellow artist, I must say that the illustrations are just stunning!"
            Marian O'Neal, Specialist in Educational Publishing, Monterey, CA

Asa and the Holstein Queen

YOLO
COUNTY
CALIFORNIA

Almonds are grown in a very few sections of the United States. In Yolo County almonds lead all other orchard crops, a testimonial to soil and climatic supremacy. The industry pays well.

YOLO
COUNTY
CALIFORNIA

A Yolo County world's record Holstein dairy herd. In the foreground is Tilly Alcartra holder of the world's milk production record, 30,452.6 pounds in one year. Dairying is a big industry here.

Tilly Alcartra, the Holstein Queen
Pictured on a 1914 pamphlet for Yolo County

Asa
and the
Holstein Queen

An American Story

Written and Illustrated by

Lynne Gough

Asa and the Holstein Queen
Copyright © 2016 by Lynne Gough
All rights reserved
This book or any portion thereof may not be reproduced or used in
any manner whatsoever without the express written permission of
the publisher except for the use of brief quotations in a book review.
Scanning, uploading, and distribution of this book via Internet or
via any other means without the permission of the publisher
is illegal and punishable by law.

Written, illustrated, and designed by: Lynne Gough
Edited by: Janet Marchant

This is a work of historical fiction. Other than actual persons and events
portrayed according to the author's interpretation and understanding,
all characters and events appearing in this work are fictitious.

Printed in the United States of America
Gorham Printing, Centralia, Washington
First printing 2016
10 9 8 7 6 5 4 3 2 1
Library of Congress Control Number 2015921265
ISBN 978-0-9969939-0-6

Published by:

Wit & Wisdom
Publishing

Books may be purchased by contacting the publisher at:
www.asaandtheholsteinqueen.com
Volume discounts available

In memory of
Margaret Morris Duncan
"Auntie Marg"
1922-2012

CONTENTS

PART FOUR
Tilly Alcartra

ILLUSTRATIONS BY THE AUTHOR

PART ONE

My Great-Grandfather

Tales from My Ancestors

Everybody's life is a story.

When I was in grade school and the teacher said, "Class, please take out your history books and turn to page 43," there was a loud groan from my classmates. History always meant an hour of memorizing names, dates, and events printed in an outdated, dog-eared text book. When the teacher turned her back to write on the blackboard, my classmates rolled their eyes at each other and whispered, "History is so BORING!"

I never told anybody—because I would have been laughed out of school—but I actually LIKED history; in fact, it was my favorite subject next to recess. One day I realized that the word *history* meant "his story" and it wasn't just about long ago events—it was personal.

When I understood that my own *ancestors* had actually lived during the times I read about in my history book I was fascinated. Ancestors are all our family members who have lived before us, like our grandparents and their grandparents and so on.

If you ask your older family members to tell you their stories about the old days, you can pretend you walk in their shoes, and you can see what they have seen. You'll be surprised how different the world looks through someone else's eyes. And, as simple as that, you are learning real history!

This story is about my ancestors who came to California in the *nineteenth century*; that means the 1800s, and it was a long time ago. The Morris family members were all real people, and Tilly Alcartra was a real Holstein cow. I have heard this tale since I was a little girl, and now I pass it on to you.

A Special Partnership

Some of our best friends have four legs.

More than a hundred years ago in Yolo County, California, near the town of Woodland, lived a hardworking dairy farmer named Asa Warren Morris. Asa was my great-grandfather and he was a proud, successful man. His loving wife Mary had given him four fine sons named Frank, Charley, Harry, and Asa James, and a beautiful daughter named Zella May.

Asa owned over a thousand acres of prime Yolo farmland where he and his four sons successfully raised champion Holstein cattle. And the queen of his herd was a very special cow named Tilly Alcartra.

Asa Morris was a hard-boiled, self-made man: tough, shrewd, and feisty. A goal-oriented person, he took calculated risks and made plenty of mistakes—but he never gave up. Asa understood that success could only be earned by his own efforts, and he was grateful to live in America, a nation that offered him the freedom to choose his own destiny.

Appearances can be deceiving, and inside this tough little dairyman lived a heart of gold. That heart was full of *integrity*—which means honesty and strong moral principles.

Asa believed in the old saying, "A man's word is his bond." That meant if he made a promise, he kept it.

In the times that Asa lived, an honorable *character* was a person's most valuable asset. Character is who we really are—our innermost thoughts, feelings, and the actions we take. It is also the ability to stand up for our beliefs and do the right thing even when it isn't popular.

Many people of strong moral character like Asa also have *idiosyncrasies*—meaning they have their own peculiar quirks. Asa had plenty of them! On the one hand, he was generous, reliable, and fair; but on the other hand, he was outspoken, opinionated, and *domineering* (a great word for bossy). Such are the contradictions of being human.

At the age of twenty-two, he left his home in Pennsylvania and traveled 3,000 miles west to Yolo County, California, to seek his fortune. Over many years he worked his way up from laborer to landowner, from dairyman to champion cattle breeder. Asa built his career from scratch, and he reaped the rewards of his own efforts.

Asa was already fifty-two years old—with an outstanding reputation in the cattle business—when a stroke of luck changed his life. He purchased a Holstein yearling named Tilly Alcartra, instantly sensing she was something special. He knew when he bought her it was his lucky day. It was Tilly's lucky day, too, because Asa was just the man to develop her full potential. Under his loving care, Tilly exceeded all expectations and became famous as a world champion milk producer.

For more than a decade, Asa and Tilly were a well-known and inseparable team in the American dairy industry. There was a special partnership between the old dairyman and his remarkable cow, which carried them to the peak of fame and fortune—far beyond Yolo County.

CALIFORNIA COW HOLDS WORLD'S RECORD

TILLY ALCARTRA, who became the world's champion milk producer over all breeds November 13, 1914. A year's semi-official test was completed with a production of 30,452.6 pounds of milk. Tilly Alcartra is the property of A. W. Morris & Sons of California.

Tilly Alcartra, world champion milk producer

Yolo County, California

A good and broad land,
a land flowing with milk and honey.

Exodus 3:8

 Yolo County is the very heart of Northern California's Central Valley. Its curious name came from the Patwin Indian word *yoloy* which means "a place thick with bulrushes." Bulrushes are cattails, but in Yolo County they are called *tules* (too-lees) and they grow in the marshy wetlands near rivers and streams.

 Woodland was named for her splendid native oak trees, and since her founding in 1871, her citizens planted all kinds of different trees that grew tall and broad. Their vast branches still arch gracefully over her historic streets forming dense canopies of shade—a welcome relief on a hot summer day.

 In Asa's time, Woodland was the wealthiest small town in America and it was an important center for *agriculture*, which is the science of growing food. Dairy farming was big business, and herds of dairy cows that grazed on Yolo pastures kept the valley supplied with delicious milk and butter. Woodland's farmers owned vast acres of land where they grew all kinds of crops and raised all kinds of animals to feed the people of Northern California. They worked very hard and made lots of money. To show off their success they built grand, beautiful homes in every imaginable style.

Yolo County land is mostly flat, but on a clear day—if you stand in the middle of a country field and look around—you can see mountains in three directions. To the west is a low range of mountains that hide behind a distant haze on a sunny afternoon and look dusty blue. They are called the "Blue Ridge." To the east are the mighty Sierra Nevada Mountains crowned in winter by jagged snowcapped peaks and easily seen from the valley floor. To the north is the world's smallest mountain range: rugged little mounds called the Sutter Buttes. The Maidu Indians called them "Esto Yamani" or middle mountains, since they sit between the two larger ranges. To the south the Central Valley stretches for over a hundred miles, and the great Sacramento River wends her way along the eastern Yolo border—gaining depth and power en route to the delta of San Francisco Bay.

In springtime, late winter rains paint the Yolo landscape a beautiful bright green, and amidst the fields in wayward patches, orange California poppies and vivid yellow mustard bloom. When the land is plowed and the sun warms the fertile soil, it is planted with the promise of abundant crops.

When summer comes, the green grasses turn golden brown. The sun shines almost every day from May to October and it hardly ever rains. It can be very hot and the fields get so dry they must be irrigated. Row after row of sunflowers, tomatoes, corn, and alfalfa cover the Yolo landscape like a patchwork quilt of green, red, and gold.

Autumn brings dry north winds, and a faint smell of wood smoke lingers in the chilly air. It is harvest time for summer's crops and the fields are alive with activity. When harvest is finished, certain fields are ploughed under and lie

Yolo County, California

LAND OF AGRICULTURE

Peaches

Sunflowers

Wheat

YOLO
COUNTY
→
→Woodland

Sugar
Beets

Tomatoes

CENTRAL
VALLEY

Nuts

Grapes

Rice

Honey

Corn

fallow, which means they take a rest; but other fields are waiting to be planted with crops that thrive in winter— because it hardly ever snows.

Winter's cold, rainy days make muddy lakes in the fallow fields. Sometimes, when the winds are still, dense Tule fog forms near the river and hovers low over the fields in a thick misty blanket. For weeks, the sun peeks through the fog and teases with a secret smile. Then, out she comes full-faced and blazing, the land sheds her winter coat, the almond trees blossom, and the cycle of seasons begins anew.

Majestic old oak trees with gnarled trunks stand like sentries amidst the fields where they watch over the crops, and their heavy twisted limbs bow down with the weight of age.

Most farms have modern houses that were built in the last half century, but here and there the scenery is dotted with beautiful nineteenth century homes and the skeletons of old

Yolo oaks watch over fields of crops.

wooden barns—relics of an earlier time. The once thriving dairy industry is gone now, but Yolo County is still fine, productive land with a proud history.

Asa Morris began his career as a Yolo County dairyman and cattle breeder in the last decade of the nineteenth century. By 1920, he and Tilly had reached the peak of fame. Let's travel back in time—to the 1850s—to meet Asa as a boy, in a place very distant from Yolo County.

PART TWO

A Pioneer, a Soldier, and a Boy Named Asa

Greene County, Pennsylvania

Wherever you are born and raised
is part of who you are.
Those who love and inspire you
lay the foundation for who you will become.

The Morrises are an old American family and a very long thread in the tapestry of the United States. They have always been an independent, hardworking lot who practice the saying "God helps those who help themselves." They are quirky, hardheaded, and stubborn, but like the nation they helped build, they have endured. Like many early settlers, they sought opportunity to improve their lives, and they traveled long distances to find it. They took big risks and sometimes they failed, but their finest qualities were their determination and their common sense.

My great-grandfather Asa's life began almost three thousand miles from California in the southwestern corner of the state of Pennsylvania. His family lived in Greene County, just west of the Appalachian Mountains. Two hundred and fifty years ago, Greene County was the western edge of the American Colonies, a forbidding wilderness full of wild animals and hostile Indian tribes. Today, it is lovely wooded

Greene County, Pennsylvania

country with rolling hills and valleys, tamed by generations of settlers. The people of Greene County, like the land on which they live, have a long, eventful history. The Morris family lived there for generations.

Asa Warren Morris was born on May 8, 1857, and he opened his eyes for the very first time in the same house where his father first saw the light of day. His family lived in the countryside a few miles west of Waynesburg. This historic American town was founded in 1796, and Asa's ancestors were some of its original landowners.

The Morris family were *yeomen,* an Old English word for landowning farmers who are neither rich nor poor. Their farm sat amidst the rolling hills near the banks of Tenmile Creek, so named because the mouth of the creek was exactly ten miles from Fort Redstone, built by the early settlers to protect themselves from the Indians. Long before state borders were settled, these pioneer lands were called the "Tenmile Country."

Asa was the oldest son of John and Sarah Morris and his birth was cause for celebration. In those days, the first son was a guarantee that the family name would live on. Baby Asa had wisps of reddish hair and the promise of light blue eyes, inherited from his father's side of the family. He was named in honor of his uncle who was called Asa Warren Morris, too. When a younger person is named after an older person he is called a *namesake.* Uncle Asa Morris was 30 years older than his namesake nephew, and he would have a big influence on his life.

Generation after generation of Morris children were namesakes. They were called Sarah, Martha, or Phoebe; Asa, John, or James. Asa's large, extended family was full of them and it was very confusing. So, when all the Sarahs and Marthas and Phoebes got married, they used their *maiden name*—their surname before marriage—as a middle name. Asa's mother became Sarah CHURCH Morris and his grandmother became Martha ROSEBERRY Morris.

Asa was sandwiched in between an older sister, Martha Ann, and a younger sister, Arta Mace, who he nicknamed Sis and Artie. Sis was spirited and bossy, so Asa could always count on her for a good argument. Artie was quiet and gentle with soft brown eyes and a smile that could warm the sternest heart.

Asa's father John was a tall man for his times and stood five feet eleven inches in height. He was slim and long-legged with black wavy hair, a fair complexion, and clear light blue eyes. John and his four brothers all had broad, high foreheads that arched over a low brow bone, and long well-formed noses which gave them a distinguished appearance. Most of his life John wore a moustache and beard that changed in size and shape depending on the fashion of the day.

Like many men of his generation, John learned his skills at his father's knee. His opinions were formed by the time and place he lived and by the company he kept. He was plain spoken and honest, two traits that earned him the respect of his friends and the resentment of his enemies. Behind his calm demeanor lived a lively sense of humor that made his eyes dance and his moustache twitch when something tickled his funny bone. Those same eyes could shoot fiery blue sparks when he was angry. John worked sun-up to sun-down every day and he enjoyed the simple pleasures his life allowed.

Asa's mother Sarah was a lovely woman with a delicate bone structure and a creamy complexion. She had soft brown eyes and glossy chestnut brown hair which she smoothly pulled back and pinned at the nape of her neck.

Her fine soprano voice brightened somber church services and sang soothing lullabies to her children. Sarah

Asa's parents John and Sarah Church Morris

taught Asa to sing and he belted out his songs with enormous gusto, a trait that would follow him throughout his life. Sarah was a caring mother, a good listener, and a wise counselor. Her wisdom didn't come from book learning; it came from experience and common sense.

John Morris raised *livestock*, which is the proper word for domestic farm animals like horses, cows, pigs, and sheep. He bred Shorthorn cattle, a dual-purpose breed that was used for both meat and milk. He had a pen full of hogs that made tasty ham and bacon; as a sideline, he bred racing horses.

John had trained as a carriage-maker, but with his talented hands he also worked as a stone mason, a carpenter, and a skilled blacksmith. He forged horseshoes, wagon wheels, and hand tools from hot iron bars—using a hammer and tongs over an open fire. Blacksmiths were in great demand since one horse or another in the neighborhood always needed new shoes.

Farming families like the Morrises lived close to the land. They made their living with their hands and by their wits, and their survival depended on Mother Nature's bounty.

Their old farmhouse was a plain, square structure with a simple peaked roof, built by hand from sturdy whitewashed brick and local timber. Thick walls and stout oak doors had withstood harsh Pennsylvania winters for three generations. Within those old walls lived many family memories, stored for safe-keeping from the passage of time. But memories notwithstanding, John had a never-ending job keeping the roof from leaking, the chimneys from collapsing, and the frigid winter winds from seeping through the wavy glass window panes.

Tenmile Creek was part of Asa's childhood adventures. It flowed through a gulley below the farm, meandering and gurgling over its rocky bed in the heat of summer and freezing solid in winter. Beyond the creek on the rolling hills, were woodlands and grassy meadows to play in on bright, sunny days. When snow blanketed the countryside, there was a warm hearth waiting at home.

*   *   *

Greene County was chock-full of old pioneer families who had settled the land before America even became a nation. They had intermarried for so many generations that most of the county was related one way or another. Everybody knew everybody and who all their folks were. It was like a big extended family, and young Asa had relatives all over the place. His grandparents, aunts, uncles, and cousins lived nearby, and they visited one another so often that Asa was never lonely.

He was an energetic little fellow and as soon as he learned to talk, he had a lot to say. Whether anybody cared to listen was another matter. He drove his mother crazy with his endless chatter, and sometimes Sarah put her fingers in her ears and exclaimed, "For heaven's sake, Asa! Would you HUSH?" As soon as he was old enough, his father put him to work—mostly to keep him quiet.

Most Greene County families had many children; this came in handy because there was always plenty of back-breaking work on the family farm. If you wanted to eat, you had to work; even youngsters were expected to do chores.

One of Sis and Artie's chores was to tend the chickens. They fed them grain, gathered the hens' eggs every morning and shooed them in and out of the chicken coop flapping their little cotton aprons and chanting, "HERE, CHICK, CHICK, CHICK!" The worst part of the chore was cleaning the smelly coop, so Asa made himself scarce when that job came due.

Asa was not fond of chickens. All that clucking, crowing, and wing flapping was really annoying. Besides, laying hens could give you a really nasty peck when you reached under them for their eggs, and roosters had been known to fight to the death over a feather-brained hen.

Silly creatures! Sometimes they stood on one leg and cocked their heads over sideways so that one of their glassy little eyes could get a good look at you. Then, they would SQUAAAWWWK with annoyance that you had the nerve to look back at them. But none of them was a match for Sis. Hands on hips, she looked a bad-tempered bird straight in one eye and shouted, "SCRAM!!! You midget!" That was usually enough to make the offender skedaddle. Chickens are rather stupid birds. Asa's Grandpa Ephraim liked to quote the old saying, "When God handed out brains to the animal kingdom, the chicken was behind the door!"

The family had a black and tan hound dog named Sam who trekked along with Asa's father on hunting trips. Sam bayed loudly whenever anybody approached the farm. Baying is unique to hounds; it's a throaty, musical howl that sounds like AAAHHHOOOOO! Sam had long, floppy ears and deep, soulful eyes. Asa loved to tickle the side of Sam's muzzle which made him draw up his big droopy lips and look like he was smiling. Sam was devoted to Asa and followed him wherever he went. As a pup, Sam had tangled with a ferocious red rooster whose claws had left deep scars on the side of his head. He was a loyal and brave dog with one big exception: no amount of coaxing could make him go near the chickens.

Besides his Shorthorn cattle, Asa's father kept a few dairy cows and Asa learned to milk them before he learned to write. Milking three cows before breakfast and supper were his special chores. He was very fond of his cows because they had PERSONALITY—not like those dumb chickens! Even though he struggled to get out of bed on bitterly cold winter mornings to tramp through the snow to the barn, he knew his cows depended on him. Even at a young age, Asa felt a solemn responsibility to keep the cows under his care safe and healthy.

Dairy cows are generally calm animals but they can get impatient while they are waiting to be milked. They stomp around in their stalls and kick up a fuss, and once one starts, the others carry on, too. Cows act this way, because the pressure of milk building up in their udders causes discomfort. An *udder* is a big milk sack which hangs below the cow's belly; it has four long nipples called *teats* which function like faucets to let out the milk. When you milk a cow you sit on a low stool at the cow's side and alternately work two of the teats at a time, using a rhythmic squeezing and pulling motion which releases the milk into your bucket. You get cramps in your hands and calluses on your fingers. Sometimes, just to annoy you, an ornery cow will give you a good hard kick in the shins. Milking is hard work, but to a dairyman, it's as natural as breathing.

Some cows are not very bright and they don't smell so nice first thing in the morning. But, the more you get to know them, the more they grow on you. Their soulful mooooooing gets to be a pleasant part of the background noise of your day. They roll their big, soft brown eyes, swat flies expertly with their tails, and give you a big wet lick up the side of your face with their long, rough tongues. In these simple ways, they work their magic on you. Farmers can't afford to get too attached to animals that are their living, but for a child it's almost impossible, and some cows can be real charmers.

Asa's favorite cow was a fawn colored Jersey named Marigold whose doe-like brown eyes and friendly manner won his heart. She was always glad to see him, and she was

a good listener. Asa and Marigold often carried on one-sided conversations while he milked her, and sometimes he even trusted her with his secrets, because he knew she would never tell—at least not to another human.

Most mornings while Asa was milking, Sam the hound would station himself just beyond the cow's kicking range and whine. This was his signal for Asa to turn one of the cow's teats and give him a squirt. Sam was so practiced at catching the warm stream of milk that he seldom missed, but the barn cats watched silently from a distance just in case there were any leftover drips.

Early one autumn morning while Asa was milking Marigold, she could tell he was upset, so she turned her head to look at him and blew a gentle snort of acknowledgment. Asa took this gesture as a chance to unburden his troubles, so he leaned his head against her warm flank and confided, "I made a big mistake, Goldie. I took Pa's best saw without asking when I was cuttin' up branches for my fort in the woods. When the dinner bell rang, I laid the saw up against a tree and forgot about it. It sat there for three days in the rain before I remembered, and by that time the teeth were rusty and the handle was warped.

"Pa was MAD! He frowned and said to me, 'Son, NEVER take my tools without my permission. That saw is ruined because of your forgetfulness and it will take me hours to clean off the rust, sharpen it, and make a new handle. I can see that you're sorry and I know that you meant no harm, so I won't paddle you this time. Instead, you will give me all your pocket money, and for the next week you will shovel manure for one extra hour every day after school.' "

Asa leaned in and whispered in Marigold's big ear, "Goldie, I know you girls can't help making lots of manure and I don't really blame you, but I sure hate shoveling it!"

Marigold gave an understanding snort, nodded her head up and down, and gave Asa a big sloppy kiss. Cows can be very forgiving.

Many years later, when Asa was a grown man with his own cattle herd and his own naughty little boys, he never forgot Marigold and he still talked to his cows.

The Old Storyteller

Grandpas have many talents
and one of them is telling stories.

In the old days FAMILY was the most important part of your life. Asa's grandparents, Ephraim and Martha Roseberry Morris, had lived in Greene County their entire lives and they knew all sorts of local history. After Sunday supper the children always asked Grandpa Ephraim to tell them a story.

Grandpa Ephraim was a wiry man, withered by hard work and stooped by old age. His skin was leathery and some of his teeth were missing, but he still had lively blue eyes, a long white beard, and a full head of wavy white hair. Inside that old head lived a stash of terrific stories and he loved to tell his grandchildren hair-raising tales about the old Greene County Indian days.

Grandma Martha was short, stout, and as tough as an old shoe. She had borne ten children, buried one, and helped to deliver at least a dozen more babies in the neighborhood. Martha had a large round head with a double chin and green eyes that could fire silent warning shots whenever anybody got out of line. She was a practical, no nonsense woman who wore the same old cotton apron every day except Sundays.

For church she wore her best green woolen dress and arranged her graying hair in two fat, sausage-shaped rolls on either side of her pink, wrinkled face. Those rolls bounced up and down when she talked, and made her grandchildren giggle. Martha knew absolutely every old family in Greene County, and she could tell you exactly where each one had come from and when. Ephraim loved his dear old wife and called her "Mother."

*   *   *

One Sunday evening after a fine roast beef supper, Ephraim pushed back from the table, patted his stomach and said, "You've raised some prime beef, Johnny. And Sarah, my dear, that was as fine a meal as any man could ever want. Your horseradish sauce was superb—hot enough to melt the buttons on my waistcoat! Mother, your apple pie was delicious as always—just enough spice. What do we say, children?" A loud chorus erupted, "THANK YOU!"

"Now for some fun," said Ephraim as he stood up, hitched his britches, and made a beeline over to the fireplace. He sat down in his favorite spindle-back rocker while Sam turned in circles before plopping down at his feet on the hearth rug. Ephraim watched Sam with a chuckle and asked, "Do you youngsters think that if I turned around as many times as old Sam before I sat down, I could tell a better story?" Little heads nodded, so Ephraim rose, turned around several times and grinned as he plunked himself down again. He reached for his pipe, filled it with moist tobacco from a metal canister, then lit it and began to puff. Once the pipe was smoldering and wisps of fragrant smoke circled his head, he began:

"My granddad, Richard Morris, was born in 1748, on

the shores of the Chesapeake Bay in the old Maryland Colony. He and his brothers worked on vast plantations, planting and *priming* tobacco. Priming means removing the leaves from the stock of the plant. It was very hard work—they were poorly paid and it was hard to make enough money to get ahead. They had little to show for their labors except stained fingers from the tar in the tobacco leaves. The Chesapeake climate was miserable, and the crowded living conditions were even worse. Granddad was one of twelve children, and when his parents died, he saw little reason to stay in Maryland. More than anything, he wanted a better life and he wanted to own his own land.

"In the early 1770s new lands were opening up for settlement west of the Appalachian Mountains. The cost per acre was so cheap that settlers jumped at the chance to claim 300-acre plots for their families. Some of Granddad's neighbors decided to leave Maryland to settle these new lands which were part of our Tenmile Country. A few of the men made a scouting trip just to see what the terrain was like, and being satisfied that they could build a new life there, they returned to the Chesapeake Bay for their wives and children.

"Together with their families, they faced a two hundred fifty mile trek through vast forests and across the steep Appalachian Mountains. The settlers tied all their worldly goods to pack saddles on their horses. Some people had to walk and younger folks often rode two to a horse. Granddad decided to join these pioneers, leaving behind his home and the tobacco fields forever. He was the only one in his family to venture westward—he had a streak of *wanderlust* which runs in our family."

"What's wanderlust, Grandpa?" young Asa asked with a puzzled look. Ephraim replied, "Well, Asa, it's the need inside a man to see what's over the next hill, a curiosity to go

places and experience new adventures. Your Uncle Asa inherited Granddad's wanderlust, and *he* travelled three thousand miles, all the way to California! But that's another story.

"When the travelers arrived in the Tenmile Country, they found a densely forested wilderness inhabited by wary Indians. Granddad claimed a plot of land by chopping the boundary marks on trees with a *tomahawk* which is an Indian version of a hatchet. The settlers called this *tomahawk rights,* but for the native Indian tribes, it was a threat.

"Granddad cleared a patch of land and built a log cabin near Tenmile Creek. He married his neighbor Mary Seals and eventually they had seven children. Their first child, my father James, was born in 1773. Sadly, I don't remember him, since I was just a baby when he fell off the roof of a house he was building in Waynesburg, and was killed.

"The Indians didn't take kindly to the settlers building cabins on their ancestral hunting grounds, and they grew even angrier when some of them were needlessly killed by the newcomers. So, the Indians watched in secret and plotted their revenge. Since they knew the land, its trails, and hiding places better than the settlers, the Indians became a constant threat. They could silently sneak up in their soft deer-skin moccasins and attack from behind before anyone knew they were there.

"One day a band of Indians came upon three of Granddad's neighbors who were making maple syrup outside their cabin. The Indians ambushed, tomahawked, and scalped them—killing all three of them on the spot. Scalping their enemies was the Indians' bloody revenge and it was a very nasty business! They hung the scalps on their belts in triumph and also as a warning.

"Sometimes they forced their way into the cabins and stole everything they could carry. Then they slaughtered entire families, and even little children like you weren't spared. So Granddad and his neighbors had to build forts where they could go in times of trouble; they became Indian fighters to save their homes and loved ones. They bought rifles that cost more money than they had paid for their land—just to defend themselves.

"I'll bet you children didn't know that your great-grandma Jane was one of the only members of her family who survived an Indian massacre when she was just a youngster! Her father was away on a hunting trip when the Indians burst into his cabin and attacked his family. He arrived home to find most of his family killed. Jane was tomahawked, scalped, and left for dead. She hid under some covers until the attackers cleared out, was rescued and nursed back to health. Without her bravery and endurance, you wouldn't be here today."

Asa and his sisters looked at each other, their eyes wide with astonishment. Ephraim saw their expressions and paused for a moment to tap his pipe ashes into the fire. He didn't believe in sugar-coating history for children and just told it the way he knew it. Asa ran his small hand over his head just to make sure his scalp was intact, and with a shudder he asked, "Did Jane's father do things to the Indians for revenge, Grandpa?" Ephraim looked up from the fire and nodded, "Believe me Asa, there was plenty of bloodshed on both sides. Some say that Jane's father never gave up looking for those Indians who slaughtered his loved ones, and legend has it that he tracked them all the way to Ohio.

"Along about 1775, came the Revolution. Remember when I told you children about old King George III of England who ruled the American Colonies?" Sis piped up, "You said he was a real stinker of a king!" Ephraim grinned, "That's right and he was greedy to boot. He taxed the colonists unfairly and when they'd had more than enough of him, they rebelled by dumping more than forty tons of the King's tea into the Boston harbor. That made old George REALLY mad and he sent his huge army of Redcoats from England to put down the rebels.

"On July fourth, 1776, our Declaration of Independence was signed in Philadelphia and the War of Revolution broke out across the Thirteen Colonies. Our Tenmile Country was the western frontier of the colonies and those were treacherous times for the settlers, so my granddad Richard joined the Frontier Rangers. The Rangers were our only defense forces who routed out the hostile Indians. You see, King George's sneaky Redcoats were paying the Indians to attack the settlers.

"Granddad went out with the Rangers on an expedition to the falls of the Ohio River in Kentucky. He was a crack shot and he killed more than one Indian. In the following years, he also volunteered as a soldier in the Pennsylvania militia. Many backwoodsmen were skilled sharpshooters, and when they joined the American Continental Army, they shot and killed several important British army officers. That helped turn the tide of the war for the colonists. They were all brave, tough men who did their part to settle this land and win our independence from England. Every Fourth of July was special for them because it marked the day that the United States of America was born.

"About twenty years later, new territories were opening up for settlement in Ohio. Granddad's old wanderlust kicked up again, so he sold his land and moved with some of our family to Pickaway County—that's in central Ohio—and that is where he died. Someone in each generation moved even further west. So you see children, our family have crossed this great land from coast to coast, all the way from Maryland to California. Always be proud of America and remember that your ancestors helped to make her a nation."

"Oh please, Grandpa, tell us another Indian story," Asa

begged. In the background Sarah silently shook her head. Ephraim glanced at his pocket watch and said, "I think you youngsters have had enough storytelling for one evening. I promise that next Sunday, I'll tell you the story of your Uncle Asa, who went to California on a wagon train before any of you were born. Now it's time for bed so Grandma will tuck you in and hear your prayers."

The following Sunday, Grandpa Ephraim kept his promise, and told the children about their Uncle Asa, the California pioneer. The story was retold many times over the years, and became a proud chapter in the Morris family history.

Uncle Asa Morris, the Pioneer

Gold rush pioneers opened the flood gates
for American westward migration.

In January, 1848, almost ten years before young Asa was born, gold was discovered in the American River in the foothills of California's Sierra Nevada Mountains, and newspapers all across America shouted,

"GOLD, GOLD, GOLD
California Strikes it Rich!"

Word spread like wildfire around the world and thousands of men and women dropped what they were doing and rushed to California to find riches for themselves. In 1849, so many hopeful people came for the gold rush that history calls them the "forty-niners."

When the news about the California gold strike reached Greene County, Pennsylvania, John's older brother, Uncle Asa Morris, caught the gold fever. He was thrilled by the notion that he could travel to California and make himself a very rich man, but his parents were none too pleased that their 24-year-old son was determined to go west. There were plenty of heated protests with his mother leading the pack.

After several attempts to talk some sense into his son, Grandpa Ephraim remained calm as he confronted him one last time. "Well, Asa, you're a grown man," he said, "and you must make your own way in this world, but I still think your scheme is foolhardy. Many good men with great ambitions have perished on lesser journeys. Whatever you decide, rely on your common sense and trust in your Maker."

Grandma Martha, on the other hand, let loose the full fury of her feelings. "Asa, have you lost your mind? Do you know the risks you would be taking? You might starve or freeze to death. Indians might capture you and scalp you. Looters might take everything you have and shoot you. It's happened, you know! We might never see you again and it would break my heart to lose you . . ."

Martha went on and on but made no headway with her son. The Morris family have a stubborn streak that surfaces in almost every generation, and Uncle Asa had it. He had made up his mind: he would join the thousands of adventurers rushing to California to try their luck.

In the winter of 1849, Uncle Asa helped to organize a wagon train called the Jefferson California Company. Jefferson was a Greene County town where many of these pioneers had been born and raised. Bills were posted around the county to encourage worthy men to join the venture.

From dozens of applicants, twenty-nine men were selected for their good character. Dr. George Read, a 31-year-old medical doctor, was elected the captain of the company. Before they departed, Dr. Read addressed the men: "Gentlemen, we are about to embark on a risky journey. We shall be leaving the boundaries of civilization and traveling into the lawless lands of the frontier.

We must trust in one another if we are to survive. Each of us must pledge our belief in the laws of Man and of God and His *Ten Commandments*. We know not what lies ahead on our journey; it is dangerous and full of pitfalls. With a majority agreement, any man who fails to follow these laws may be cast off into unknown territory. Are we all agreed?" Everyone nodded in solemn assent, taking Dr. Read's words to heart.

Many people, who were lured west by the gold rush, were completely unprepared for the severe hardships of the trip. Some perished in remote and barren places with only rough-hewn boards to mark their graves. But western Pennsylvania bred tough, resourceful men and they were not about to be casualties of their journey.

On March 21, 1850, the Jefferson California Company bid farewell to their loved ones on the banks of the Monongahela River in eastern Greene County. They faced a daunting journey of three thousand miles into dangers known and unknown. They had planned carefully, mapping out their route in two stages: river and overland.

The first stage of the journey was via four rivers. The Monongahela took them north to Pittsburgh where they boarded a steamer crowded to overflowing with adventurers and their animals; then the long Ohio River carried them west to the state of Missouri. On a paddlewheel boat, they chugged up the Mississippi River to St. Louis where they bought saddles and food for the journey. Another riverboat took them west across the Missouri River to the town of Independence. They had already traveled a thousand miles from home. River travel was by far the easiest part of their journey.

Independence, Missouri, was a launching pad for hundreds of wagon trains. The Jefferson Company bought seven lightweight *Conestoga* wagons. Conestoga wagons were a specific type of covered wagon, introduced about 1720, by German settlers from Conestoga Township in Lancaster County, Pennsylvania. The floors of these wagons were tilted upwards to prevent the contents from shifting during travel. They had wooden frames and the seams were stuffed with tar to prevent leaking when crossing rivers. They had wooden wheels rimmed with iron which made for a very rough ride. Conestoga wagons were used during the Revolutionary War and throughout the nineteenth century.

To pull each wagon, the Jefferson Company bought six draft mules and one horse. Since most of the members had experience with animals, they knew that mules would be more reliable than horses or oxen. Draft mules have a donkey father and a *draft horse* mother—a draft horse is a very large work horse—and they have the best and worst characteristics of both species. They are strong, tough, and nimble, but sometimes they can be stubborn and ornery. They make up for their shortcomings with intelligence, great endurance, and funny personalities.

The mules came at a high price and by the time the party bought all the necessary supplies, they had spent more than $650.00 per wagon (that's about $14,000 today). Each wagon carried 800 pounds of food, 200 pounds of clothing, animal feed, and equipment. A few days before they left Independence, one member became ill and had to be left behind.

They traveled four men to a wagon and many of them were related. Uncle Asa drove wagon #6 with his uncle James Roseberry and his cousins Frank Gray and William Black. William was their cook and he kept a diary of the trip. On the morning of May 2, 1850, twenty-eight men rose at dawn and "jumped off" into the Great Unknown.

                    *   *   *

AMERICANS WERE ON THE MOVE. The Oregon Trail was crowded with hundreds and hundreds of wagons that crossed the frontier in one continuous stream. Thousands of wagon wheels had beaten deep ruts into the trail. Survival depended on the health and strength of the animals pulling the wagons, so the Jefferson Company was careful to not overwork their mule teams.

Near the end of the first week, William Black said to Asa, "Have you ever seen such scenery? Why the folks at home wouldn't believe how grand the land is out here!"

Uncle Asa drove his wagon through all kinds of weather, wearing homespun shirts, scratchy woolen britches, and a raccoon cap which got more tattered and smelly the further he went. He walked many miles in his knee-high leather "Stoga" boots that had hobnailed soles an inch thick.

A Bowie knife was strapped inside his boot and he carried a shotgun slung over his shoulder.

"Would you look at that!" exclaimed Uncle James Roseberry pointing to a riverbed laden with hundreds of dead animals and broken wagons. "Looks like a graveyard. Why, if that isn't a warning of what's to come I guess those fellows approaching us should be." Returning miners with haggard faces and tattered clothes trudged by as proof that not everyone's gold adventures turned out well.

Some of the company members got sick along the route so it was a good thing that they had a doctor as their captain. Uncle Asa got the mumps, an illness that causes fever and swelling below the jaw. His cousin Frank Gray took one look at him and remarked, "Asa you look like a giant squirrel with a full load of nuts in your jowls! Better do as the captain suggested and rest in the wagon. I'll ride your mule until you're able."

The Jefferson Party crossed many rivers and streams. Sometimes they had to pay ferrymen to float their wagons across fast moving water while their animals swam. They weathered the vast, stark prairie with its endless miles of flat land. Each night, while most of the men slept, one man in each wagon armed himself with a rifle and kept watch for Indians or looters who preyed on travelers.

In Nebraska Territory, they passed through Pawnee Indian lands and watched as a Missouri wagon train ahead of them was forced to surrender one of their group, a young man who had foolishly shot an Indian for sport. One hundred and fifty Pawnee warriors surrounded the wagon and demanded his life, threatening to attack if he was not handed over. They tied the young man with ropes and marched him over the hill never to be seen again.

The company trekked over the Rocky Mountains and

through the South Pass in Wyoming. The South Pass marked the Continental Divide, a natural boundary line separating waters that flow into the Pacific Ocean from those that flow into the Atlantic or the Gulf of Mexico.

They reached Fort Laramie, Wyoming, where most of the men wrote letters to send home to their families. Weeks later, back in Greene County, Grandpa Ephraim came running to the house as fast as his old legs could carry him waving a letter in hand. "Mother! You'll never guess—a letter from Asa sent from Wyoming! Says he's alright and halfway to California!" Martha burst out, "Thank the Lord! For heaven's sake, read it to me will you?" As Ephraim read Asa's words, Martha exclaimed, "Mumps! Well he did pick a fine time to have the mumps. Good thing I made him pack a bottle of my homemade tonic. It cures anything that ails you. Go tell the others!"

The Jefferson Company had good times and bad times. The boring diet of dried meat and hard-tack biscuits was not at all like Mom's home cooking, and they were constantly on the lookout for fresh game and healthy drinking water. The further they went, the long days and dwindling supplies sorely tested their tempers. The bitter dust on the California Trail was so nasty that the men had to tie kerchiefs over their noses, but their skin cracked and bled anyway.

Towards the end of July the company agreed to split up. An advance crew of twelve members would go on ahead to buy supplies and return to the train. Three wagons were abandoned, and the advance crew packed their belongings onto mules. THEY NEVER CAME BACK.

By early August, Uncle Asa and the fifteen remaining members reached the dreaded Carson Desert of northern Nevada. It spanned forty miles of deep sand with no water. It was so hot that they had to cross in the middle of the night

and, even so, the mules almost gave out from the heat. The men were shocked to see that the desert had become one continuous animal graveyard. The scattered bones were so well preserved by the phosphorous chemical in the soil that they gave off an eerie glow.

The last leg of the trail into the Sierras was steep and difficult. The mules struggled mightily to drag the wagons over the jagged rocks and on one haul up the mountainside, Uncle Asa's wagon completely broke down. He said to his cousins, "What say we dump this crate and pack on the mules from here on?" The others agreed and abandoned their spent wagon in a wooden bone yard with hundreds of others.

The Jefferson Company crossed two thousand miles— the overland part of the journey—in 109 days. After a twelve mile drive on the morning of August 18, 1850, they arrived in Placerville, California, in time for breakfast. Nicknamed "Hangtown," Placerville was a rough miners' camp where criminals were hung from a big tree in the center of town, giving the place its ghastly name. Sixteen of the twenty-eight Jefferson Company members, seventeen mules, and three horses all arrived alive in California.

In Hangtown the new arrivals came face to face with their advance crew. Instead of returning with food, the crew got caught up in the gold fever and ignored their responsibilities to their wagon mates. This made the new arrivals MAD!!! There were loud arguments, fistfights, and plenty of cussing!

On that hot August morning, none of them knew that three weeks later on September 9, 1850, California would officially become the thirty-first state of the United States. Hoards of gold miners never guessed what future greatness lay ahead for the new state; nor did they care. There was only one thing on their minds:

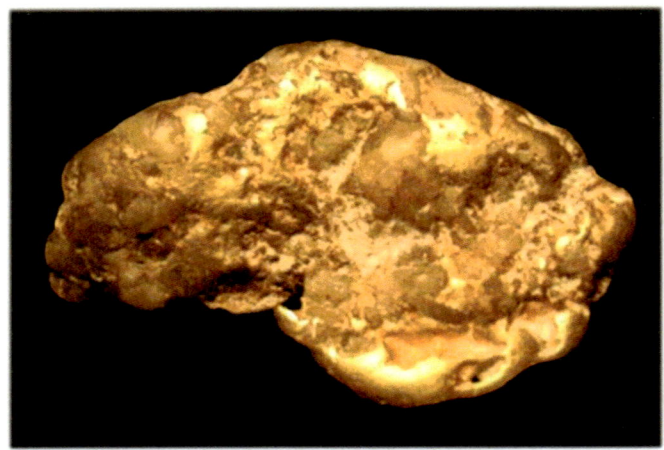

GOLD!

The Diggings

"I have seen the elephant!"

People came from all over the world to prospect for California gold, and most were unsuccessful. "I have seen the elephant!" became a well-worn phrase that meant a miner had seen the meanest, hardest times anyone could imagine and his hopes for riches were dashed.

But the Jefferson Company members had not yet glimpsed the elephant; they were high on enthusiasm. Rumors spread as to the richest diggings. Some said, "Go north to the Yuba River." Others said, "Go south along the American." It was anybody's guess where the gold would pay off. The members split into groups and went their separate ways.

Uncle Asa and ten others from the company traveled northwest fifty miles to the Deer Creek Diggings. Deer Creek was a tributary of the Yuba River, and it ran through the town of Nevada City. It was the richest gold strike in the state at that time.

The men were completely astonished to find a thousand miners already at work, and nearby American Hill was covered with tents and brush houses. Each miner had staked a claim along the river, which meant they marked an area with wooden stakes. Riverfront claims were tiny, just thirty by thirty feet in size, and sometimes miners had to defend their claims at the point of a gun.

Early miners panned the river for *placer* gold. Placers were the easiest pickings that had settled in the water from mountain erosion. The miners filled a flat, round pan with mud from the riverbed and swirled it, tipping out the water. If they were lucky, tiny flakes of gold shone brightly in the bottom of the pan. If they were *really* lucky and found a big nugget they shouted, EUREKA! That's a Greek word meaning, "I have found it!" But they took care not to shout too loudly or others might hear and want to horn in on their discovery. *Eureka* became the motto for the new state of California.

By the time Uncle Asa arrived the placer gold was nearly exhausted. Long wooden troughs called *sluice boxes* had replaced the gold pan. Shovels full of earth were washed down in the sluice box, and any bits of gold were trapped in rows of slatted screens at the bottom. Finding a few grains of gold each day was barely enough to feed yourself.

The same year Uncle Asa arrived, the first gold *lodes* were discovered. A lode is an underground vein of ore that is trapped inside hard quartz rock. No technology existed to retrieve it so miners dug into the hillsides by hand. Then they invented the *quartz mill,* a hammering machine used to crush the rock. Uncle Asa and a couple of partners invested in a mill, but it was inefficient and not very successful.

Gold mining was dangerous. Miners labored day in and day out in the dust and the mud, burrowing down into the earth with their pickaxes. Mining camps were filthy, lawless places plagued by disease, accidents, and fire. Greed drove some to commit violent acts—including murder—and when-ever liquor flowed, disputes erupted, and out came the revolvers and the knives.

Gold is a very dense, heavy metal and just a little bit can be worth a fortune. For safety, a miner kept his gold in a small bottle inside a leather pouch; he slept with it and always carried it with him. Sometimes a criminal would *jump* your claim by taking your land and your gold at gunpoint and leaving you with nothing.

"I have seen the elephant!"

The land along the Yuba River was rough and rocky with heavy clay soil the color of rust. Summers were very hot and to make matters worse, there were rattlesnakes, mountain lions, and poison oak. Uncle Asa lived in a canvas tent and always checked his bed roll for snakes before he got into it. His tent was adequate in warm weather, but when the winter snows began he almost froze solid!

One afternoon, Asa's uncle James Roseberry was hauling spent gravel with a team of mules. When he bent down to adjust the saddle, one of the mules kicked, struck him in the head, and killed him. James was just thirty-three years old. Uncle Asa and his cousins were devastated and had to bury James in a makeshift graveyard. The sad news didn't reach Greene County for months.

By the following year, many from the Jefferson Company had seen the elephant. Three of the members had died of accident or illness, and one was murdered. Most returned to Greene County wiser, but not much richer.

Uncle Asa Plants New Roots

The West was settled by ordinary people
who gambled everything they had to start a new life.

—◦⫶◦⫸◦◆◈◆◃◦⫷◦⫶◦—

By 1852 Uncle Asa had labored for a year and a half in the diggings without success. He got wet, sunburned, and sore, but had found only enough gold to feed himself. So, when a March storm flooded Deer Creek and his mill was destroyed, his mining career came to an end. He was broke, it was time to move on, and he summed up his experiences in a few words: "A poor man can do no good at gold mining!"

Ever resourceful, Uncle Asa left the gold fields and rode his horse down into the Sacramento Valley. When he'd gone about twenty miles west, he found himself in Yolo County, where he looked around. He liked the mighty oak trees and was so pleased with the fine, flat land that he decided to make his home there.

He staked a claim on 160 acres of Yolo land seven miles north of present day Woodland where he built a small cabin. As fast as he could clear the land, he sowed wheat in the *rich and fertile soil*. That's a fancy phrase for really great dirt and in Yolo County, it was almost as valuable as gold. After five years of hard labor, fine farmland emerged.

Uncle Asa missed his family and there was a shortage of suitable brides in Yolo, so in 1857, he returned to Greene County by ship to find a wife. While visiting his family, he met his namesake nephew, my great-grandfather, Asa, who was just six months old.

Uncle Asa was introduced to nineteen-year-old Jane Zimmerman, and after a whirlwind courtship, he convinced her to marry him. He was twelve years older than Jane—with a lifetime's more experience—and Jane had absolutely no idea what challenges she would face if she married him.

Her parents didn't approve of their young daughter going west, so Jane climbed out of a window and *eloped* with Uncle Asa. (To elope means to have a secret marriage without telling your family beforehand.) On January 13, 1858, they were married by a justice of the peace, an official who can legally perform marriages outside of church.

Uncle Asa brought his new bride to California by sea, a difficult journey lasting several weeks. In New York City they boarded a ship bound for Panama in Central America. Jane had never been on a ship before. The cabins were tiny, the food was awful, and the stormy Atlantic weather made her terribly seasick.

Panama is a small Central American country of hot, tropical jungle and so much rainfall that anything made of metal quickly gets rusty. The ship docked at Aspinwall on the Atlantic coast, and the Panama Railroad carried passengers for forty-seven and a half miles across the *Isthmus of Panama.* That's the narrowest piece of land between the Atlantic and Pacific Oceans. In Panama City, on the Pacific side, Uncle Asa and Jane boarded another ship that sailed up the west coast and through the Golden Gate to San Francisco. Years later, the Panama Canal was built to replace the railroad, so that ships could sail through from one coast to the other.

Uncle Asa and Jane Zimmerman Morris

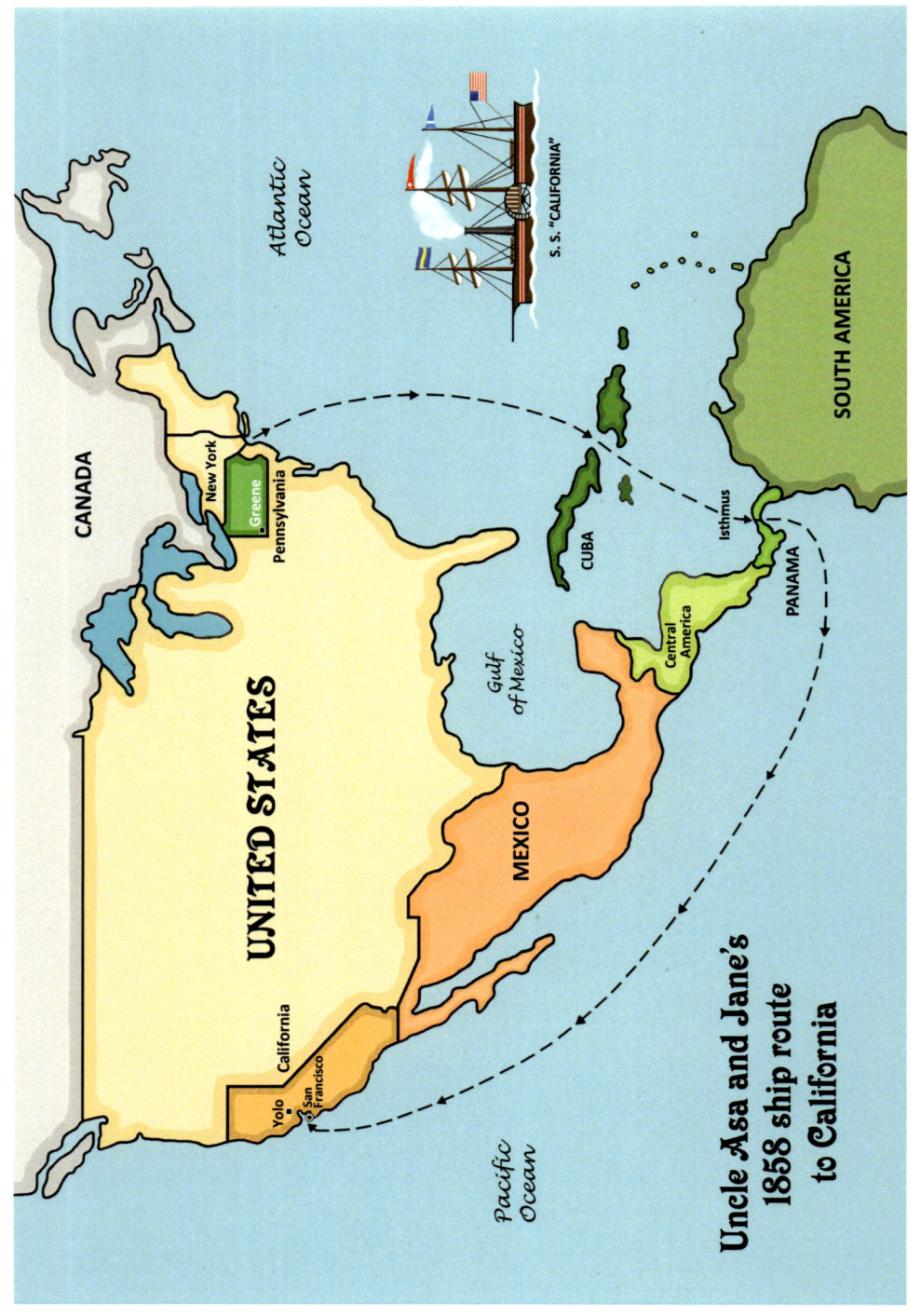

Uncle Asa and Jane's 1858 ship route to California

San Francisco was a booming city thanks to thousands of gold miners who had come and gone. They were a rowdy bunch of greedy adventurers who had left their mark in a rough part of town known as the Barbary Coast. Uncle Asa took Jane on a carriage tour of the city, and as they drove by that notorious area, she was astonished by its bawdy saloons and gambling dens. From every saloon doorway, a cloud of cigar smoke wafted out and lingered in a smelly blue haze while stale whiskey fumes permeated the streets.

Standing on a street corner, was an older lady in a gaudy purple satin gown, and a big hat trimmed with peacock feathers. She waved to Jane and called out, "That's a good-lookin' man, honey! I'd hang on to that one!" Jane blushed, Asa grinned, and he clasped her hand.

San Francisco was already an international city. The gold rush had brought twenty-five thousand Chinese to California, which they called, *Gum San* or Gold Mountain. Many of them later made their homes in *Dai Fow* which meant Big City. Older Chinese merchants still wore customary robes with their long hair tied in a traditional pigtail that fell to their waists; they withstood more than their share of scorn.

Mexicans had lived in California for two centuries. Russians had come decades earlier to trade furs, and a host of other nationalities also worked and lived in the city. With its stew of such diverse cultures, San Francisco had major problems. Vicious criminal gangs roamed the streets, the hastily built town burned down five times, and there were unsettling earthquakes. But San Francisco flourished and was a world away from the quiet Pennsylvania countryside Jane had left behind.

In those days, there were no big bridges spanning the San Francisco Bay, so Uncle Asa and Jane had to cross it by ferryboat. On the opposite bank they boarded a paddlewheel riverboat that chugged north through the delta and up the Sacramento River. The boat docked in bustling downtown Sacramento, called *Yee Fow* or Second City, by her Chinese residents. After unloading passengers and cargo, the boat continued north to Knights Landing where Uncle Asa hired a horse and wagon for the last few miles to the ranch. Jane Zimmerman Morris arrived at her new Yolo County home on March 21, 1858.

*   *   *

"It's not exactly the way I'd pictured it, Asa," Jane remarked as she saw her new home for the first time. "It's rather small and rough, but I think we can make it nice." If Jane had been an older or more demanding bride, she might have gone straight back to Pennsylvania rather than live in such a place but, instead, she and Uncle Asa got to work.

He whitewashed the walls, built cupboards, hung pictures, and bought new furniture. She scrubbed the cabin from top to bottom, sewed checkered gingham curtains, and covered the oak plank floors with hand-braided woolen rugs.

She planted flowers in the window boxes, and Uncle Asa made her a rocking chair for the front porch. The cabin began to look quite civilized and Jane said to her husband, "I think we've a fine place here to invite company for Sunday supper. Why, if she weren't so far away, I'd even invite my mother!" Uncle Asa laughed and promised her that when they had saved enough money, he would build her a much grander house.

Gradually, they settled into a daily routine of a farmer and his wife, and they were happy. Jane kept very busy cooking, scrubbing, and sewing, as well as raising chickens and growing vegetables. Sometimes in the summer, it got so hot in the cabin that Uncle Asa had to bring her cook stove out on the front porch. At harvest time, he went to Sacramento and hired a Chinese cook to help Jane feed the work crews who labored in their fields. Every evening she wrote a detailed record of each day's events in a tiny leather diary.

In 1859, Jane gave birth to a son they named Leroy, and Uncle Asa was very proud of his boy. To their great sorrow, Leroy died when he was only fifteen months old, and Jane never had any more children. When they buried their baby in the graveyard down the road, part of Jane's heart went with him; such was the sorrow borne by many pioneer women.

*   *   *

Uncle Asa was very *frugal*. That means he was careful with his money. He bought more and more land until he owned six hundred and forty acres. He planted wheat and barley, stabled several horses, and kept a herd of cows, pigs, and sheep. His orchards were full of peach, apricot, and black walnut trees and near Jane's vegetable garden, table grapes were staked to a trellis. He and Jane hived their own bees and made delicious honey. Jane sold eggs from their laying hens and hand-churned butter. She was a small woman, but she had strong arms; in one single year she churned over 500 pounds of butter!

Uncle Asa was a real American pioneer. He planted hardy old Greene County roots in the California soil where they thrived. The land was plentiful and he grew his way to wealth. As an early Yolo County settler, he opened the door for his namesake nephew to follow him.

Trouble Ahead

Sometimes, big historic events happen around us
that shape our lives and teach us important lessons.

My great-grandfather Asa was just a little boy when
America faced the looming threat that became the Civil War. A
civil war means that two armies within the same country fight
against each other. Everybody in his family was uneasy and
he heard the tension in the quiet, worried voices of his parents.

One cold November day in 1860, Asa's uncle Thomas
Morris and his family came for a visit. Uncle Tom was nine
years older than his brother John and he lived nearby in
Marshall County, Virginia. He was a *distiller* by trade which
means that he made and sold whiskey. Uncle Tom brought
along a jug for his father Ephraim, whose eyes lit up when he
saw it. He smacked his lips and called for a taste.

Uncle Tom, Grandpa Ephraim, and John huddled
together by the fire. The whiskey warmed their bellies and
loosened their tongues, as they spoke earnestly to one another
about serious national matters. In a corner of the room Asa
was busy building a tower out of wooden blocks with his
cousin James, but he overheard the older men as they spoke
about the coming war, and he knew it was bad news.

Abraham Lincoln had just been elected sixteenth President of the United States, and big trouble was brewing for the country. John was very direct and asked his brother, "Tom, you've got a better sense of how things stand, so just how much stock should we put in this rumor of war?" Uncle Tom's face darkened; he shook his head and said, "The South has threatened to leave the Union immediately, and I believe one spark of rebellion could set this country ablaze." Ephraim looked at his oldest son with dismay and asked, "How long before things get really ugly?" Uncle Tom frowned, "Well, Father, I'd say not more than a few months at most, and if we're forced to go to war against our fellow Americans, God help us all."

Uncle Tom was right. Five months later on April 12, 1861, the newly formed rebel army fired the first shots on Fort Sumter, South Carolina. When John Morris picked up his local newspaper his heart sank. In three inch tall letters was a one word headline:

WAR!

By nightfall the terrible news had traveled all around Greene County. The long-feared fight to save the Union of the United States had begun.

*   *   *

The Civil War was sparked by the spread of slavery. At that time, the eastern states of America were divided by an east-west boundary called the Mason-Dixon Line which ran along the southern border of Pennsylvania, and just below Greene County. Above the Mason-Dixon Line, the northern

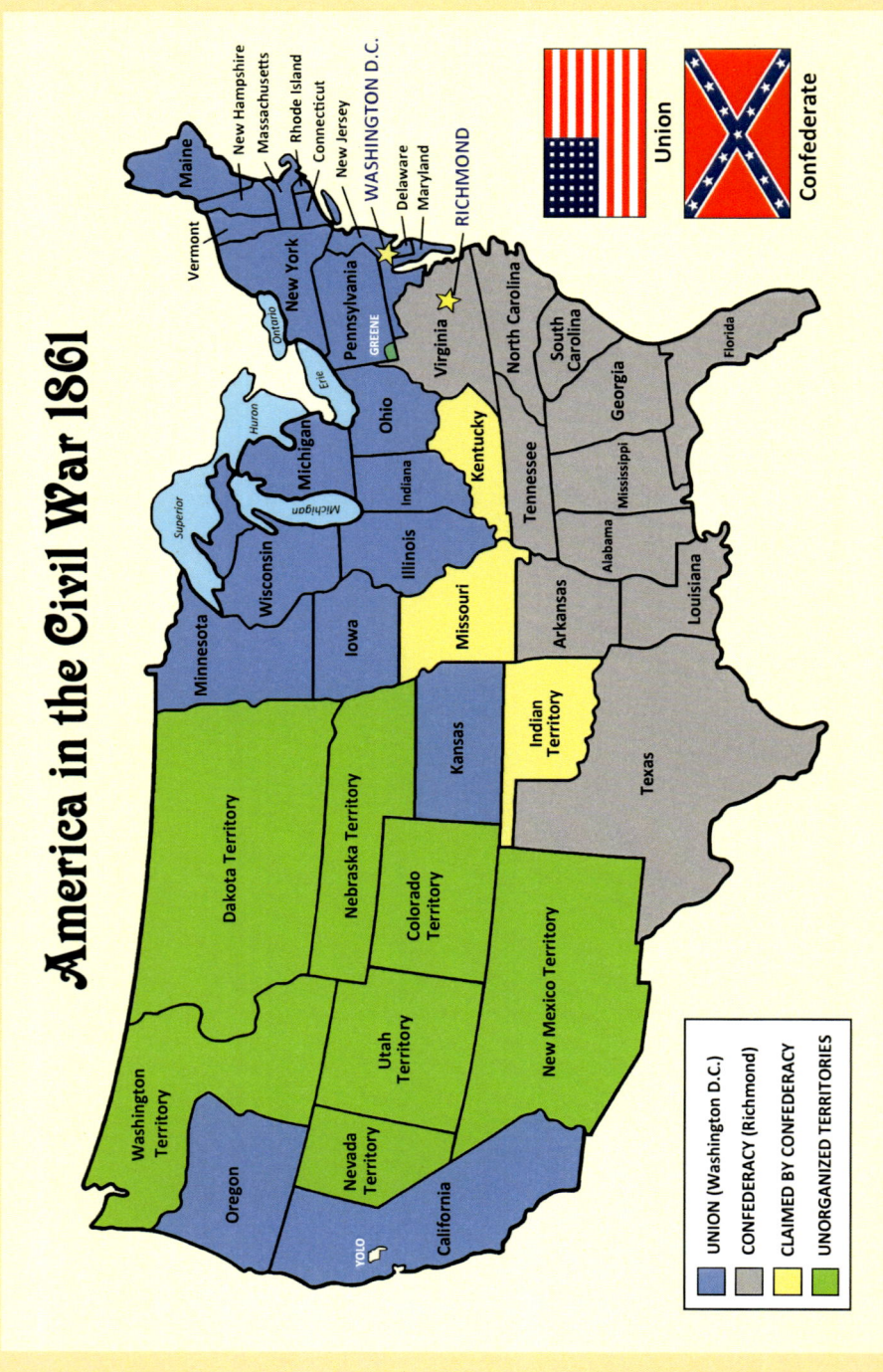

America in the Civil War 1861

Union

Confederate

UNION (Washington D.C.)
CONFEDERACY (Richmond)
CLAIMED BY CONFEDERACY
UNORGANIZED TERRITORIES

WASHINGTON D.C.
RICHMOND

New Hampshire
Massachusetts
Rhode Island
Connecticut
New Jersey
Delaware
Maryland

Maine
Vermont
New York
Pennsylvania
GREENE
Virginia
North Carolina
South Carolina
Georgia
Florida

Ohio
Michigan
Indiana
Illinois
Wisconsin
Minnesota
Iowa
Kentucky
Tennessee
Mississippi
Alabama
Arkansas
Louisiana
Missouri

Ontario
Erie
Huron
Superior
Michigan

Washington
Territory
Oregon
California
Nevada
Territory
Utah
Territory
Dakota Territory
Nebraska Territory
Colorado
Territory
New Mexico Territory
Kansas
Indian
Territory
Texas

YOLO

states had ceased to own slaves. Below, in the southern states, it was still legal for a white person to OWN a black person. In fact, the entire southern way of life depended on the back-breaking labor of its slaves.

Slaves were auctioned off, just like cattle. They were treated as property, not as people, and their masters were sometimes cruel and heartless. It was illegal for slaves to learn how to read, and if they ran away and were caught, their punishment was terrible. Slave mothers and fathers were frequently separated from their children, who were sold to the highest bidder—even if that bidder lived miles away. They often led miserable lives and were powerless to change them. Slavery was a destructive institution that left generations of broken families and broken hearts.

As America expanded westward and acquired new lands from Texas to California, the southern states wanted slavery to expand, too. Some people, called *abolitionists*, felt that slavery was wrong. They wrote about its evil practices, wanted to abolish it, and their repeated calls for action made them unpopular even in some of the northern states.

By the time Abraham Lincoln became president, disagreement about slavery was so fierce that slave-owning states *seceded*, which meant that they left the union of the United States. America splintered into two separate nations. The North was called the UNION. Abraham Lincoln was President, and he aimed to keep the country united. The South was called the CONFEDERACY. The Confederates elected their own President named Jefferson Davis, who fought to create a separate, slave-owning country. There was no easy solution to a divided nation, and the problem just got worse. Northerners called Southerners *Rebels* and Southerners called northerners *Yankees*, and they attached insulting words to both names to show their hatred for each other.

War is always a terrible event; good people die and there is great suffering. But the Civil War was especially terrible because Americans fought Americans, and some even fought their own kinfolk. The Union and the Confederacy raised armies that totaled more than three and a half million men, and over the following four years of war the United States was very nearly destroyed.

Captain John Morris, Union Soldier

A well trained army is essential
to preserve a free nation.

At the time of the Civil War, Pennsylvania was not a slave-owning state. Most of Greene County was solidly behind preserving the Union but their views on a war to free the slaves were conflicted. Many hoped that a compromise could be made with the South to avoid bloodshed, but that didn't happen.

President Lincoln called for volunteers to help fight for the Union alongside the Regular Army. Asa's father John Morris answered the call and helped to recruit other Greene County men. On a June morning in 1861, as John prepared to leave his young family, he gathered Asa, Sis, and Artie close to his heart and told them, "I must go now, but every day that I am gone, remember that I love you. Mind your mother, be brave and strong, and think of me when you say your prayers. I am counting on you."

When Sarah kissed her husband goodbye, she didn't know if she would ever see him again. She hid her fears behind a brave face. Sis and Artie buried their heads in the folds of their mother's long skirt and wept. Grandma Martha's double chin trembled and she couldn't stop the tears from running down her cheeks. Ephraim took her hand and simply said, "Buck up, old girl—he'll come back." Martha nodded uncertainly. Their eldest son, Asa's Uncle Tom, was already fighting in the Union Army so it was heart-wrenching to send a second son off to war.

Asa watched silently as his father rode his horse down the road and disappeared in a cloud of dust. He ran off to the barn, threw himself down on a pile of straw, and cried his heart out with only Marigold for company. She nosed him with concern and he knew she understood.

Throughout the summer and autumn of 1861, the war raged through neighboring Virginia and into the southern states. Greene County was bordered by the Confederacy, and though her land was spared, her young men were not. Each time a battle was fought, anxious families hoped that their loved ones would not be among the casualties. Asa missed his father so much that every morning he sat at the window and watched for John to come riding up the road. He never came.

*   *   *

Early in the Civil War, volunteer soldiers elected their own officers, and John—like his brother Tom—was chosen by his men to be their leader. John became a captain, a middle ranking officer, in the Union Army. Captain John served with the Eighty-fifth Regiment of Pennsylvania Volunteers, and he trained for the job for several months. A *regiment* was an organized group of about one thousand soldiers. More than two thousand regiments from many northern states made up the Union Army. The Eighty-fifth was part of the Union forces called the "Army of the Potomac," commanded by General George McClellan.

There were three kinds of Civil War army regiments: infantry (or foot soldiers), cavalry (or horse soldiers), and artillery (or cannon soldiers). The Eighty-fifth was an infantry regiment and all her troops were from southwestern Pennsylvania. A regiment was usually subdivided into ten *companies* — A through K — and Captain John commanded the one hundred soldiers of Company F.

The Union Army issued each soldier a dark blue Union uniform (the Confederates wore grey) and a rifle. Infantry officers like Captain John also carried long steel swords on their belts. Officers rode on horseback, while their troops marched on foot.

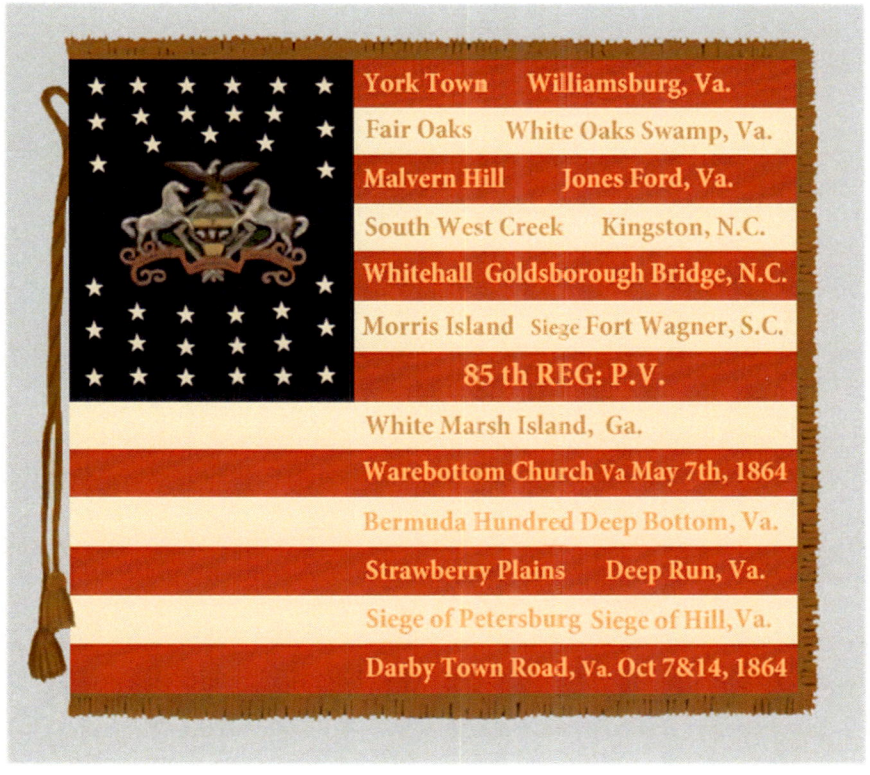

85th Regiment Pennsylvania Volunteer Infantry Flag

The army supplied food, tents, and blankets, and issued small amounts of paper and quill pens so that the men could write letters home to their families. A surgeon was also assigned to each regiment.

In November of 1861, the Eighty-fifth Regiment was ordered to Washington D.C. to guard our nation's Capitol Building. Armed troops were everywhere and so were threats on President Lincoln's life. During the time that Captain John's regiment camped in Washington, he watched the new Capitol Dome being built over the Houses of Congress. The dome rose like a crown atop the symbol of American democracy—which was fighting for its life. And, serving inside that magnificent building was Captain John's cousin, Ohio Congressman James Remley Morris.

Every week Captain John wrote to Sarah, telling her about life in camp. Asa waited eagerly for his father's letters, but by the time they made it to Greene County the news was old and sometimes the regiment had moved.

My Dearest Sarah,   *January 12, 1862*

I hope that you and the children continue in good health. Our regiment has moved once again and is established at Camp Good Hope near Washington. We drill every day and the men are busy building earthworks to protect the Capitol. I cannot complain too much about camp life. Colonel Howell sees to it that his men are well looked after. Thus far, the Company is in good health save for a few cases of measles.

Last week Colonel Howell and 200 men from our regiment led a raid in nearby Maryland to arrest a Rebel spy. They found guns and ammunition in his barn and one of our men picked up a sack of Rebel bullets called 'minie balls.' Tell Asa that I put a few in my knapsack for him. Someday, I hope he will understand why this terrible war was necessary.

Please tell Father that I have written to our cousin James. Congress is very busy but I hope to have a chance to meet with him before we leave this place. With any luck this war will not last beyond the year.

I love you very much and each day away from you and the children makes my heart ache for the sight of you.

Your loving husband,

John

In early spring, 1862, the Eighty-fifth Regiment was ordered south from Washington to the rebel state of Virginia. Nine hundred and fifty men were crammed shoulder-to-shoulder on a little steamship called the Daniel Webster. They sailed down the Potomac River and down the Atlantic coast, landing at the tip of southeastern Virginia, enemy territory. This was the start of a Union operation called the "Peninsular Campaign" launched in March, 1862, which was intended to capture the Confederate capital city of Richmond.

For weeks the Eighty-fifth marched northwards with other Union regiments through the wet swamplands towards Richmond. The weather was awful! It rained so much that the horses stumbled and the cannons got bogged down in the sticky mud. The heavy wooden supply wagons that carried food and tents did not fare much better. It was a slow, miserable journey made worse by wood ticks, poisonous spiders, and fever.

Sometimes the Eighty-fifth went hungry because the supply wagons had not caught up with them. On cold nights, when the soldiers made camp in a remote field, they had to hunt for dry kindling wood and chop down fence posts for campfires to keep themselves warm. If their tents hadn't arrived, they leaned up against a tree trunk or lay on the damp ground, and they slept in their itchy woolen uniforms. The daily life of a Civil War soldier was extremely uncomfortable and sometimes very scary.

As they marched along their route towards Richmond, for the very first time, the soldiers from Greene County saw slaves working in the fields. The slaves watched silently from a distance, hoping that the army had come to set them free. But there would be many terrible battles fought before they were granted their freedom.

At the end of April, the Eighty-fifth made camp near one of America's oldest towns, Williamsburg, Virginia. Not more than five hundred yards away, the entrenched Confederates waited. Each day as the Union troops practiced maneuvers, warning shots were fired at them from across a river. Tensions increased and combat was soon to erupt.

On May 5, 1862, the Eighty-fifth, along with other regiments, came face to face with their Confederate enemies at the edge of a wood. The Union commanding officer gave his men a rousing speech to bolster their courage; then he gave the order: "Fall in!" The men of the Eighty-fifth were placed near the front lines and steeled themselves for the battle. "Forward Eighty-fifth!" shouted the commander. The regiment slowly advanced across a field of ankle-deep mud towards a densely wooded grove. Most of the soldiers had never been in combat before and they were very frightened.

"FIRE!" The crack of a thousand Confederate guns and the thunder of cannons shattered the silence of the quiet Virginia countryside. Shells flew overhead exploding in every direction, and cannon balls hit the ground with tremendous force, making craters of destruction. The Union forces returned fire with everything they had.

Captain John had just begun to lead his company forward when—suddenly—an artillery shell burst very near his head. A large piece of hot metal struck his left cheek, broke his jaw, and made a deep, ugly wound. The impact of the explosion knocked him to the ground, and two of his men dragged him to the rear where he lay senseless. He was the very first man wounded in his regiment.

While the battle raged on around him, Captain John regained his senses and managed to crawl under some shrubbery for protection. The side of his face was a bloody mess, so he wound his neck cloth around his jaw and he waited. He felt responsible for his men and helpless that he couldn't lead them.

For hours, thousands of troops from both armies fought the Battle of Williamsburg. When it was finally over, hundreds of soldiers from both armies lay dead in the fields, and crews of soldiers were sent to bury them where they lay. The Union Army held its ground and the Confederates retreated northward towards Richmond. The battle was a *stalemate* (which means that neither side really won), and before long the two armies would face one another again.

For the Eighty-fifth, the night after the battle was horrendous. The wounded were covered with every available blanket, and inside a waterlogged tent, the surgeon operated as fast as he could. Cries of pain and suffering pierced the surrounding darkness.

Most of the soldiers had no overcoats, and their uniforms were completely drenched from the incessant, drizzling rain. They shivered and their teeth chattered from a penetrating cold that rose from the wet, swampy ground. The supply wagons had been delayed, so there was no food and no hot coffee to ease their discomfort. For many, sleep was impossible.

When the surgeon finally dressed his wound and set his broken jaw, Captain John lay exhausted in his tent; his injury was terribly painful. Pain medicine was in short supply and only used for the most critically injured, so if you were wounded, you took a swig or two of whiskey and you toughed it out. The whiskey was just a temporary fix, but it finally numbed Captain John's pain and he slept.

The following morning, he dragged himself to his feet to report for duty, but he felt so unsteady that he had to retreat to his tent. Wave after wave of dizziness made him nauseous, and a loud ringing in his ears was maddening.

At home his family heard about the Williamsburg battle and prayed that he was safe, but days passed before Sarah received word about her husband. When a letter finally arrived, it was not written in John's handwriting and she looked at it with dread. Grandpa Ephraim urged her to open it. It read:

My Dearest Sarah,   *May 9, 1862*

Our cousin, Private Tom Roseberry, kindly offered to pen this letter for me. We have met the enemy in Williamsburg and have lost two of our brave men. The battle was vicious and sickening with so many casualties that I am at a loss for words.

I have been wounded, though not mortally. I was hit in the left side of the face by a piece of shell and have a broken jaw and a sorry wound which causes me much pain. My hearing is gone in my left ear and I am having trouble writing as my hand shakes very badly. The battalion surgeon has patched me up and says that time will likely heal my face, though my appearance will be frightful for a while. I want to prepare you so that when I return to you, God willing, you will not be afraid. We march northward soon and I may not be able to write again for some time. Please tell Asa and our girls how much I miss them and love them as I do you. Give my love to Father and Mother.

Your loving husband,
John

A Fevered Battle

The horrors of the Civil War
were compounded by fever and sickness.

A few days later orders came to march north. Captain John rode his horse at the very front of his company, but the constant jolting of the ride aggravated his wounded jaw. Towards the end of May, the Eighty-fifth reached a place called Seven Pines, just a few miles south of Richmond. Confederate spies, hidden in the woods, carried advanced warning to their commanders that the Union Army was approaching. The Confederates lay in wait.

May 31, 1862, was a sultry, grey day. The ground was waterlogged from the previous night's rain; supply wagons were late, and a hasty breakfast was all the men received. Around one o'clock, the Confederates launched artillery into the Union camp, taking the soldiers by surprise. The Battle of Seven Pines had begun!

The Eighty-fifth Regiment was part of General Silas Casey's 2nd Division on the first line of defense against the attackers. The soldiers took up their positions in newly dug rifle pits protected only by *pickets* — which are wooden stakes with sharp points on the end. The rifle pits were muddy and the dampness seeped into the soles of their boots. Due to illness amongst the Union troops, the Confederates out-numbered them by a wide margin.

As the Confederates advanced, the ground was choked with smoke from cannon fire. Hails of minie balls flew thick and fast, and artillery shells sent sparks and pieces of metal flying everywhere. Captain John's heart pounded and sweat poured down his back, but he could not let his men see that he was afraid. Part of being a leader is going forward even when you are frightened. After three solid hours of fighting, Casey's Division was ordered to fall back to the secondary line of defense. Reinforcements arrived and the two armies fought late into the evening.

The following morning the battle continued; soldiers grew exhausted, and bodies of the fallen lay all around. Casualties for both armies totaled more than 11,000 men. Yet, the Battle of Seven Pines (also called The Battle of Fair Oaks) was another stalemate.

Casey's Division, including the Eighty-fifth, retreated to camp near White Oaks Swamp. Conditions in camp were terrible: the low-lying swamp bred fever, and soon half the soldiers were ill. With his jaw aching like blazes, Captain John collapsed in his tent. He was so cold and shaky that as darkness closed in, he couldn't remember anything more.

The next morning, one of his men found him lying on the ground outside his tent. His whole body was paralyzed. Alarmed, the soldier bent down and called, "Captain Morris, Sir! Can you hear me?" Captain John's eyelids fluttered but he didn't speak; he was only aware of a faint voice and blurry face that hovered above him. "Can you move your legs, Sir?" No response . . . no movement. "Send for the surgeon!" cried the same urgent voice.

Later, another voice was heard, "Sir, he's in surgery and

says we best get the Captain onto a plank to move him. Be careful not to bend his neck, he says. Just carry him to his tent and cover him with blankets. Doc said he will be along as soon as he can get away!" When the surgeon finally came and examined his patient he said, "It's a paralysis in his spine but we can't move him until that fever comes down. Keep him covered, give him lots of water, and we'll just have to wait."

Captain John lay on his back for an entire week, before he was put aboard a troop train which transported him 250 miles to hospital in Philadelphia. The captain's cousin, Private Tom Roseberry, who thought the world of Captain John, had to blink back his tears as he helped carry him aboard the train. "Godspeed, Sir," he said as they parted.

Captain John spent three weeks in a Philadelphia hospital. He couldn't move and his nerves were so raw that he couldn't sleep. He lay hour after hour on his hospital cot and stared at the cracked ceiling. The smell of battle lingered in that room amongst the wounded, and he would never forget it. All he could think about was Sarah and his children. How would he ever be able to take care of them? His doctors finally declared that he could not rejoin his regiment and might never walk again, so he did his duty and resigned from the Union Army. His hands were so weak that he could barely sign his own name on his resignation letter before they sent him home.

Captain John Comes Home

For a wounded soldier,
his loved ones mean everything to him.

When the news reached Greene County that Captain John was alive, his family was overjoyed and Asa was so happy that Papa was coming home. But Sarah spared her children the worst of the news. Captain John's letters, written by a nurse, were very sad. He told Sarah that he was as helpless as a baby and needed round-the-clock care. His mind played tricks on him and he relived his battles every time he slept.

Asa wanted to go to the station to meet his father's returning train but Sarah said no. She knew that her young son was not prepared for the sight of his injured father. The captain's brothers, James and Mathias, met the train and looked at each other with dread as they carried Captain John on a stretcher to their wagon. They drove him home lying down on a straw mattress, swaddled in blankets, but every bump and jostle along the miles of road caused him agony.

When they carried him into his house, he looked so awful that his family was deeply shocked. He was no longer the robust man who had left them the year before. He was rail thin, pale, and very weak. His face had a jagged red scar and his broken jaw was still swollen. He could barely move.

Sarah ran to him and kissed his forehead while stroking his hair. She didn't let her children see her fears. Instead, she reassured them, "Papa is hurt but he will get well, and each of you can help by being good and kind to him." Asa pulled away at the sight of his injured father, but Captain John whispered to him, "Don't be afraid, Son." Sarah placed his limp hand atop Asa's small hand. It was the very first step in a long recovery.

The next few weeks were just plain miserable. Captain John slept most of the time in a downstairs room that had been converted into a makeshift bedroom. Sarah kept very busy nursing him, and Asa and his sisters had to tip-toe around to avoid making noise.

Grandma Martha took over the cooking and Asa's aunts came to help. Sis and Artie helped their grandmother gather herbs from the garden to prepare *poultices*—which are homemade medicines for wounds. They picked bouquets of wildflowers and brought them to their father's bedside. They sang songs their mother had taught them in their reedy little-girl voices to cheer him, and even though he could barely hear them, they were rewarded by a warm smile.

The house was chilly in the early mornings so Asa carried a steady supply of small logs for the fire to keep his father comfortable. Grandpa Ephraim sat at his son's bedside every day and read the newspaper to him; the Captain's brothers did the farm chores and chopped wood. Sam the hound slept next to Captain John's bed and would only leave his side when absolutely necessary.

Captain John had great willpower. Every time he opened his eyes and glimpsed his children's anxious faces he knew he had to recover. Slowly, he improved and as he gained strength, he was able to spend less time sleeping and more time with his youngsters. He often asked Asa to sit next to his bedside and talk to him.

Asa had discovered that his father couldn't hear very well when his head was turned so he shouted his questions. "Whoa there, Son. I'm not totally deaf, so you can tone down your volume and save your voice," said his father. "Sit on my right side so I can hear you better."

Like most little boys, Asa was full of curiosity about the war. He asked, "Pa, when you were in Washington D.C. did you meet President Lincoln?" Captain John smiled and replied, "No I didn't, Asa, but one afternoon, I did see him riding his horse down Pennsylvania Avenue. He is a giant of a man with a long, craggy face, a grizzled beard, and kindly eyes. The President was wearing his signature stovepipe hat, which rises a good eight inches or so above its brim, and makes him seem even taller. As he passed by, he tipped his hat at the Company F troops, who were very gratified by his acknowledgment.

"President Lincoln's son Tad was riding alongside him on a pony. Tad is a just a few years older than you are, Asa, and I've heard that sometimes he is a real prankster in the White House. Apparently, Tad likes to review the army troops with his father, and sometimes he wears his very own Union Army uniform."

Asa thought an army uniform was a grand idea. He was so enthusiastic about it, that Grandma Martha sewed a blue jacket and cap for him from an old woolen blanket, and Grandpa Ephraim whittled a toy rifle from a piece of scrap wood. When Asa was fully outfitted, his father raised a weak hand, and saluted him.

Asa proudly wore his uniform, and liked to pretend that he was a Union officer like his father. He kept busy marching up and down the yard wielding his rifle and giving orders, "Fall in. Forward Eighty-fifth; Heeuupp, two, three, four, heeuupp, two, three, four."

While he was marching, Asa often burst into song. He knew all the Union Army battle tunes by heart, but his favorite was the chorus from *The Battle Cry of Freedom:*

> *The Union forever Hurrah boys, Hurrah!*
> *Down with the traitors, up with the stars;*
> *While we rally round the flag boys,*
> *Rally once again,*
> *Shouting the battle cry of freedom!*

Marigold, the cow, could hear him from as far away as the barn, and smiled to herself. Grandma Martha heard him from the kitchen, set down the big wooden spoon she was using to stir the evening stew, and closed the window. She looked at Sarah and exclaimed, "I'm proud that my young grandson is so patriotic, but he does make a racket!"

When Asa tried to recruit his sisters, they just laughed at him, but the local boys were only too glad to play army games. Asa informed his friends that since he was the proud owner of REAL Rebel minie balls, he should be the Union commander. The others insisted that he produce the proof, so Asa reached into the pocket of his britches, held out three bullet-shaped lumps of lead in a grubby hand and asked with some annoyance, "Any questions?" One of the boys spoke out, "Yeah, Asa, just how do we know those are actually Reb bullets? "Asa looked disgusted and replied, "Because my Pa brought 'em all the way from Virginia and he NEVER lies!"

The pint-sized army built forts in the woods out of fallen tree limbs, hid behind them, and ambushed each other hollering, "KERPOW! I got you; you dirty Reb. You're dead!"

Whoever lost had to wave a white flag of surrender, a dingy old handkerchief tied to a branch. They notched their victories with a pocket knife in the bark of an old oak tree, and the older boys—who had learned to write—also cut their initials, just in case any future historians might like to know who fought in the imaginary Battles of Greene County.

*   *   *

Six long months passed before Captain John was strong enough to move his arms and legs. His face healed and he grew a beard to cover the long scar on his jaw. For a while he had terrible nightmares and woke everybody up when he shouted out, but gradually the peaceful countryside soothed his nerves and his children made him laugh.

One day a political rally was held in Waynesburg. Captain John was able to hobble about with crutches so he went to the rally with his brothers. The crowd that gathered around the speakers' platform cheered as Union supporters gave their patriotic speeches. But in the midst of the rally, a young Confederate sympathizer showed up and demanded to be heard. He was a hot-headed young college man, and when he spoke against the Union he really riled up the crowd. Murmurs of disagreement flared into a roar. Captain John got so angry that before his brothers could stop him, he moved forward, raised his arm, and beat the fellow with his crutch! No Rebel sympathizer, young or old, would ever make trouble as long as Captain John had the strength to put him down!

In April, 1863, Greene County had a close call with the Confederate Army. Fifteen hundred rebel troops invaded nearby Morgantown, West Virginia, less than thirty miles south of the Greene County seat, Waynesburg. They destroyed a railroad bridge and killed several Union troops. The Rebels burned homes and stole all the dry goods, supplies, and horses they could lay their hands on. Waynesburg quickly summoned her defense forces. Several tense days passed before her citizens learned that the Rebels had turned and were marching away. Greene County was once again, safe.

Aftermath

Wars never have a happy ending.

For four long years, the war dragged on, and more than six hundred thousand soldiers died. Parts of the South were burned to the ground and families fled for their lives. There was great hunger and suffering, and hardly any Union or Confederate family escaped without the loss of somebody they loved.

In July, 1864, a messenger on horseback arrived at the farm bringing tragic news to the Morris family. Asa's uncle, Lt. Colonel Tom Morris, had been shot and killed by the Rebels at Snicker's Ferry, Virginia, in the Battle of Cool Springs. He was buried where he fell on the battlefield, and he left behind a wife and five young children. Uncle Tom had seen three hard years of service in the Union Army, and his death was a great blow to his troops in the 14th West Virginia Infantry Regiment.

The family took his loss bravely, but for weeks Grandma Martha could barely speak without weeping. Her oldest son had given his life to save the Union. Uncle Tom's photograph was placed on the fireplace mantle opposite a picture of President Lincoln and, on the wall above, hung Captain John's sword. That sword would proudly be passed down to Asa's descendants for five generations, as a remembrance of the Captain's service to his country.

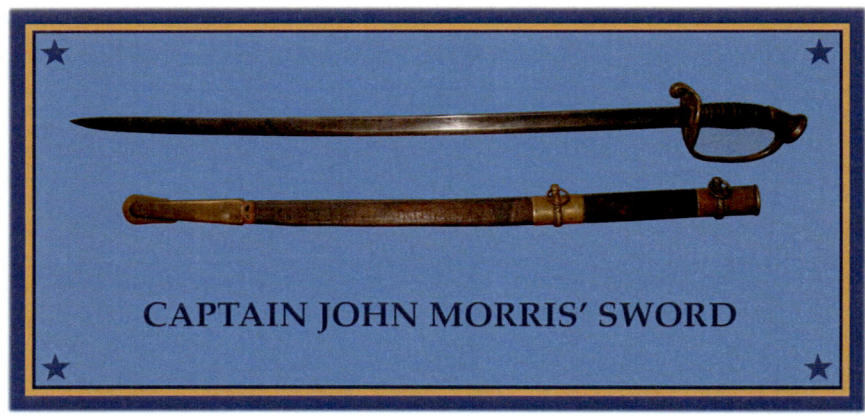

CAPTAIN JOHN MORRIS' SWORD

Asa was just a month shy of eight years old when the Civil War finally came to an end. The Confederates had lost the war. On April 9, 1865, Confederate General Robert E. Lee surrendered to Union General Ulysses S. Grant at Appomattox Court House, Virginia. President Abraham Lincoln had freed the slaves and reunited the United States as one nation. But the end of the war was not the end of hatred between the victorious North and the defeated South; there was one final tragedy.

On the warm evening of April 14, less than a week after the war ended, President Lincoln and his wife Mary enjoyed a stage play while seated in a special balcony at Ford's Theater in Washington D.C. They never suspected that close behind them, an evil man was about to change American history. Fueled by vicious hatred, the diehard Confederate rebel secretly entered the balcony where the President sat and shot him in the head from behind at close range. President Lincoln was *assassinated* — which means that he was killed for political reasons. His killer was an actor named John Wilkes Booth.

In the Ford's Theater audience that evening sat Captain John's cousin, Congressman James Remley Morris, who had just finished his second term in office. James was an eyewitness to the assassination. Hearing the pistol shot, he saw Booth leap from the President's balcony to the stage below and the President slump over against the railing. For a moment there was dead silence in the audience, then complete chaos. Realizing what had happened, James leapt to his feet and cried out, "Hang the scoundrel!" But Booth escaped and was on the run for two long weeks before he was cornered and killed by a posse of lawmen.

The entire Morris family and most Americans were shocked by the Lincoln assassination. Two days later, on Easter Sunday in faraway Yolo County, California, Uncle Asa and Jane Morris heard the terrible news. President Lincoln, who had saved the United States, was dead.

Asa never forgot the Civil War; its tragedies were branded on his young heart. Some of his Greene County neighbors returned missing arms and legs, and others never returned at all. Asa learned not to take life for granted, because it could end in a single heartbeat on a battlefield. He watched his father suffer, and he knew that terrible things could happen even to really good people like Uncle Tom. As the oldest son, Asa had to work very hard to help his injured father support the family. Life was difficult and money was scarce, so he learned to take charge and depend on himself.

*   *   *

Over time, Captain John recovered, though he was never as able-bodied as he had been before the war. His family increased by three more sons: John Roseberry Morris, James Madison Morris, and Elijah Ephraim Morris. He pushed himself to succeed by any possible means. By his actions and his positive attitude, he taught his four sons and two daughters to be courageous, to persevere, and to work hard.

His neighbors admired him, and in 1876 they elected him as a *Commissioner* of Greene County. (A commissioner is responsible for building roads and bridges and spending tax money wisely.) Captain John was honored to serve his community.

Perhaps because he had fought in the Civil War as a young man, wanderlust came late in Captain John's life. In 1892, when he was sixty years old, he left his Greene County farm in the care of his brother, and moved one thousand miles west to Jewell County, Kansas. He was keen to try his hand at crop farming on flat land. But after eight years, he grew weary of the desolate, endless prairie and returned home to Greene County where he spent his remaining years.

Captain John with twins Joe and Sadie and second wife Elizabeth
Jewell County Kansas, 1894

Captain John outlived his wives and two of his children. He had twins by his second marriage, more than thirty grandchildren, and his descendants spread all across America. He never became a wealthy man, though if you had asked him, he would have told you that his family was his wealth.

In his long life, Captain John witnessed a tremendous expansion of the United States. He also saw the dawn of electric lights, telephones, automobiles, and airplanes. Like many of his Morris ancestors, who were tough old buzzards, he lived to be almost ninety years old!

Captain John Morris 1832-1922

Asa Meets His Legendary Uncle

A legendary person is someone who has
done something remarkable. Uncle Asa risked his life
on his journey west and lived to tell the story.

In June of 1866, Uncle Asa and Aunt Jane returned east
to Pennsylvania by ship to visit their families in Greene
County. When the man and the boy—both named Asa Warren
Morris—met face to face, Uncle Asa had a chance to relate his
fascinating adventures to his nine-year-old namesake.

Uncle Asa was a lean, energetic man with dark wavy
hair laced with grey. He wore a long grizzled beard and had
the same broad forehead and low brow as his brother, Captain
John. His complexion was deeply tanned since Yolo County
had so many clear, sunny days. His piercing blue eyes warned
that nobody could fool him and only a fool would try.

Aunt Jane was a small woman with a round face, brown
eyes, and dark hair drawn back in a roll at the nape of her
neck. She wore little pendant earrings, and a delicate bracelet,
finely crafted from genuine California gold. No one who
looked at her petite form, dressed in the enormous hoop skirts
of the day, would ever suspect that she was a pioneer woman
from Northern California.

Uncle Asa had a forceful personality. He sized up his young nephew with a penetrating gaze, looked at his brother, and said with a broad grin, "Fine-looking boy you've got, Johnny!" Asa looked his uncle straight in the eye, grinned back, and they shook hands. They were more alike than either of them knew; both were strong-willed, hard-headed, and full of energy.

When they sat down for a chat Uncle Asa said, "You don't remember me, do you Son?" Asa shook his head and Uncle Asa continued, "You were just a little sprout the last time I saw you. Let me see your hands." Surprised, Asa held out his small hands palms up. Uncle Asa took a look and commented, "Good . . . good. I see you're developing the calluses and strength you'll need to be a fine farmer. The other skill you'll need is a good head for figures. Keeping up with your arithmetic, are you?" Asa nodded. "Excellent!" said his uncle. "And how many cows do you milk before breakfast? Three, you say? That shows endurance for a young lad.

"I hear you're interested in California, Asa. Well, let me tell you, gold mining is a miserable way to make a dollar. In the days of gold the miners used to say, 'I have seen the elephant.' That meant they'd finally faced failure. Well, I saw that elephant, so I wised up and moved on.

"Now, farming is another matter. California is called the Golden State, not just because there is gold in her hills, but because there is so much promise in her land. Our cabin sits in a long, flat valley with the Sierra Nevada Mountains on the east side and the Pacific Ocean over the hills on the west side. Our Yolo County soil is as fine as you'll ever see, and with hard work, it brings forth a tremendous bounty. Did you know that the winter is so mild I can grow different crops all year long?" Asa glanced out the window at the late Pennsylvania snowfall and had his doubts.

"Don't get me wrong, Nephew," explained Uncle Asa, "It's not an easy life as Jane can tell you firsthand, and she works as hard as any man I know. We've had our share of droughts and floods, crop failures, and sickness but we've persisted haven't we, my dear?" He smiled at his little wife who looked up from her sewing and smiled back. "But, it's been worth the struggle to see our land increase and we've been happy in California."

Uncle Asa continued, "When I first came to Yolo County my friend George Sharpnack from the wagon train rode with me. George's farm is about a mile from us and we lease his pasture for our horses. For months George and I slept on the ground at the foot of a big oak tree while he helped me build a cabin." Uncle Asa rolled up his shirt sleeve and showed his nephew a long scar. "You see this? Acquired it in mortal combat with a stubborn oak tree that refused to yield. Tore me up something awful!" he chuckled. "But I finally felled that giant and now it's the floor of our cabin.

"Early on, the Yolo oaks grew very thick and Grizzly bears lived there. Grizzlies can be real monsters and some of them weigh seven hundred pounds! One of them chased me when I was out exploring and—lucky for me—I shot him dead!" Asa's eyes grew round with astonishment.

"Before my time, trappers came from up north in Oregon to trap beaver for their fur called *pelts*. Beaver pelts are very valuable for coats and hats and such, especially in the East. Each trapper hid his pelts in his own secret hiding place called a *cache* along the creek near my cabin, until he was ready to take them away to sell. So, that creek was named Cache Creek because of those crafty trappers."

"Do you have Indians nearby Uncle?" Asa asked. Uncle Asa pondered a few moments and replied, "Yes, we do, Asa. Sometimes they camp near the creek for a spell and then they move on. Indian tribes in California are not like the ferocious Iroquois that we had here in Pennsylvania. Out West they're usually not prone to making war; they're content to live in the valleys, weaving baskets and grinding acorns into meal for their supper. When California was settled, some tribes like the *Yosemite* were forcibly driven from their lands. Some died from disease and others just disappeared into the hills."

"Do stagecoaches come to Yolo County?" Asa asked. "Sure do!" Uncle Asa answered. "A few miles north of us is a small town called Knights Landing that sits alongside the Sacramento River. It has a ferryboat dock and a stagecoach stop. Jane often gets her packages sent from Sacramento by stage, and we sell our eggs and butter at the General Store in Knights Landing.

"Yolo City (Woodland) to our south is really a booming town. Jane likes the shops, and they always do a nice Christmas celebration. Someday, the railroad they're building across the country will go all the way to Yolo County, and you can come and see our place for yourself."

Asa loved Uncle Asa's California stories, even the scary ones. He figured there was a huge world beyond Greene County, with all kinds of adventures to be had. He realized that his uncle had taken a big risk yet had come through very successfully. Asa knew then and there that he wanted to follow in his uncle's footsteps. But first, he had some growing up to do.

*   *   *

In 1868, back in Yolo County, Uncle Asa kept his earlier promise to Jane, and they broke ground for a grand new house. He was determined that the house be not only beautiful but also strongly built. Uncle Asa told his builder, John

McKenzie, "I want you to have each of the vertical timbers milled all in one continuous length. That way if we have an earthquake and the house comes off her brick foundation, she will be all in one piece and can be rolled right back onto the bricks." That request made for some VERY LONG pieces of lumber, as it was to be a two-storied house.

Jane had been chronically ill for several years with typhus fever, a disease that lay hidden on old ships and in tropical countries. Typhus caused terrible headaches and there was no cure. Like many pioneer women, Jane had persevered through many hardships but the typhus finally drained her life away. Tragically, in August, 1869, she died; she was only thirty-one years old.

Uncle Asa was heartbroken. He had loved Jane deeply and was so sad that she hadn't lived to see her new home completed. In the little country graveyard near their home, Uncle Asa buried Jane next to their infant son and he grieved for her. Today, the beautiful house he built still stands as a gracious, silent witness to more than 140 years of Yolo County history.

*   *   *

Five long years passed and Uncle Asa's splendid house was a lonely place for a widower. In 1874, he chose a second wife, Mary Alice Campbell, who was twenty-seven years younger than he was. Mary Alice brought six new lives into the big house: two sons, Lindsay and William, and two daughters, Jennie Belle and Kate. Two other children died young. Uncle Asa was almost fifty years old when his first surviving child was born.

Like his brother Captain John, Uncle Asa served his community. He was a County Supervisor who laid out the roads in northern Yolo County. He was also a prominent member of the local *Grange*, an organization of farmers that helped get their products to market at less cost. He and Mary Alice were pillars of their small Yolo community, and their descendants lived in the old family home for one hundred and twenty years. Uncle Asa had come to California with not much more than hope, but by his own efforts and tough pioneer spirit, he prospered.

Mary Alice Campbell Morris 1853-1944

Another Asa Morris Heads West

After the gold rush, Americans discovered
the great agricultural opportunities California offered,
and another whole generation moved westward.

Not long after Uncle Asa's visit, Grandma Martha passed away, followed two years later by Grandpa Ephraim. They had lived good, long lives but time had worn them out. Their absence left a big hole in Asa's heart. His grandparents had given him something important called *tradition*. They taught him to know and respect the lessons of the past, and by so doing, to go boldly forward and seize the future.

Ephraim and Martha were laid to rest in the old Roseberry family cemetery, set peacefully on the side of a hill overlooking a wooded green valley, and another generation of Asa's family became part of history.

As the years passed, Asa grew into a handsome young man. He was middling in height, wiry and strong, with the broad Morris forehead and intense, bright blue eyes. Mother Nature must have put extra spark plugs in Asa's engine because he had tremendous physical energy. His wavy brown hair curled around his *cowlick*. That's the part of your hair that grows like a swirl. It's a funny word that came from the fact that when cows lick their newborn youngsters, they flatten the hair into swirls. Whenever Asa got really mad his cowlick stood straight up, just like the hair on a dog's back.

Asa Morris as a young man

His family knew that when Asa's cowlick stood on end, fireworks followed. Sarah did her best to tame her son's fiery temper—with limited success. Sis didr.'t help matters when she compared her brother to a *banty* (bantam) rooster. These roosters are small, spirited, and feisty.

Asa had plenty of courage and a temper to match; he never walked away from a fist fight and sometimes sported a black eye to prove it. Fist fights among young men weren't unusual in those times. They settled their differences with a minimum of bloodshed and, generally, nobody got arrested. The outcome was far less deadly than shooting each other with dueling pistols as earlier generations had done.

Asa went to the nearby Holbrook School during the winter term, but in the warm months he helped out on the farm. He was a hardworking young fellow with all the strength and the skill of his yeoman heritage; he was intelligent, capable, and ambitious. For generations of Americans like Asa, hard won independence had given them a tremendous drive to succeed by their own hands.

Every year, Asa raced his father's horses at the Greene County Fair. He was a good horseman, with a flair for showmanship, and he caught the eye of a young lady of the neighborhood. Her name was Mary Elizabeth Call and she was a schoolteacher. Mary thought that Asa was a fine-looking fellow but maybe just a bit too daring. Asa thought Mary was the nicest, prettiest girl he knew, and before long they were *courting* — which is the old fashioned word for dating.

Asa still believed in his childhood dream to go to California, and like Uncle Asa, he wanted to own land and work for himself. Greene County was very hilly, so the area for growing crops was limited; also, most of the prime farmland was already owned by old, well established families. There were only so many possibilities for an energetic young man with little money. Yolo County, California, offered plenty of flat land and unlimited opportunities.

When Asa was twenty-two years old, Uncle Asa wrote offering him a job as a farmhand on his Yolo ranch. In exchange, Uncle Asa would have a reliable young family member as his employee. That sounded like a pretty good deal to Asa, for more than one reason. He suffered from asthma, a lung condition which sometimes makes it hard to breathe. Western Pennsylvania had humid summers and hard, cold winters, which made his asthma worse. The mild, dry California climate might be just the ticket to cure him.

*   *   *

For some time, Asa's mother Sarah had been ailing with consumption, a disease of the lungs that was not curable. Today it is called tuberculosis and there is medicine for it. Sarah coughed and coughed until she was exhausted; she gradually wasted away and, sadly, in March, 1879, she died. Sarah was just forty-two years old and Captain John, who was forty-seven, was left to raise their three younger sons—a difficult task, even for an old soldier. The day that Sarah was laid to rest next to Ephraim and Martha, Asa's life changed forever. His mother would no longer be a gentle guiding presence in his life, but she had taught him well and he could guide himself.

At first, Captain John was reluctant to let Asa go to California, but he wanted his son to better himself and he decided he wouldn't stand in his way. Captain John knew that Asa would be in the capable hands of Uncle Asa so he gave him his blessing. As a parting gift, he gave Asa one of his best shotguns. He figured that his son might need a reliable gun out west.

Asa had courted Mary Call for two years, and he followed proper tradition by asking Mary's father for permission to marry her. When approval was granted, Asa proposed to Mary, and he couldn't believe how lucky he was when she said, "Yes!"

Asa's bride Mary Elizabeth Call

As a token of his love, he gave Mary a simple gold band that had belonged to his mother, and they were officially engaged.

Mary came from a fine old Greene County family and her father, James Call Jr., was a Justice of the Peace. She was twenty-one years old with curly strawberry blonde hair, a fair complexion, and soft, heavy-lidded blue eyes. Mary was well mannered and calm, but she was no pushover.

Captain John took Mary aside after Sunday supper and said to her, "My dear, my son is as fine a fellow as can be found anywhere, but he is stubborn and sometimes his temper gets the better of him. He needs a wife with a firm hand. Do you think you can keep him in line?" "Don't worry, Captain," Mary replied with confidence. "I have four brothers. There's not much I haven't already seen!"

So, on September 20, 1879, Asa and Mary were married, and soon they were off to California to start their new life together. The last great frontier in the continental United States beckoned, and another Asa Warren Morris headed west.

A Railroad Adventure

As steel ribbons of track
were laid further and further west,
America was transformed into a modern nation.

On May 10, 1869, ten years before Asa married Mary Call, the *Transcontinental Railroad* was completed, connecting the Union Pacific and the Central Pacific Railroads together at Promontory Point, Utah. Transcontinental meant that trains could travel from one side of America to the other, and it took six years to complete the huge project.

Beginning in Sacramento, thousands of Central Pacific workers laid tracks eastward, blasting through the solid granite walls of California's Sierra Nevada Mountains using dynamite and *nitroglycerine*—a dangerous liquid explosive. On the other end, thousands of Union Pacific workers laid tracks westward from Nebraska, across the great expanse of prairie and the Rocky Mountains. The two railroad companies had a contest to see who could lay the most miles of track in one day. The Central Pacific workers laid ten miles and won!

Where the railroad ran, so did another new invention, the telegraph, and messages could be tapped over the wires from coast to coast. That same year, 1869, a *branch line*, or offshoot of the main railroad line, connected Yolo County with the rest of the country.

Early trains had big problems: exploding engines, buckled tracks, and head-on collisions were just a few of the dangers that plagued railroad travelers. By 1879, when the newlyweds crossed the nation by rail, many problems had been remedied. Plus, there was a railway station in almost every town. So, Asa and Mary Morris were able to travel safely to Yolo County, California, by train—just as Uncle Asa had predicted. Best of all, crossing America by train took just over a week.

Locomotives are the engines that pull train cars. The earliest ones were called Iron Horses because just one of them could pull more weight than hundreds of real horses. Locomotives in those days were driven by steam. They had huge water boilers heated by burning coal or wood, and the fires made a lot of sooty, black smoke.

It took several men to run a train. The engineer was the driver, the fireman stoked the boiler, and the brakemen manually operated the brakes. One brakeman rode in the locomotive, one in every other passenger car, and two in the *caboose* (the very last car). Inside the train, the conductor was responsible for the passengers, and he was assisted by several porters, who also loaded and unloaded baggage.

Trains chugged along, sometimes reaching 50 miles an hour top speed. The rail cars were built mostly of wood, and they creaked and swayed as the wheels rolled over the seams in the tracks with a rhythmic clickety-clack. Train travel had its drawbacks, but even the poorest accommodations beat riding in a covered wagon or getting seasick on a ship.

There were three classes in railroad travel. First Class was the best and the most expensive. The cars were steam-heated, lit by several gas lamps, and had two roomy washing facilities. Wealthy ladies and gentlemen traveled with all the luxuries of home, and there were plenty of porters to fuss over them. The ultimate in First Class comfort was the "Pullman Palace Car." Invented by George Pullman in the 1860s, these cars were beautifully furnished with plush sofas, luxurious carpets, and private sleeping compartments. Palace cars were positioned near the end of the train to keep their passengers as far away as possible from locomotive noise and smoke.

Second Class cost less but was also less luxurious. The car furnishings weren't as fancy but were still comfortable, with steam heating and reclining padded seats.

Third Class was simply called Emigrant Class. An *emigrant* is someone who is moving to a new country or region, to start a new life. Travelers in these cars were generally poor and usually bought one-way tickets to their destination. Emigrant cars were positioned at the front of the train, just behind the locomotive, the coal car, and the baggage car. They took the brunt of the impact if the train had a wreck. Crossing America in an emigrant car was not a trip most passengers cared to repeat.

Accommodations were very basic; there was one gas lamp at each end of the car, one wood-fired stove for heat, and one tiny bathroom facility. Hard wooden back-to-back benches faced one another, and made up the seating. Smoke from the locomotive seeped into these cars making them very dirty, and passengers got grime and soot all over their clothes.

At nighttime, the railroad company sold long boards and rough mattress cushions filled with straw or wood chips that could be placed crosswise on the boards between the benches. With loud snoring and crying babies, it was cold, noisy, and uncomfortable—even for the hardiest traveler.

Since dining cars were not yet widely available, the train stopped about every eight hours at designated dining halls. Passengers were given only twenty minutes to have their meals, so when the train pulled into the station and the doors opened, a hungry mob rushed into the hall. A meal cost a whopping 75 cents, and many passengers were still clutching part of their meals when the train got rolling again.

It was not a simple feat for Asa and Mary to travel from Waynesburg, Pennsylvania, to Woodland, California. In those days there were many individual railroad companies, and each one covered only part of a cross-country route. So, Asa and Mary's trip required seven different trains! Most trains were either a *local,* which stopped at every little town along the route, or a *limited*—an express train that only stopped at big cities. The newlyweds took a local, which made their trip two days longer.

*   *   *

The *Waynesburg and Washington Railroad* was a narrow gauge train that ran on rails three feet apart, instead of the standard four-feet, eight-and-a-half inches. Fondly known as the "Waynie," this little train only covered the twenty-eight winding miles between the southwestern Pennsylvania towns of Waynesburg and Washington.

In Waynesburg, on the autumn morning the newlyweds departed, Mary's father James, hugged his daughter in a rare public display of affection and whispered, "Good luck, my dear. Remember to write to us as soon as you arrive. We will be counting the days." As he shook Asa's hand he cautioned, "Take care of my girl, young man, and don't let her want for anything. I'm depending on you." Asa smiled, "I'll do my best, sir."

Mary's mother Martha, a tiny stern-looking woman, didn't easily betray her feelings, but when her daughter kissed her goodbye, a big solitary tear rolled down her cheek. Martha dabbed her handkerchief to her eyes and Mary felt her own tears well up. She gently took her mother's hands in her own and whispered, "I love you, Mama."

Before Asa and Mary boarded the Waynie, a porter loaded their trunks and household goods into the baggage car. He tagged their baggage so it would be checked through to California. Then, the couple stepped up into the train car. Mary carried a big basket of food, packed by her mother for the journey. Passengers with little money brought their own meals and supplemented them at the dining halls along the way. They settled into their seats and poked their heads out the window. As the train began to roll, they waved goodbye to Mary's parents who quickly became tiny specks on a distant platform. They were off on the adventure of a lifetime!

At Washington, Pennsylvania, Asa and Mary changed trains and traveled north to Pittsburgh on the *Pittsburgh, Cincinnati and St. Louis Railroad.* In Pittsburgh, they changed again and boarded the emigrant car on the *Pennsylvania Railroad* westbound for Chicago.

Soon after they were seated, the conductor came along the aisle and punched their tickets. He was a tall, skinny fellow with a pasty face and cold grey eyes. His railroad uniform was spotless and he sported a waxed, pointy moustache. He took Asa and Mary's tickets and made a hole in them with a big metal punch, which proved that they had paid their fare. He surprised everybody with a big booming voice and spoke his words so precisely that after he had passed by, Asa snickered and said to Mary, "Did you hear that fellow who took our tickets? Looks like a string bean but sounds like a foghorn!" Mary grinned, "Oh, Asa hush, before he hears you!"

Before the train even left the station, the conductor passed by again and offered each passenger a feather pillow.

He gave Asa two and charged him 25 cents apiece. For the newlyweds that was a lot of money.

Asa and Mary looked over their fellow passengers and nobody looked very prosperous. Most were young families, clad in clean but shabby clothing. Some had come from distant lands and they jabbered at each other in foreign tongues. Like the newlyweds, they were off to places unknown to begin a new life.

Mothers clutched their squirming youngsters while the littlest ones screamed at the top of their lungs. Down the aisle from Asa and Mary, two small boys squabbled loudly with one another while their father was distracted with the family's baggage. Both boys had runny noses which they wiped on the backs of their sleeves. They couldn't sit still, so they lurched up and down the aisle grasping at the backs of the benches with their dirty little hands. When they passed Asa and Mary, one of them gave a huge, sloppy sneeze which blew all over Asa. The offender grinned at him and quickly moved on. Disgusted, Asa took out his pocket handkerchief, wiped the side of his face and announced to Mary, "A week of that and I just might clobber those two! Promise me that when we have our own children they will learn better behavior."

On their third pass down the aisle, the conductor finally grabbed the boys by their collars and ordered, "SIT DOWN!" He turned to their father and said, "Sir, would you please control your sons, or I will have to ask you to get off the train."

Doors slammed, baggage men scurried about the platform, and the signalman swept his flag to clear the tracks. "ALL ABOARD!" cried the Conductor. The giant locomotive engine fired, and steam hissed out from under the huge wheels as they began to turn in tandem. Thick smoke billowed out of the smokestack, and the engineer clanged a very loud bell as the train chugged out of the Pittsburgh station, slowly

picking up speed. A short while later, as the scenery went whizzing past, Asa exclaimed, "Who would have ever imagined we'd be traveling at such an astonishing speed!"

When the newlyweds crossed America for the first time, each day dawned in a new place with new scenery. Autumn's artistry had painted the countryside brilliantly. Across Ohio and Indiana, the trees were colored orange and scarlet, yellow and gold, with the falling leaves whirling about in the breezes.

After many hours, the train left the countryside behind and approached the outskirts of a very big city. "CHICAGO, ILLINOIS, next stop!" cried the conductor. "Passengers headed west will please change trains. Consult your timetables!" Grabbing their bags, Asa said to Mary, "We'll have to hurry. Ready? Let's make a run for it!" He took Mary's hand and they ran as fast as they could across the station to the other side and down a long platform to their next train. The *Chicago and Northwestern Railroad*, bound for Council Bluffs, Iowa, was steamed-up and ready to depart. Out of breath and giggling, the two of them plopped into their seats with just moments to spare.

On the rails again, Asa and Mary noticed that Jack Frost had already waved his icy hand over the Great Plains, leaving the remains of harvested crops flattened and discolored. Twenty-two hours later the conductor cried out, "COUNCIL BLUFFS, IOWA, next stop! This is the Pacific transfer station for all passengers headed to California!" The newlyweds made another mad dash to catch the *Union Pacific Railroad* train to Ogden, Utah.

For the next thousand miles, as they crossed an endless vista of flat prairie, Asa remembered that Uncle Asa had traveled this route to California in a covered wagon. Just thirty years later, he and Mary were rolling over the very same route, pulled by a big iron machine! It was remarkable!

Asa and Mary's 1879 Railroad Route

2,780 Miles
9 Days

Pennsylvania

3 Pittsburgh
2 Washington
1 Waynesburg

60 miles

Pennsylvania Enlarged

Railroad Lines

1 Waynesburg & Washington
2 Pittsburgh, Cincinnati & St Louis
3 Pennsylvania (Main Line)
4 Chicago & Northwestern
5 Union Pacific
6 Central Pacific
7 Central Pacific (Marysville Line)

The prairie lands of Iowa and Nebraska gradually gave rise to the rugged foothills of the Rocky Mountains where trees were a welcome sight. An early winter storm had swept across Wyoming and the Great Salt Lake of Utah, dropping snowy bundles on the highest peaks of the Rockies.

"OGDEN, UTAH, next stop! End of this line, Ladies and Gentlemen." For the sixth time, Asa and Mary changed trains, this time boarding the *Central Pacific Railroad* bound for Sacramento, California. Mary noticed that the cars on the Central Pacific were newer, cleaner, and more spacious than the previous emigrant cars, many of which were leftovers from the Civil War era.

The mountains of eastern Utah flattened into expansive salt flats that stretched for miles. When the train finally crept into Nevada, it stopped at a large dining hall in Humboldt—an isolated town where the scenery was nothing but desert. Asa managed to buy one dried-out ham sandwich before the train left again.

"RENO, NEVADA, next stop!" Fierce winds blew clouds of dust and tumbleweeds across the sagebrush and sands of northern Nevada. The train couldn't leave Nevada fast enough for Asa and Mary, who had grown weary of desert scenery.

When they reached the Sierra Nevada Mountains, the engineer kept the locomotive in a slow but steady climb. As the train finally crossed into California, Asa and Mary grew more and more excited. Almost there!

At the Truckee station, they had breathtaking views of the Sierras with their rocky peaks and dense pine forests. Someone opened a window and gusts of frosty, pine-scented air flowed into the stuffy car. Mary nudged Asa and said, "Did you get a whiff of that delicious fresh air? What a relief from the stale air we've been breathing. I already like California!"

Approaching Donner Summit, at an altitude of 7,227 feet, the train passed through dark snow sheds built on the side of the mountain by Chinese laborers. These sheds resembled long tunnels, were made entirely of wood, and they protected the train from avalanches and rock slides. Then the train began to descend, and responsibility shifted from the engineer into the capable hands of the brakemen. By coordinating their efforts, and manually applying the brakes around curves and declines, the brakemen kept the locomotive from becoming a runaway train. Railroad men took their jobs very seriously as their passengers' lives were entirely in their hands.

The train continued its descent into the Sierra foothills with their rusty red soil. It stopped at the old gold mining towns of Alta, Dutch Flat, and Gold Run, all now diminished in size and vitality since the end of the gold rush. A final descent brought them down into the flat Sacramento Valley with its endless vista of prime farmland that one day would supply much of America with fruits, nuts, and vegetables.

"SACRAMENTO, CALIFORNIA, next stop!" cried the conductor, as the train pulled into Sacramento, California's capital city, which sat along the bustling waterfront of the Sacramento River. On her docks, merchandise of all sorts in barrels, crates, and pallets was being loaded and unloaded from small boats and barges. Riverboats carried cargo and also took passengers back and forth regularly to San Francisco. The busy streets, where merchants sold lumber, hardware, and dry goods, were clogged with horse-drawn wagons and pedestrians trying to avoid getting run over. Off in the distance, Asa and Mary could see the newly completed, white California Capitol building with its magnificent golden dome.

Their final train change was in Sacramento to the *Central Pacific Railroad* Marysville Line which went west over a long wooden trestle to Davisville, and then headed north. Only a few miles left to go, and then... "WOODLAND, CALIFORNIA, next stop!" cried the conductor. Asa lowered the train window and they poked their heads out for a closer look. As far as the eye could see, acres and acres of crops grew in flat spacious fields, guarded by stout Valley Oaks standing like sentries. Fruit and nut orchards thrived in the loamy soil. Sheep and beef cattle grazed on vast ranches, each with its own fine house. The sun was shining and the crisp autumn air was filled with the scents of harvest. For a Pennsylvania farmer's son, it was the next best thing to heaven.

As the train approached the station at the east end of town, a conductor reappeared and told Asa that he must return the pillows he had paid for at the beginning of the journey. Apparently, Asa was supposed to have turned them in at the end of each railroad company line, but he had unknowingly put them inside his bag and carried them from train to train instead. This conductor assumed they belonged to his Central Pacific line. "Sir, I must insist that you return the pillows," the conductor repeated. This didn't set well with Asa as nobody had said anything about RENTING the pillows. After a week of use, he thought the pillows were his own property.

He confronted the conductor, "Do you mean to tell me that you expect me to return these pillows I paid good money for, carried on five different trains, and used for a week? Why, they're all grubby and smelly and who would want them?" The conductor shifted from one foot to the other, looked Asa in the eye and boomed, "You weren't supposed to do that, Sir. Besides, it is company policy!" Asa didn't like the sound of that. He grew red in the face and his cowlick stood straight up. "I don't care what company policy is. I paid for these pillows and I intend to keep them!" "But, Sir . . ." cried the flustered conductor, "you *can't* KEEP those pillows. I'll have to report you to the management!"

With temper in full throttle Asa shouted, "The heck I can't. If I can't keep them, neither can you!" With that, he pulled out his pocket knife, held the pillows over the open window, and ripped them from one end to the other. Chicken feathers flew everywhere, and a cloud of them blew down like snow on the tracks next to the train.

Mary did her best to keep from giggling at the sight of the conductor's shocked face. The two of them high-tailed it off that train in a hurry and didn't look back! When they had made their way down to the other end of the station, they both burst out laughing. "It'll be awhile before that fellow forgets *us*!" Asa declared.

They looked at each other and grinned—they were both very dusty and rumpled from the trip. Asa gave his bride a broad smile and asked, "Well, what do you think?" Mary, who was always practical, said, "It certainly is very flat here, but I like all the big oak trees and the mountains in the distance. I expect we'll get used to it."

So, on November 7, 1879, with just fifty dollars and sixty cents in his pocket, a strong back, and a willing heart, Asa and his bride arrived in Woodland, California.

PART THREE

The California Farmer

Uncle Asa's Ranch

Success is not defined only in terms of money;
it is a measure of a person's character.

Relieved to finally be off the train, Mary fussed with her bonnet, smoothed her skirts, and wiped a smear of dirt from Asa's nose with her last clean handkerchief. She looked at their wrinkled, sooty clothes and asked, "Whatever will your uncle think of us, looking so dirty and untidy?" Asa looked at her shining eyes and wisps of curly hair escaping from her bonnet and smiled. "Don't you worry—he'll think you're the prettiest niece an uncle ever had."

Down the road a distance, a horse and wagon were approaching, which soon pulled up next to the tracks. "Asa Morris?" asked a young man wearing overalls and a plaid cap. He jumped down from his seat and doffed his cap at Mary. "Howdy do, Ma'am. My name's Sam Maxwell. I work for your uncle and he sent me to fetch you. Let's put your trunks in back and then you sit up here on the bench so you can see the town."

Sam drove them slowly down Woodland's thriving Main Street. It was an impressive town. The Bank of Woodland rose tall and strong, guardian of the community's wealth, and nearby, a Wells Fargo and Co. Express office transported goods and merchandise all across the nation. In front of the general merchandise store were barrels of autumn pumpkins, gourds, and ears of Indian corn. Next door, a harness maker displayed tooled leather saddles and sleek riding crops in his shop window. The grand looking Craft Hotel covered a whole block and dominated the center of town.

As they passed by, Asa pointed to a drinking saloon and shook his head. He didn't approve of drinking liquor—EVER! From its earliest beginnings, Greene County had manufactured and sold thousands of gallons of whiskey. Growing up, Asa had seen enough drunkenness amongst his neighbors to last a lifetime. He thought a clean and sober life was the only remedy. Little did he know, as he saw Woodland for the first time, that the town had almost forty saloons which caused plenty of trouble and that a battle was brewing to confront this issue.

Mary noticed the covered wooden walkways along Woodland's storefronts that kept pedestrians off the dusty road. Many well-dressed ladies and gentlemen strolled along looking in the shop windows. On the north side of Main Street was the Opera House where actors, musicians, and singing groups called *minstrels* performed. Woodland was a cultured, well-to-do town and the newlyweds liked it. And, growing in front of the courthouse, they saw their very first palm tree! Asa pointed to that curiosity and exclaimed to Mary, "Have you ever seen the likes of that!" Years later he would grow them in his own front garden.

Sam turned north just outside of town. As they bumped and jostled over the rutted road, the wind came up suddenly and almost blew off Mary's bonnet. "Watch that north wind Ma'am," Sam cautioned. "It can blow something fierce here, hot in summer and freezing in winter." During the seven mile drive to Uncle Asa's farm, Sam continued to chatter away about the area, but they didn't hear much of what he said, as they were both overcome with anticipation.

When Sam turned the wagon left onto a lane lined with black walnut trees, Asa and Mary were completely astonished to see Uncle Asa's grand and beautiful house. It was designed in the decorative style of the day called *Italianate*—which means it was really fancy—and it was surrounded by a long picket fence, beautiful flowers, and shade trees.

The house sat on a foundation of bricks made on the farm. Its walls were built of strong mountain fir completely faced with California redwood, which was painted light green and trimmed in shades of dark green and burgundy. It was two stories tall, and the broad front porch was framed with six distinctive square wooden columns, clustered near the center. Above the porch, beneath a large central *gable*, was a balcony with a railing of scrolled woodwork. (A gable is a small peaked roof that juts out from the main roofline.) Ornate woodcarving surrounded the roofline, the corners, and all the windows, and wide stairs led to massive double front doors with an etched glass window above. The quality and size of Uncle Asa's house showed the wealth of its owner; Asa and Mary had never seen anything like it.

Next to the house stood a tall, square water tower, and nearby was a cast bronze dinner bell atop a long pole. Behind the house stood two barns, a carriage house, a chicken coop, and tidy, fenced pastures where horses and cattle grazed.

The land was cultivated and planted with wheat, barley, and other crops. It was an outstanding ranch, and the young people couldn't believe that the older man had achieved so much for himself in the years since he had left Pennsylvania.

Uncle Asa's grand house

When they pulled up, the front doors burst open and Uncle Asa stepped out onto the porch. He was still a lean, tanned, and energetic man but he looked much older than Asa remembered. His hair was almost completely white and he wore a long full beard. At first glance he looked like a weather-beaten Santa Claus, but his bright blue eyes were kindly and they lit up when he saw his nephew. His large hands had the thick calluses of a hardworking man, and his handshake was very firm. In a hearty voice he exclaimed, "Well, well, well! So you've finally arrived! How was the trip? Easier than coming the way I did, I'll bet! I dare say you're much taller than the last time we met! What were you, nine or ten?"

The two Asas grinned at each other. "And this lovely lady is your new bride? How do you do my dear? I remember your father, James; knew him well when we were boys—a very good fellow indeed."

Mary extended her little white hand which was dwarfed in his. "Call me Uncle if you like," he said as he patted her hand. Mary blushed and said, "Uncle Asa, I hope you will forgive our appearance. The train was very dirty." Uncle Asa gave her a warm smile and chuckled, "You should have seen me when we pulled into Hangtown on the wagon train! Talk about dirty—filthy was more like it! Why, I was so smelly that even a skunk would have disowned me!"

"Ah, here is your aunt." Uncle Asa gestured to his dark haired young wife, Mary Alice, who was only about five years older than Asa's bride—making them more like sisters than aunt and niece. She had a long face with high cheek-bones, very dark hair, and dark eyes; her distinctive features showed her strength of character. Uncle Asa introduced them with a twinkle in his eye. "Mary Morris, meet Mary Morris! Now what shall we ever do about that?" Not only were uncle and nephew both named Asa Warren Morris, but their wives had the same first and last names, too. It was bound to get confusing! The younger Asa solved the problem. "Mary's family has always called her Mollie," he explained. So, from then on, Asa's bride was known by everybody as Mollie Morris.

Uncle Asa's two youngsters, Lindsay and Jennie Belle, hid behind Mary Alice's long skirts, giggling and peeking at the newcomers. They were introduced, and then took off running around the yard, squealing and jumping up and down with excitement. A small dog and two nanny goats joined in their romping.

The younger couple was given a tour of the house, which was as magnificent on the inside as it was on the outside. The parlor, dining, and sitting rooms had imported Italian marble fireplaces and were filled with fine furniture. A sweeping staircase with a hand-carved walnut banister led to the upstairs rooms. Uncle Asa had even installed gas lanterns for nighttime lighting.

After the tour, Uncle Asa said, "Go ahead upstairs now and wash up, first room on your left. Afterwards, we'll have some refreshments and a visit."

When they came back down, he gestured to the porch chairs, "Have a seat here and rest yourselves. Mary Alice, my dear, can we give these young folks a glass of lemonade to wet their whistles?" They settled on the porch where the view of prime farmland was inspiring for a hopeful young man. "Well now, Nephew," said Uncle Asa, "you know California is destined to be a great state, so you've come to the right place. What do you think of the ranch?" Asa was so impressed he didn't know what to say.

Later, Uncle Asa escorted Asa and Mollie to a little white house which sat alongside the main road. It was a simple structure with a lopsided sloping roof and small rooms but it was perfect for the newlyweds. Mollie stood on the steps and smiled at Asa. "Can you believe it? We're finally here! A few flowers, a vegetable garden, and we'll have ourselves a very nice home," she said confidently. "We're so lucky that Uncle Asa offered us this opportunity." Asa nodded, and put his arm around her shoulders. Then he gave her a tender kiss, and said, "I'm the lucky one—to have you as my wife." Mollie's face glowed with happiness.

As they stood together on the porch of their new home, Asa took a good look at the miles of fertile fields surrounded by the distant mountains. He hoped that one day he, too, might be as successful as Uncle Asa. The following day, he began a new life to make that possible.

Asa and Mollie's little white house on Uncle Asa's ranch

The Farmhand and the Missus

Farmers are special people, who see endless potential
in a field of dirt. But farming is a never-ending job
that doesn't care if you're tired and doesn't wait
for sunshine and good weather.

"Always remember, respect this land and it will repay
you in kind," Uncle Asa advised his nephew as they toured his
ranch on horseback the following morning. "This is God's
country and if you can't make it grow here it probably won't
grow anywhere!"

Asa remembered those words when he was up to his
eyeballs in corn and the wheat crop was so dense that he had
to beat a path through it to find the road. Crops certainly did
grow splendidly in Yolo County. It was also a great place to
raise animals, and the ranch had plenty of livestock that
needed daily tending.

Even though he was Uncle Asa's kin, Asa didn't expect
any special privileges. He worked just as hard as the three
other farmhands employed on the ranch. Sam Maxwell, who
had collected them from the train, was from Missouri. Tom
Fern was from England and he uttered many curious
expressions that Asa simply couldn't make out. One morning

as they were talking about what to do with a big pile of leftover potatoes from the garden, Tom told him, "Me Mum made the best 'Bubble and Squeak' in the county." Asa laughed and asked, "What on earth is that?" Tom replied, "It's a sort o' mash with leftover veg and potato fried up with a bit o' meat. It's jolly good!"

Jim Dan (Chen Dan Ho) was from China. His folks had come to California when Jim was a youngster so his father could work building the railroad. Jim had a difficult time speaking English, and Asa often had to ask him to repeat himself just to get the gist of what he was saying. Despite their different backgrounds, they were all hard-working, good-hearted fellows.

Every day, Uncle Asa supervised his farmhands who worked from dawn to dusk. Motorized tractors hadn't been invented yet, so all the heavy farm machinery such as plows, threshers, and harvesters were pulled using draft horses and large mule teams. Draft horses are gigantic and very powerful. Fortunately, they are usually good natured and gentle—which is a good thing because they often weigh over 2,000 pounds and can easily squash a man if they get riled up.

Asa's jobs varied depending on the season. He plowed fields, planted seeds, harvested crops, and baled hay. He milked fourteen cows every morning before breakfast. He cleaned the barns, and fed, groomed, and saddled the horses. He chased down runaway livestock, mended fences, and shot coyotes and foxes with his shotgun. He was REALLY tired by the end of the day!

Asa was a big thinker. He was able to look ahead for new opportunities, and during the years he worked as a farmhand he became interested in breeding dairy cattle. Beef cattle had grazed Yolo County pastures for some twenty years, but the dairy industry was still in its infancy and Asa realized its future potential. Since his boyhood days with Marigold, he had always liked dairy cows and could see ways to improve them. He set a goal for himself to breed the finest quality dairy

Uncle Asa's Ranch
Cutting sorghum and harvesting wheat with draft horses

cattle in the state, maybe even the whole United States! But many years would pass before he had enough experience and money to make that happen.

Uncle Asa had a wealth of practical experience and common sense, so Asa paid attention and learned everything he needed to know about growing crops and raising cattle. He worked very hard and didn't miss a single day's labor in five years. At the end of each day, when he looked down at his callused hands, he knew that every blister and splinter he got was bringing him closer to his goal.

Nobody's life is without troubles. Some days everything went wrong and Asa was just plain discouraged. The barley crop showed signs of insect damage; a highly valued animal unexpectedly died despite his best efforts; it rained so much that preparations for planting were ruined in a muddy mess. It didn't really matter what it was—sometimes, a farmer's lot is disappointing.

He would go home to Mollie at the end of the day with a scowl on his face. Mollie was a patient woman but she didn't put up with that nonsense. She would give Asa a *pep talk*— which is like a swift kick in the pants, only with words. "Remember why we came here, Asa? OPPORTUNITY! You know there is nothing better for us back in Greene County and at least we don't have to dig our way out of the snow. Besides, we both knew it wouldn't be easy here, so buck up and tomorrow will be better, you'll see."

In the summer of 1880, Asa and Mollie were expecting their first child. Uncle Asa suggested that the baby be born in the soft surroundings of his big home where Mollie would be more comfortable. So, on June 20, 1880, Mollie gave birth to their son Frank Leslie Morris in Uncle Asa's ornate, high-backed mahogany bed. Asa was thrilled with his boy who gave him one more reason to succeed. Like all proud papas, he thought his new son was the handsomest, smartest baby in the county. Uncle Asa gave his nephew a cigar, and the fellows on the farm gave him their warmest congratulations and a hearty slap on the back. Then, they all went back to work.

Asa and Mollie missed their families in Pennsylvania. Letters were mailed back and forth between Yolo and Greene Counties so everybody could keep up to date with family news. They wrote pages and pages about baby Frank and about Uncle Asa's new son William Campbell Morris, who was born just three months after Frank. Plus, there were always interesting things happening on Uncle Asa's ranch.

There was lots of news from Greene County, too. Captain John had remarried and wrote that he and his wife Elizabeth had welcomed twins named Joseph and Sadie— which meant Asa had a new half-brother and half-sister the very same year he himself became a father! They wrote back and forth that the weather in Pennsylvania was exceptionally warm, that the wheat crop in Yolo was taller than anybody could remember, and that old Mrs. McGlumphy, who lived down the road from Captain John, had died during a terrible rainstorm and the ground was too waterlogged to bury her!

Asa's brothers and sisters wrote to him as well. Artie had married Mr. Goodwin Hunt the previous spring, and brother John was inventing some interesting things out in the barn. James had plans to study for the ministry, and Elijah was getting top marks in school. Sis wrote that her son Clyde had just lost his first front tooth, and the tooth fairy had been very good to him. They wrote about all the ordinary things that mean so much when families are far apart.

After five years of labor on Uncle Asa's ranch, Asa took Mollie and four-year-old Frank back to Greene County for an extended family visit. They stayed with Mollie's parents and everyone was very pleased to have them back.

Frank was the center of attention. His grandfathers, Captain John Morris and James Call, were delighted with their young grandson, and each one claimed that the lad was the spitting image of himself at that age. Like two old roosters they crowed about Frank to all their neighbors. Mollie was amused by their antics and said, "Maybe you two should wait until he grows up to decide which one of you he looks like. Besides, you will soon have another grandchild to brag about." Sure enough, on February 7, 1885, Asa and Mollie's second son, Charles Call Morris, was born. Asa was a proud father once again and the grandfathers crowed more than ever!

But, as the months passed, the comforts of family and the familiar scenes of his Pennsylvania boyhood just weren't enough for Asa. California had gotten under his skin. She was in his blood, and she called him back.

Adventures of an Entrepreneur

Entrepreneurs are people with a lot of brains and spunk.
They take big risks to build their own businesses from
scratch, and they generally try several things
before they succeed.

Back in Yolo County, Asa longed to spread his wings,
so he leased a piece of property and began farming for himself.
He didn't have enough money to start up his own dairy farm
yet, but he had enough to raise crops on his leased land, and
part of the time he still worked for Uncle Asa. He was always
on the lookout for new ways to make money.

One day Mollie held up the stump of a straw broom
and complained that it was hard to find a decent broom; they
just fell to pieces even though they cost good money at the dry
goods store. So Asa got the notion to make brooms himself. He
bought a broom-making machine called the McCombs "Old
Reliable" which he set up in the barn, and he trained himself
to work it. It ran by peddles using foot power, not electricity.
He grew sorghum, a grain crop with many uses—one of which
was broom straw—and he also designed improvements in the
structure of his brooms. His designs were road-tested by
Mollie, and after several flops, she declared them the best she

had ever used. Asa sold his brooms to the local farmers' wives and the dry goods store in Woodland. It was just a side business, but it helped pay the bills and he developed another valuable skill.

The "Old Reliable" McCombs Machine

is sold outright for cash, or is placed on lease on monthly payments for a definite number of months until paid for. The monthly payment plan enables you to make the saving over hand sewing pay for the machine.

WRITE US FOR INFORMATION ABOUT IT.

Our power tieing machines are fast replacing the old style "squirrel cage" foot tieing machines (and other makes of power machines, too, for that matter), and there is nothing else on the market quite so well made and so durable. We keep them in stock—both right and left hand.

Our power burl cutter is also a favorite machine—especially in the small shop where the attached sizer is not a necessity.

Hand Stitch Broom Sewing Machine Company
1215 House Building, ∴ **PITTSBURG, PA.**

Asa's broom making machine

Asa experimented with several newer crops like sugar beets. Yolo County had just the right soil and climate, and the beets grew like crazy. The Spreckles Sugar Company heard about the great success that Yolo farmers had been having and came to investigate the rumors. In the following years, the sugar beet industry really took off and Spreckles built a sugar processing plant north of Woodland.

Meanwhile, in the little white house, Mollie was busy. On July 31, 1887, a third little boy was born. They named him Harry Van Wey Morris. Asa beamed when he saw his new son and said, "Three of them, Mollie! My grandmother always said that the Morrises had a LOT of boys!"

Harry was barely in short pants before Asa grew restless again. He came up with a scheme to open a butcher shop in Fresno County, so he talked to his uncle about his ideas. Uncle Asa was a living example of the entrepreneurial spirit and rather than express concern about possible risks, he encouraged his nephew to pursue new opportunities. He also cautioned, "Remember, Nephew, I served my time in the gold mines and it wasn't the great success I'd hoped for. But every man should be free to take his chances and make his own mistakes. It's part of the tradition of our great country. Go ahead with your plans, but remember that I'm getting to be an old man. I had always hoped that you would take over and manage the ranch for my boys when I'm gone. If things don't work out, come back to Yolo County."

So, Asa moved his family to Fresno, California, about two hundred miles south of Woodland. It was drier, hotter, and even flatter than Yolo County, and Mollie didn't care for the place at all. Asa opened his butcher shop and as a sideline he began to deal in dairy cattle. Within a year, the butcher shop was very successful, but Asa discovered that he didn't really like butchering; he preferred cattle on the hoof.

He decided to sell the shop, but kept on with the business of trading dairy cattle. Then, still exploring new business ideas, he took his profits and bought a raisin vineyard. Asa didn't know the first thing about raisins, but that didn't stop him! He was a fast learner and eager to get ahead.

Asa Morris about 1890

Table grapes, when picked and dried, become raisins. They grew exceptionally well in Fresno County where they were becoming a popular crop. Prices for them had sky-rocketed and there was fierce competition between growers. Mollie wasn't keen on the raisin farm idea and told him so in no uncertain terms. "Asa, this is the last scheme I'm going to put up with. Why can't you be content to make a modest living like other men? If we go belly-up in this raisin venture, we're going home to Yolo!"

Too bad Asa didn't invest in wine grapes instead of raisin grapes, since wine became a lasting industry which thrives in California today! But Asa was so dead set against drinking, he would never have dreamed of raising grapes that could make people drunk. Within a year of his experiment, there were altogether too many raisin farmers in Fresno, and the price of raisins plummeted. Years later, Asa described his time there as, "Not one of my wiser decisions, but I did learn to buy and sell good dairy cows, even ones that other people thought were only fit for the slaughter house."

The best thing that came from Fresno was yet ANOTHER baby boy, born November 19, 1889. They named him Asa James Morris. As a little fellow, he had an ongoing problem with droopy trousers, and the family constantly told him to hitch-up his britches. The nickname "Britches" stuck.

*   *   *

In April, 1891, Uncle Asa became seriously ill. He summoned his wife Mary Alice to his bedside and whispered, "The land is yours, my dear. Hand the reigns of the ranch over to Asa until our own boys are old enough to manage it themselves. He is a good man and will do well by you." A few days later, on April 29, Uncle Asa passed away. He was sixty-five years old and had lived a very adventurous, full, and satisfying life.

An urgent telegram arrived in Fresno announcing Uncle Asa's passing. His nephew boarded the next train for Woodland and arrived just in time for the funeral. Uncle Asa was buried next to his beloved Jane. After the family had gone home, Asa stood beside the grave, bowed his head and bid a special goodbye to the man who had taught him so much.

Mary Alice was left to care for four growing children and a 640-acre ranch. She asked Asa to bring his family back to Yolo County and run the ranch for her. He accepted the job. The timing was just right, since the raisin farm in Fresno had failed. The whole family returned to Yolo County, and for the next thirteen years, management of Uncle Asa's ranch rested in Asa's capable hands.

A Passel of Boys

In the old days, a man with four sons
was considered a lucky fellow.
Boys provided a built-in labor force,
but they also caused a lot of trouble.

    Asa was a good manager. He trained his four boys and
Uncle Asa's two boys, Lindsay and Will, to farm the land and
care for cattle, just as Uncle Asa had taught him. He increased
crop yields by improving irrigation, so the ranch's fertile soil
truly became "pay dirt."

    Asa kept his passel of boys busy, but even with all their
chores they still had time to make mischief. Frank was five
years older than his brothers, so while they were still too little
to be any fun, Frank played outside with his cousin Will
Morris, and with Will's cousin, Charley Campbell. Uncle Asa's
ranch was very large with lots of places for games like Hide
and Seek. Sometimes the boys dreamed up their own games,
specially designed to scare the living daylights out of each
other!

    As an agricultural experiment, some well-meaning fool
had planted bamboo in the field south of Uncle Asa's big
house. Bamboo is a bushy, tropical plant which grows in tall,

The four young Morris brothers on their best behavior
Charley, Britches, Frank, and Harry

thick canes that are very strong. Once you plant bamboo, you can never get rid of it, because it spreads underground and soon you have a big grove. That old bamboo grove is still there today even after one hundred and twenty years!

One day Frank, Will, and Charley sat behind the barn picking their teeth with straws. They had exhausted every game they knew, and they were just plain bored. Charley Campbell came up with a new idea, and with a gleam in his eye he said, "Say fellas, you see that tall stuff growin' over there? What say we make a race for it? First one out the other side wins." Without warning Frank spat out his piece of straw and yelled, "You bet! C'mon fellas, I dare ya! LET'S CRASH THE BAMBELINAS!"

This outburst prompted a mad dash towards the bamboo with all three running at top speed, screaming like banshees. BAM!!! Head first into the grove they went, forcing their way through the dense canes. But, bamboo is not afraid of little boys. In fact, it saw them coming and made sure that it tore their clothes and scratched them plenty.

The three burst out on the other side of the grove screeching with laughter and rubbing their wounds. Charley, whose leg was scraped and bleeding, claimed victory. Frank had a shaft of dried leaves sticking out of his hair, a bloody scratch running up the side of his nose, and a big hole ripped in his shirt. Will didn't fare any better. They don't call it "BAM" boo for nothing!

When she saw the boys coming across the field, Mollie just shook her head. Their games always resulted in some sort of bloodshed. "Frank!" she scolded, "At it again, I see. I just wish you would wear the same shirt each time so I don't have to keep mending them. Better yet, why not leave the shirt behind next time and run naked? And don't you dare come crying to me when you're all scratched and bleeding!"

Like most boys, the Morris brothers were sometimes naughty, especially when the other three got big enough to cause trouble, too. One afternoon, they decided to try smoking. Most of the grown-up farmhands rolled their own cigarettes and they looked really *sophisticated*—which means worldly—when they smoked. Since the boys had no money for real tobacco, they used corn husks for wrappers and "corn silk," which is the stringy part under the husk, for tobacco. The corn silk was damp so it took lots of matches to get their cigarettes to burn, and they cast each burnt match on the ground.

The nasty smelling smoke wafted out from behind the barn, and the four of them coughed so much that they made a lot of ruckus. "Phew! Tastes awful!" Harry exclaimed. "The real stuff must be better than this or they wouldn't bother with it." Frank looked around and cautioned, "Keep it down, would you fellas, or Pop will hear us, and you know what that means . . . Uh Oh! I think he heard us. Yep! Here he comes and his cowlick is sticking up, so LOOK OUT!"

Asa had gotten wind of their smoking experiment and he wasn't at all amused. He marched around the corner of the barn with a face like thunder and exclaimed, "What in Sam Hill are you boys doing back here?" He looked down at the ground and saw the litter of burnt wooden matches. "This is a disgusting business and to top it off, you've darn near set the barn on fire! Have you any idea of the consequences if you burn down the barn?" He saw Harry with a guilty look on his face holding one of his hands behind his back. "And Harry, give me those matches! Frank, I hold you responsible for this as you're old enough to know better. Where are your brains, Son? I'm ashamed of you all." The next stop was the woodshed for a paddling!

As the boys grew older their pranks got wilder. Old houses in those days had no indoor plumbing, so toilets were placed in an *outhouse*. Mothers called it the *privy* because that was more refined. The privy was a small, wooden building built over a smelly cesspit some distance from the house for obvious reasons. Inside, was a wooden seat, sometimes two, and a stack of old newspapers instead of modern toilet paper. You had to be really careful that the seat was kept smoothly sanded or you might get a splinter in your backside. Plus, it was easy to get distracted reading the funny papers in the scraps of newspaper. Cartoon characters were always getting into trouble, sometimes providing the boys with further inspiration for mischief.

One day Lindsay and Will Morris cooked up a secret plot to move the family privy. The way they chose to move it was not only reckless, but downright dangerous!

All four of Asa's boys were in on the plot. Lindsay, the oldest, had discovered a stash of dynamite stored in a crate in the barn. Dynamite was not regulated in those days, and Asa occasionally used it to remove tree stumps, big rocks, and hard pan—which is very compressed soil. Dynamite required both a wick and a percussion cap to make it explode, and in the wrong hands it was deadly. Lindsay managed to remove a single stick from the stash, hoping that Asa wouldn't notice.

One Saturday morning, Mary Alice and her daughter Kate decided to go to Woodland for the day leaving Lindsay and Will at home. Before she drove off in the buggy, Mary Alice warned, "Now you boys be good while I'm gone and don't you dare make any trouble!"

Her warning went unheeded. Asa was busy plowing out on the north portion of the ranch, and Mollie had gone to the neighbor's house to have tea, so the six boys thought they were in the clear.

Lindsay was the ringleader and declared that since he had seen it done before, he would place the dynamite. He crept up to the privy, looking over his shoulder all the while. The others hung back, hiding in and around the barn, hoping nobody would see them.

Uncle Asa had built every ranch building very strongly, even the privy, which sat on heavy skids so it could be moved when necessary. Lindsay figured the dynamite would be most effective right down inside the hole. Holding his nose, he placed the cap and lowered the dynamite stick down by its wick until it caught on a cross timber. He lit the wick and ran away as fast as he could, throwing himself head first into a pile of straw. The others covered their ears and waited. Several tense minutes passed and nothing happened.

Lindsay had just poked his head up out of the hay when suddenly there was a terrific BOOOMMMM! It shook the ground where the boys were hiding, and they saw the privy blow straight up in the air. WOW!!! What a sight! The boys howled with pride. But, after such a rocketing success, the privy landed exactly where it was before! Oh Dear! What a disappointment! They looked at each other and Will shouted, "This is all your fault Lindsay! You should have put the dynamite on the outside instead of down the hole. What a dumb idea!"

From across the road Asa heard the boom; he raced to the scene and quickly assessed that nobody was hurt. Despite a big scorch mark in the field, a blackened privy door hanging by one hinge, and some lingering smoke, the damage was minimal. It didn't take him long to figure out that a privy does not just shoot into space on its own; it needed a bit of help, and he was pretty sure where that help was hiding!

Asa found them up in the hayloft, whispering to each other. He marched them down the ladder and stood all six of them in a row. For a few moments he was completely silent. Next he squinted at each one and tugged at his moustache. His

cowlick stood straight up and his face grew redder and redder. Then he completely blew his stack, which was much scarier for the culprits than the dynamite!

The boys got a tongue lashing the likes of which they had never had before and a belt lashing that their backsides would not soon forget. They were put to work filling in the smelly old hole and digging a new one. Then they had to move the scorched privy with a pulley and ropes and repair it.

When Mary Alice returned home she was dumbfounded by the exploits of the six hooligans. She groaned to Asa, "Where in the world do they get these ideas? They can't be left unguarded even for a few hours."

But the story didn't end there. The "rocketing privy" became the stuff of family legend, and each succeeding generation passed the story down to their children and their grandchildren.

*   *   *

Many of the Morris ancestors were inventors. They had logical minds and clever hands that developed new farming and irrigation methods, new types of machinery, and time-saving dairy techniques.

Asa's boys, particularly Harry, inherited this talent for invention. The crowning achievement of their youthful follies was the invention of a homemade roller coaster. This creation made Mollie's heart jump into her throat every time she looked at it.

The boys got the idea to build a ramp from the upper barn door in the hayloft down to the ground, a drop of about twelve feet. They planned to run a small cart on wheels down the ramp with one of them riding in it. Construction of this wonder took all the *ingenuity* (creative inventiveness) they could muster, as well as all the scrap lumber and spare nails around the ranch.

Since this project was out in the open, Asa was aware of his sons' intentions. He was secretly proud that his four boys had enough gumption to tackle such a project. But he cautioned, "You have my permission as long as it doesn't interfere with schoolwork or chores, and as long as you don't kill yourselves in the process. Your mother wouldn't like that!"

Mollie was so upset when she saw what they were planning that she cornered Asa and said, "Are you really going to let them do this? I'll never forgive you if one of them is badly hurt or worse." Asa replied, "At least this time their antics are out in the open and I can check on them. Besides, maybe one of them will become a structural engineer!"

So, the ramp was built. It was about two feet wide and twenty feet long with low boards nailed on the sides to keep the cart on course. Since the lumber was a collection of scraps, the result was a rickety structure held up by old fence posts and barn boards. The cart was about two feet long by fifteen inches wide, built from an old fruit crate. Harry made the wheels in the woodshop from wooden spools, metal rods, and bolts. The finished product was a sight to behold, and the four rascals proudly christened their work, "The CHUTE." Asa looked it over carefully and pronounced it workable.

"Hey fellas," said Frank, "Which one of us is goin' to be the test pilot? Since I'm the oldest I think it should be me." Harry countered with some common sense, "Seems to me that you're also the heaviest and maybe we should have the lightest one of us try it first to see if it works." All eyes turned to Britches. "How 'bout it Britch?" Frank asked. "Want to be the first fella to Shoot the Chute?" The smallest and most courageous of the lot, Britches agreed. Finally, he would achieve some recognition often denied the youngest son!

So, up the ladder they went to the hayloft. Britches wore old clothes for his solo performance and tucked newspaper into the seat of his pants—since the cart was made of very splintery wood. As he climbed in he gave a thumbs-up sign to his brothers, gripped the sides and declared, "Ready to shoot!" Mollie watched her small red-headed son from a safe distance, squeezed her eyes shut, and said a prayer. Asa grinned from ear to ear.

With a simple light push the cart began to roll down the chute, bumping over the seams in the lumber and gaining speed. WHOOSH! Halfway down, a wheel caught on a nail head and the cart tipped sideways. Out flew Britches, over the ramp, hollering his head off. In seconds he landed with a thud on the dirt below and Asa came running. "Are you alright Son?" he asked as he helped the boy to his feet. Britches had had the wind knocked out of him and was a bit wobbly. When he caught his breath, he waved his fists in the air and declared with a shout, "That was **T E R R I F I C ! ! !** Mollie breathed a sigh of relief.

Fortunately, Britches had landed on his backside and no bones were broken, but for the next week his bottom was black and blue. "Shooting the Chute" was off to a rocky start, but the boys remembered the thrill of it for the rest of their lives.

A Mother's Job Never Ends

Our ancestor mothers were unpaid heroes
who raised generations of Americans.

For Mollie, raising four rowdy boys was a non-stop job. They were noisy and careless, demanding and petty, but she loved them anyway. The little white house was stuffed to the gills. There was plenty of moaning and groaning—with four young rascals underfoot—but they all made do, even if they tripped over one another. Every day Mollie rose about five o'clock in the morning, pumped water by hand, heated it on a wood fired stove to make coffee, and then cooked ham and eggs for breakfast.

Before her sons left for school, she checked to make sure that their hands and faces were washed. She buttoned up their jackets, gave each one a kiss, and handed them their *satchels* (old-fashioned leather straps that held their books together). On cold days she tucked baked potatoes into their pockets to keep their hands warm, and later they had them for lunch.

She waved to them as they tramped down the road to the Buchannan Schoolhouse. It was one large room where all the pupils sat in separate rows by grade level. The lady teacher, called a *schoolmarm,* was very strict and did not allow any nonsense. She taught reading, writing, and arithmetic. Lessons for the older pupils also included geography and history.

When they came home from school their lessons continued. With the idea in mind of a future business in dairy cattle, Asa trained each of his boys to work with the *scrub cows* that lived on Uncle Asa's ranch. These cows were mixed breeds that grazed on the scrub grasses in the fields. Britches showed a special talent with the scrubs, but all the boys became good dairymen.

The boys grumbled to their mother about the long working hours, but Asa ignored their complaints and sent them on to the next chore. He said firmly, "Get your overalls on and get out to the barn. Those cows can't wait, you know." When Asa was well out of earshot, Charley griped to his brothers, "Cows! Cows! Cows! Doesn't Pop ever think about anything else?" Mollie overheard him from the kitchen as he slammed the door on his way out. Later, when she told Asa, he laughed so hard that he popped the top button on his britches and said, "He might as well get used to it—there will be more cows in his future!"

Mollie managed all the time-consuming tasks necessary to run a household in the days before electricity. She didn't have a washing machine or a dishwasher, and instead of a refrigerator, she had an ice box. The ice man came regularly with his wagon to deliver big blocks of ice packed in straw. Ice came from winter's frozen lakes and streams, not your freezer. Foods that spoiled easily like milk and meat were kept cold in the ice box.

Mollie had a lot to do to feed her family. She grew her own vegetables and spent lots of time storing and preserving them. Firm fruits and vegetables like apples, carrots, and potatoes were stored in a root cellar under the house where it

Mollie Morris about 1890

was dark and cool all year. Peaches, apricots, and tomatoes could be dried in the sun, or canned to carry the family through the winter. Canning involved cutting up hundreds of pounds of fruit and vegetables and cooking them in a big boiling kettle. The hot mixture was ladled into glass "Mason" jars, and when they were closed with rubber seals and screw-on metal lids, you could hear the lid contract with a peculiar "schuuuuppppp" sound. This meant the jar was sealed air tight and the food lasted a good long while.

*   *   *

During the day Mollie mended shirts and trousers, baked bread, cleaned house, and cooked meals. She washed endless piles of clothes in a big metal tub and hung them out to dry with wooden clothes pins on a long clothesline. The boys tended to accumulate a lot of interesting things in their pockets so Mollie never knew just what to expect when she emptied them out: live lizards, dead bugs, earthworms, foxtails, pieces of string, blackboard chalk. . . the list went on. She took to having a rolling pin close at hand just in case something nasty popped out that was still alive! Sometimes washing took all day, but if there was any time leftover she went over to visit Mary Alice in the big house to have a cup of tea and a chat.

On Saturday night all her sons had a bath in the big washtub—whether they wanted it or not. Mostly NOT! They used a stiff, horsehair back-brush with Mollie's homemade lye soap, which was so strong that it practically took your hide off, and it didn't smell like perfume, either! Every time they bathed, there was so much caterwauling that Asa remarked to Mollie, "You'd think they were about to be boiled alive like lobsters!"

Since hot water had to be heated by the kettle-full, there was only so much to go around. Frank was first in the tub and each successive bather griped loudly about the previous occupant's grime. Britches was always last in the tub, and by the time it was his turn, the water was murky and lukewarm.

At the bold age of five he declared to his mother, "Just ONCE, I'd like to be the first one who spoils the water!" Mollie told him that come next Saturday, if he was good as gold, he might get his wish.

Whenever any of them was sick or hurt, Mollie soothed their fears, tended cuts and bruises, and nursed fevers. She loved her children so much she would have done anything for them. She worked tirelessly all day long until her family went to bed, and nobody paid her for her labor. Sometimes, if she thought Asa was being too strict, Mollie would say, "Actions speak louder than words, Asa. The boys will remember what you do far longer than what you tell them." Many times her sons silently thanked her for sparing the seat of their pants.

Asa and Mollie taught each of their children that hard work and self-reliance make our lives worthwhile. None of the Morris children grew up expecting anybody to solve their problems for them. They learned to forge their own paths, make mistakes, and learn from them, just as their ancestors had done.

Country People

In times past, country people often lived miles apart. They knew that in times of trouble they might need their neighbors, so they didn't take them for granted.

Our ancestors' lives were not easy. Crops failed, houses burned down, and many people died from illnesses that today are quite curable. Religious faith was especially important to them, and every child learned to say his prayers before going to bed, because nobody knew what the next day would bring. It was a comfort to place your trust in God's eternal care.

Down the road a mile or so from the big house, next to the graveyard where Jane and Uncle Asa were buried, was a little church, and every so often a *circuit preacher* came to hold services. He rotated his visits, sometimes preaching in three or four churches on his circuit in a single day.

Going to church was a challenge for the four active young Morris boys. Even if they had misbehaved all week long, they put on their best clothes and their best manners for Sunday service. They sat with their parents in the hard wooden pews and were warned not to whisper or squirm, which was practically impossible. They sat as still as they could and stared at their shoes until one of them—accidently on purpose—elbowed his brother in the ribs. This provoked a glare from Asa and a stern, "Shuuuuusssh," from Mollie.

Each time a prayer was finished, the boys made sure everybody in church could hear them say, "AMEN!" They sang hymns slightly off key with their finest voices and tried not to fall asleep during the sermon. The preacher generally got a word in about man's sinful nature, which they figured didn't apply to them. After church they tipped their caps at the preacher, grinned at their neighbors, and since one of them was usually missing a tooth or two, this added to their charm. Then they went home, ate too much at Sunday supper, and did their chores before falling into bed.

One day in 1898, the church caught fire and burned to the ground. For the little Yolo community, it was an enormous loss. Mary Alice Morris helped her neighbor, Mary Cross Pockman, raise money for a new church, completed in 1900.

Mary's Chapel and Cemetery

Since then, the little white Yolo church with its towering steeple has been called "Mary's Chapel" and the adjoining old graveyard "Mary's Cemetery." It seems fitting that both Mary Morrises are buried there.

Church was not the only place where neighbors mingled. One June evening Mary Alice held a dance in Uncle Asa's big barn to celebrate the return of her daughter Jennie Belle and son Lindsay from *boarding school*. (That's a school where you live full time.) The rough wooden barn floors were scraped and swept clean, and with the efforts of several carpenters, the barn was transformed into a modern ballroom. It was beautifully lit with Japanese lanterns, decorated with garlands of flowers, and had a platform specially built to hold the "Society Orchestra" that played all the popular tunes of the day. From the inside you would never have known that you were dancing in a big old barn that ordinarily stabled twenty horses!

Young men donned their finest gabardine suits, and young ladies wore exquisite pastel party dresses. Jennie Belle looked especially pretty in her light blue taffeta and lace dress, handmade by the finest dressmaker in Woodland. There were plenty of chaperones: mamas, papas, and grandparents who made sure the younger folks behaved themselves.

They danced until midnight, whirling around the floor in a blur of color, smiles, and laughter. Then they all went down to the big house for a late supper served by Mary Alice. It was great fun and many a young man met his future wife at such a country dance.

*   *   *

The small Yolo community held large summer picnics in a grassy field on the banks of Cache Creek. They parked their carriages nearby, tethered their horses to fence posts, and spread out big blankets under the oak trees.

One July morning they gathered for an extra-special picnic. They had all dressed in their Sunday best, because a photographer from Woodland had come to take their picture. Old cameras were big, boxy things with a lens that stuck out like an accordion and a full drapery over the photographer's head to block out light. At that time, photography was a slow process, so everybody had to hold very still and say CHEESE for several minutes. By the time the film was fully exposed, their grins were frozen on their faces and everybody looked stiff as a board.

There were lots of characters at that picnic. Grey-haired grandmas in dark dresses and decorated hats chatted amongst themselves, exchanged biscuit recipes, and bragged about their grandchildren. Grandma Lucy's ample bosom swelled with pride as she turned to Grandma Emma and said, "Emma, I expect you've heard about my grandson, Grover. You know— Clyde and Mildred's oldest boy? Grover is the star pitcher for the baseball team this year, and he's struck out more batters than any pitcher in the last ten years! Grover gets his talent from my Clyde, I expect." Emma nodded in agreement.

Two balding grandpas with grizzled whiskers wore flannel trousers held up by striped suspenders. They played a mean game of checkers on a battered board set on top of an old tree stump. Grandpa Hiram and Grandpa Sam had been checkers rivals for years. As they focused on their sixth straight game of the day, Sam saw that Hiram was about to jump his last black checker with a double-decker red king. He said, "Just so you know, Hiram, I'm watching your moves carefully." Hiram grinned and jumped his red king over one more square. "VICTORY!" he crowed, "Gotcha Sam!" as he swept Sam's last checker off the board. Sam looked at the

Cache Creek Picnic 1891

empty board with dismay. "Winning six games in a row seems a bit fishy," he said, "since I've always beaten the pants off you before today." Hiram snickered, "Just can't recognize superior skill when you see it can you, Sam?"

Nearby in a sand pit, Asa was playing horseshoes. He and the other men sported flowing mustaches and long side-whiskers which were all the rage in the big cities. They wore three-piece woolen suits and round derby hats. As they took off their jackets to toss the horseshoes, they compared notes on their crops and the latest in farm equipment.

"Say, Asa," said Emmett as he tossed his horseshoe towards the post; it missed, making a thud in a cloud of dust. "I hear tell you saw one of those new-fangled machines they call a 'combine' when you were in Sacramento last month. Do you think they're liable to catch on here in Yolo?" Asa took his turn, hit the metal post with a clang, and replied, "Be a while, I expect, before they iron all the bugs out of 'em. Between you and me, our friend Joe over there is the only fellow I know with more money than sense who'd be fool enough to buy one!"

The four Morris brothers and their cousins, Lindsay and Will, were dressed in woolen britches, long-sleeved jackets, and flat straw hats. Jennie and Kate Morris wore cotton calico dresses and big sun hats. All of them wore tight leather boots buttoned high above their ankles and were cautioned by Mollie, "If you go near the creek watch out for rattlesnakes!" Mary Alice added, "And girls, for heaven's sakes don't pick any plant you don't recognize just because it's pretty. It might be poison oak and you know that means misery. Lindsay, you stay out of that field and don't climb the fence. The neighbors have an ornery old bull over there!"

The overworked mothers wore cotton aprons tied over their pretty dresses. After days of preparation, they were finally able to lay out the meal. Mary Alice called out, "All right, everybody please help yourselves!" The crowd jumped to its feet and swarmed around the feast like honey bees in an almond tree. The ladies had outdone themselves—with tall stacks of home baked bread, sliced ham and chicken, homemade pickles, potato salad, and corn on the cob. There was also a garden favorite: sliced homegrown tomatoes. They had baked fresh peach pies made from their own fruit orchards for dessert. Lemonade was king because nobody ever drank liquor—at least not when Asa was around.

The food disappeared so quickly that Mary Alice called out, "Mollie, have you got more ham in your basket? It seems to be very popular and the mustard is running low. It looks like we're going to need more bread, too." Mollie rummaged in her big basket which yielded enough ham for one more plate full. "This is all I've got left, Mary," she said, straddling the uneven ground in high button shoes while holding the ham and balancing two large mustard crocks. "We'll just have to steer them towards dessert. What say I start cutting the pies?"

There was still plenty of corn on the cob dripping with local butter. Most of the old folks who didn't have many teeth left skipped the corn and went straight for the pie. But not Grandpa Sam; he was a corn fanatic, loved the stuff and couldn't get enough. He kept the cobs coming until he had eaten five. He glanced over at Hiram, the checker king, who was patting his belly with satisfaction and commented, "Great food this year, eh, Hiram?" Hiram nodded. Sam went to work flicking his fingernail at his remaining front teeth. "Say, Hiram," he asked, "Have you got a toothpick on you? That corn is stuck in my teeth." Hiram snorted, "What teeth, Sam?" A few minutes later they were happily snoozing in the warm sunshine and nobody pestered them even when they snored.

After lunch the children ran sack races and did cartwheels and somersaults all over the grass. Charley was a bit of a show off and when he catapulted around the field, he slipped on a patch of damp grass and skinned his knee. He stood up red-faced and looked around to see if anybody had noticed. Sure enough, three giggling girls had seen his clumsiness and his Cousin Kate teased, "You're a wonder, Charley—you should join the circus!" But Charley got his revenge. He quietly disappeared toward the creek and returned a while later with a surprise for Kate. She screamed, her hat blew off, and her long braids went flying as Charley chased her round and round holding an icky, squirming lizard by its tail. Asa reached out and grabbed Charley by his collar as he made another pass and said, "Whoa there, Son. Hand it over." Charley frowned, dropped his squirming captive into Asa's big palm, and took off running. Asa let the lizard go when nobody was looking.

Off in the distance behind a large oak tree, two pimply, hotheaded teenage boys had an argument over their lovely neighbor, Charlotte. She was a real dazzler with red curly hair and green eyes. She wore a pink checked cotton dress trimmed with white silk ribbons, and her sunhat was tied with a big cherry-pink bow.

Charlotte was just fourteen-years-old, but she had mastered the art of grown-up flirting and used it effectively to pit one boy against the other. She simpered, tossed her red curls, and flashed both boys a rosy smile, which showed off her perfect little white teeth. Charlotte had shattered the dreams of several young men in the neighborhood and the boys almost came to blows over her attentions.

The end of the picnic saved them from bloody noses, but both went home brokenhearted. Everybody else had a wonderful time. As the sun set, casting long shadows beyond the distant Blue Ridge hills, they said their goodbyes, hitched up their horses, and headed for home. All in all, life in late nineteenth century Yolo County was simple and wholesome and most people were contented.

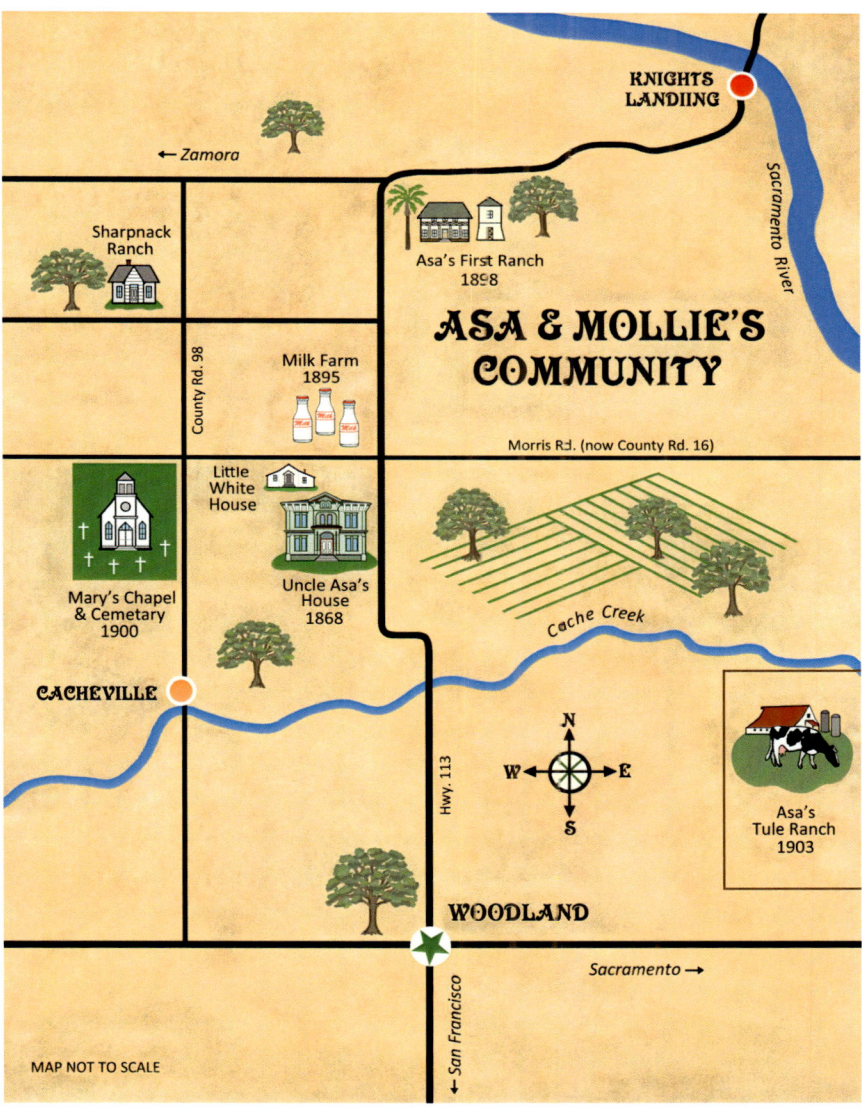

The Milk Farm

Starting a new business is a challenge
even for an experienced person.
It takes smarts, hard work, perseverance,
and a lot of luck.

Over the years, Asa had developed a lot of expertise with dairy cattle. In 1895 he started a dairy in the field across the road from Uncle Asa's big house. It was a very modest beginning, using the scrub cows on the farm to produce milk, rather than special dairy cattle breeds which were very expensive. The milk was driven by wagon to Woodland's cooperative creamery for processing. His own four sons and Uncle Asa's two sons worked alongside him.

Asa also invested in two purebred bulls—a Jersey and a Holstein-Friesian—to improve the quality of his scrub cows. Over the following five years he discovered that with careful breeding, milk production greatly increased.

Milk products needed to be priced properly (to sell for more than the cost of production) so that the dairy could make a profit. In those days a quart of milk sold for about seven cents, so you had to sell a whole lot to cover your costs and make a dollar profit.

Asa's first milk farm across from Uncle Asa's house: Asa standing (front right), Mollie (left) in buggy

In 1898, Asa purchased 320 acres of land two miles north of Uncle Asa's ranch near Knights Landing. He moved his family from the little white house to a larger house on the new property. At the same time he weeded out the non-productive scrub cows and moved the better quality cattle to the new ranch.

Asa had big plans and he was a powerhouse of ideas. One evening in early 1903, while the family sat together at suppertime, Asa announced, "Since we've improved the quality of the scrubs, I think it's time we sold the lot and invested entirely in registered purebred cattle. I believe they are the future for America's dairy industry. We'll create superb breeding stock, so we can compete with the best of them.

"The way I figure it, we've saved some money to expand but we'll also need a bank loan. There's no guarantee we'll succeed, but if we do make a go of it, we'll have some-thing to really be proud of." Everybody nodded in agreement. Asa winked at Mollie, rolled out a big wad of papers covered in numbers, and laid it on the table.

Asa continued, "We'll need more land, bigger barns, and modern equipment. Most of all, we'll need quality cattle. He looked around at the earnest faces of his sons, "You're going to have to work harder than you ever have in your young lives, but I have every confidence in you boys."

Asa impressed upon his sons the practical purpose of breeding high quality animals. "As you know by now," he said, "we're not getting into this game for bragging rights. This is a business and profit must be our driving force. We will strive for the highest quality and top production by breeding wisely. Humane treatment is our obligation, and our cows will be treated like ladies. Each animal must be evaluated by the quantity of feed she consumes versus the cash return she provides in milk and offspring."

Asa was a very practical, smart man, and he chose the Holstein-Friesian breed because it produced sturdier stock with more milk production. This breed had been imported to America from Friesland in Holland. The Dutch were justly proud of these marvelous animals and had developed them by crossing two very ancient breeds, the German Holstein and the Dutch Friesian. Later, this crossbreed came to be known simply as Holstein. The result was super milk producers who grazed on field grasses and easily adapted to many different climates.

Holsteins are large, handsome, black and white cattle who thrive in California because the sun shines a lot, it's never too cold, and there is plenty of room to roam in the pastures. There are delicious fields of food to eat and patches of green clover which is a tasty cow dessert.

Asa was one of the earliest Holstein breeders in Yolo County, but he was not the only man to appreciate the great qualities the breed had to offer. William Howard Taft, who in 1908 was elected the twenty-seventh President of the United States, liked the breed, too. During his term in office, President Taft kept a Holstein cow named "Pauline Wayne" who lived and grazed on the White House lawn. Pauline was not a champion milk producer but she provided the Taft family with all of their milk and butter needs. President Taft weighed in at over three hundred pounds, so he must have eaten the lion's share of Pauline's butter!

*   *   *

In late 1903, Asa began to implement the plan he had laid out at the family dinner earlier in the year. As the first step in expanding his cattle breeding business, he bought a 1,000-acre ranch just east of Woodland and he named it the "Tule

Ranch." It was a large, flat piece of land perfectly situated for raising cattle, and Cache Creek, which flowed across the northern boundary, was a source for much needed water.

He and the boys constructed a small dam to divert part of the creek for irrigating feed crops. They built miles of fencing, fixed up an existing house on the property for the family, and built bunkhouses for the farm hands.

Since dairy farming requires a lot of easily accessible water, Asa drilled several wells, and installed mechanical pumps to keep water flowing to the *tank house.* Every ranch had a tank house (a tall, timbered water storage tower that delivered water using gravity). There were also two existing windmills that pumped water the old-fashioned way, using wind power. These mills deposited water for the animals into big wooden troughs. With an ample water supply in place, Asa built large milking barns with concrete floors that could be easily washed down. Cleaning a cow barn is smelly work, but you have to do it if you want *sanitary* milk. Sanitary means squeaky clean and Asa insisted on it.

Asa searched far and wide for the highest quality animals. His first purchase was 35 purebred Holstein cows called the Riverside herd from the Pierce Land and Stock Company in Stockton, California. A purebred animal is one whose ancestors were all the same breed. Each of Asa's Holsteins had a *pedigree,* a document which charts the names and quality of all of the animal's ancestors. They also had special pedigreed names and numbers that were *registered* with the Holstein/Friesian Association of America.

When the Riverside herd arrived by train, Asa was ready. The dairy operation continued and the careful work of breeding purebred livestock began. It would take many years before he was ready to enter the market as a top quality Holstein breeder.

Threshing wheat with mule teams: Asa driving the buggy and the boys driving the thresher

Dairy Farming is Hard Work!

In the old days people never drank skim milk.
They liked rich whole milk, thick cream, and lots of butter.
Asa's Holsteins gave super delicious milk that made
great ice cream, and who can resist that?

Running a dairy farm is very hard work and you hardly ever get to take a vacation. Your cows depend on you day and night to keep them fed and milked. Asa's Holstein herd grew and grew until he had 300 cows that produced hundreds of gallons of milk every day.

Milking 300 cows twice a day by hand was a huge job, so Asa hired special crews of milkers from faraway places like Sweden and Switzerland. These fellows were experts and they were very fast. They used a technique called *thumb punching* where they folded their thumbs inside their palms and extracted the milk with a powerful draw. The crews saved Asa time and money, but there were drawbacks to having them as employees. They didn't understand or speak English very well and when asked any question, they always had the same reply: "Yah sure, aay betcha. Aay baint teke aay do." Whatever this meant, it was interpreted as, "You bet, I can do it." Whether they understood or not, remained to be seen.

During the week the men were good workers, but every Saturday night they went to town and drank too much liquor. They were noisy and rough when they came home drunk, and they were lazy about their Sunday chores. This meant more work for the boys who didn't appreciate it a bit, so they learned the hazards of too much drink while they were still young. Asa was a *Teetotaler* which meant that he TOTALLY— with a capital T—opposed the use of liquor. He laid down the law to his crews. "No drinking on duty and no excuses!" Those who didn't cooperate were fired on the spot.

As new inventions came along to help dairymen, Asa continued to upgrade his dairy operation. Back in 1878, a smart fellow named De Laval had invented a machine to separate cream from milk. Most dairymen like Asa used this machine. Thirty years later, De Laval revolutionized the dairy industry again with an automatic milking machine that really worked. His invention cut milking time in half, and Asa installed several of these contraptions in his barns.

He expanded his dairy business when he opened his own milk processing plant at 604 Main Street in Woodland. He named his new venture "A.W. Morris Pasteurized Milk Company." Pasteurizing was a fairly new process in which raw milk was heated to kill bacteria and make it safer to drink. Asa was the first Woodland dairyman to promote pasteurization, and he insisted on high standards for his milk and butter products.

He purchased several pieces of equipment for the new plant: a large cream separator, a pasteurizer, and a bottling machine. Milk was sold in reusable glass bottles with cardboard caps instead of throw-away waxed cartons. Bottles were sterilized using a lye solution and boiling water between each use.

Asa's dairy delivered milk twice a day by horse-drawn

wagon, so his customers could have fresh milk, cream, and butter for breakfast and supper. Milk products were packed in ice for delivery because refrigerated trucks hadn't yet been invented. The horse that pulled the milk wagon was very smart; he knew the route so well that he stopped at exactly the right houses every time. Meanwhile, the milkman concentrated on getting the order correct and picking up empty bottles.

Asa's milk bottling machine

Being a milkman was considered a really good job in Woodland, even though you had to work seven days a week, and you had only one day off a month. On the other hand, the horse never got a day off! When motorized trucks became widely available, Asa bought one, and the old horse retired to a comfortable life in the ranch pasture.

Asa's milk delivery truck

* * *

On the Tule Ranch, Asa was the boss and each of his sons had a particular job. Frank sold the livestock and he knew the history and value of each and every animal. Charley, who couldn't tell one cow from another, managed the land and grew hundreds of acres of feed crops. Britches was on a first name basis with every cow, and he managed the herd and the barns. He was even on friendly terms with the bulls.

Harry, who later became my grandpa, managed the machine shop. Harry was a mechanical genius, and he kept all the trucks and farm equipment running. He invented a device called a "row crop siphon" which was used for irrigating acres of alfalfa. Harry's siphons were long aluminum pipes with a couple of strategic bends in the middle and a special valve on one end. They were laid between irrigation ditches, and once you got the first one started, they carried water from row to row, using water pressure and suction like a water vacuum cleaner. Siphons made irrigation easier, faster, and cheaper.

The Morris Holsteins ate huge quantities of gourmet chow. Asa tried combinations of feed ingredients and finally came up with the perfect diet which included: barley, alfalfa, soy meal, cottonseed meal, sugar beets, bran, and *silage*. Silage is made from corn in a *silo,* a tall, circular tower made of steel or concrete. Farmers harvest their corn, chop it up finely, and load it into the silo from the top—where it compresses from its own weight and gets soft and soggy. Silage needs to *ferment*, or age, in a silo for quite a while before it becomes a tasty corn mush. Cows just love it!

Asa's cows grazed on the pasture grasses for four hours each day. This was a useful way to keep them happy and the grass mowed at the same time! Cattle need salt and other minerals to maintain good health, so farmers put out *salt licks* for them. Salt licks are big blocks of compressed salt that are mounted on poles in the fields, like giant cow lollypops without fruit flavoring. They attract a lot of "customers" who lick them with their big rough tongues until they are worn down to a nub.

*   *   *

Like most animals, cows display unique behavior that makes them fun to watch. For one thing, they generally do everything in slow motion. They are big, lumbering creatures who like a simple daily routine and they are seldom in a hurry. Getting a cow to move when they would rather lie down in the warm grass can be a real challenge.

Even the finest cows are very messy eaters. They munch on their alfalfa hay with no concern for good table manners — never mind taking bite-sized portions. The hay sticks out of their mouths at all angles and drops all over the place.

Cows are part of a group of animals called *ruminants*. When they swallow their partially chewed food, it goes into the *rumen*, the largest digestive compartment of their stomach. The food sits there awhile and it ferments. Then, they *regurgitate* — or bring up — the partly digested food back into their mouths, and chew it again. This is called chewing their *cud*. Their rubbery jaws and big yellow teeth move round and round from side to side until the cud is just the right texture to swallow a second time. Cud chewing can be a rather sloppy business, so it's a good thing that they do it outside!

Then there's the sport of fly swatting. On hot summer days, flies generally head straight for cattle and settle on any moist place. These nasty insects tickle and itch. In response, cows create a symphony of moooooing and wave their tails wildly to flick off the flies. All sorts of ointments have been invented for this problem, but they generally fall short and the flies triumph.

Another funny thing cows like to do is to play "Follow the Leader." Sometimes when they're out in the pasture and it's dinnertime, one cow will head off toward the barn and all the others fall into line single file. They tramp along the same path day after day and eventually they wear a deep track into the dirt. When they're hungry, cows always know the shortest way to the feed trough.

Despite their eccentricities, Asa's cows were smart. Not only did they know exactly what time to show up at the barn

for milking, but each cow knew exactly which stall was hers. Trading places in the milk stalls just wasn't done — that's what you call champion cow *etiquette,* which means good manners.

Asa's Holsteins led comfortable lives in the sunny pastures of the Tule Ranch. Another famous dairyman of the time, E. A. Stuart of the Carnation Milk Company, wrote:

The Prayer of a Contented Cow

I am a milk machine,
I ask only for proper food and care,
And I will produce rich, pure, sweet milk…
I must have good food from rich pastures.
I must have pure water,
And I must have plenty of fresh air…
I like to be petted often.
Kind words also will help make me
Happy and contented.

For Better or For Worse

Sooner or later life brings troubles
to all of us, and we discover hidden strengths
we didn't know we had.

Just before the turn of the century, on May 10, 1899, an unexpected little family addition had arrived: Asa and Mollie's daughter, Zella May Morris. She was a delightful surprise and a real beauty, with her mother's heavy lidded blue eyes and her father's wavy brown hair. Zella was a special gift to a family full of boys, and Asa made certain that his little princess never milked a cow in her life!

Mollie loved having a daughter, and she sewed frilly little dresses for Zella which was so much more fun than constantly mending torn-up overalls. She drove the horse and buggy to Woodland to have Zella's photograph taken and, unlike her four wiggly brothers, Zella always sat still for the photographer, smiled on cue, and didn't make sassy remarks.

Sometimes they played dress-up and had tea in tiny china cups before the younger boys came home from school. Zella was a gentle little presence in a household of noisy boys. She giggled when her brothers made funny faces for her, and loved to sit on Asa's lap and snuggle her head next to his.

Zella May Morris

When Zella outgrew her baby bottle, Asa bought her a sterling silver child's cup and had her initials engraved on it. Mollie looked at the beautiful little cup and said, "Asa, this is a lovely gift, but I hope you won't be disappointed if she dents and scratches it. You know what babies are like." Sure enough, the first time Zella used her cup, the milk dribbled over the edge and all down the front of her bib. She squealed with delight when it made a puddle on her tray and banged her cup on her high chair. When Mollie glanced at him from the corner of her eye, Asa was grinning broadly and chuckling. No matter what Zella did, he adored her. She was the frosting on his cake.

Several years passed. Asa's dairy was making a profit and he continued working toward his goal to breed champion dairy cattle. He and Mollie had worked hard for twenty-five years to make a good life for their family, and success was just around the corner.

One day in early December, 1905, Mollie caught a cold. She had been very busy after the Thanksgiving holiday preparing for Christmas. Her cold got worse and went into her chest. Then it became pneumonia, an illness that weakens the lungs. The doctor came but there were no modern medicines available to fight a serious infection, and there was nothing he could do to help her. Mollie ran a high fever, and Asa was very worried.

Mary Alice came and sat with Mollie for hours and hours while the boys kept the fire blazing to warm the chilly room. Even so, the damp December Tule fog seeped into the room making it cold and clammy.

For nine days Mollie lingered, and as she grew weaker and weaker, Asa made a heart-wrenching decision. One by one, he motioned his children to come into the room to say goodbye to their mother. He fought back tears as he watched each of his sons kiss their mother one last time; they were all so brave and so tender with her. He held Zella close to Mollie's face so Mollie could kiss her little cheek, and Zella whimpered when Asa handed her to her brother Frank.

Hours later, Asa was holding her hand when Mollie passed away. He sat for a long time with his head bowed looking at her peaceful, beloved face. For twenty-five years, he had loved Mollie with all his heart. Her quiet strength and common sense had guided him through many trials, and he could not imagine life without her. For Asa and his children, it was the saddest day of their lives.

Mollie left behind five strong children, nurtured and raised with a loving hand in the richness and beauty of Northern California. She had been a good friend and beloved neighbor, so the whole community came for her funeral at Mary's Chapel.

Asa and his sons sat somberly side by side in the front pew, and he held his precious little Zella on his lap. As the Reverend Picton delivered a very moving service, Asa glanced along the pew at all his children, so solemn and so sad. He well remembered the day his own mother Sarah had died, and the sorrow that no words could cure.

On that misty winter afternoon, Mollie was laid to rest in Mary's Cemetery where her children could visit her grave whenever they missed her. A huge offering of flowers, their petals singed by the frosty air, covered the gravesite along with a special wreath from her children that simply said "Mother."

As the family drove home in the carriage, Asa looked down the road towards Uncle Asa's house, and for a brief moment he thought he saw Mollie standing in the sunshine in front of the little white house. She looked just as lovely as she had the day they first arrived in Yolo County. Her curly red-blonde hair peeked out from underneath her bonnet, her blue eyes smiled at him, and she lifted her hand in a gentle parting wave. He felt his heart turn over, and when he blinked away his tears and looked again, she was gone.

Asa had been through many troubles in his life, but losing Mollie was the hardest. For the sake of his children, he would summon the strength to carry on without her.

*   *   *

For six long, lonely years Asa was a widower. He worked harder than ever, and one by one his boys grew up. One day Frank came to his father and said, "Pop, I've found the girl I'm going to marry. Her name is Therese and I hope I have your blessing." Asa did better than that. He built houses on the Tule Ranch for each of his sons, and the following year Asa's first granddaughter, Madeline Morris, was born.

Raising young Zella wasn't easy for a hard-charging old dairyman. She needed a mother, and Asa longed for the comfort of a wife. Many a fine Woodland lady had her eye on Asa, but he found his new wife on a visit back to Greene County. Cassie Black was the widow of his cousin Alexander, and Asa had known her for years; it was a convenient match for them both. In 1911 they were married and he brought Cassie back to Yolo County.

Asa moved from the Tule Ranch into Woodland. He bought an old Victorian house on First Street and completely remodeled it in the latest *Mission Revival* style; it was simple, practical, and strong. The two-storied redwood house was solid and square, with heavy tan stucco walls thick with pea gravel. An unusual bold geometric design ran all along the roofline and was painted a dark contrasting brown. The front door was wide and stout with a large, heavy iron door knob. The home faced east with a broad porch that wrapped around three sides of the house, and it stayed shady and cool on hot summer days. The porch was Asa's favorite place to sit on a Sunday morning after church.

He converted an old carriage house in the side yard into a garage. Then, he dug two parallel tracks the length of his driveway, just wide enough apart so he could back out his car without getting stuck in the mud. He filled the trenches with

Asa's house on First Street in Woodland

gravel. Each successive car got wider, so the tracks were too close together and the mud got him anyway. He planted palm trees in his front yard, not much good for shade in the hot California summers, but being from Pennsylvania, he always found them a novelty.

Asa looked at his finished house from the street and commented to Cassie, "I'd say we've got ourselves a really interesting house! None of that fussy Victorian gingerbread stuff—it's unique!" Woodland thought so, too. More than one person stopped in their tracks to study Asa's house, and some of them thought it was as eccentric as he was.

*   *   *

Asa was never an easy man to live with. The lessons of his Civil War childhood ran deep, and he knew that life was an uncertain business. He was always restless, full of energy, and he drove himself endlessly to succeed. Those who knew him best also knew that he was feisty and stubborn, that he liked a good argument—especially when he won—and that he could talk your ear off to prove his point. He was competitive and demanding but he was also a fair man and his friends, as well as his long time employees, thought the world of him. Asa held high standards for moral behavior and he stood behind his beliefs.

He had to overcome his share of hardships, and in one single year, the Tule Ranch sustained three devastating fires. There were flood and drought years, crop failures, and a constant battle to keep ahead of mounting debts. A farmer's life is never dull!

Animal breeding is not a comfortable business for a sentimental person. You must make practical choices and sometimes, whether you like it or not, you have to destroy your own animals. Success depends on healthy livestock, good management, fair market prices, and honest dealing. More than once, Asa met with dishonest businessmen, livestock auctions that were rigged to favor one of his competitors, and with animals that died young or failed to fulfill their potential. A lesser man might have given up and a chosen a more comfortable path.

Asa's Greene County relatives sent their sons to California to work for him because they knew he could turn an aimless youth into a responsible working man. He treated his nephews just like his own sons, which meant they worked HARD!

Day after day, year after year, Asa rose at dawn; he worked and worked and worked until he had achieved the standards he had set for himself. He claimed that he hadn't shaved by daylight in twenty years, since it was dark when he left in the morning and dark when he came home at night. But he was always enthusiastic about his work, and he set an example for his sons who were hard pressed to keep up with him. And—when nobody was listening—he still talked to his cows, sometimes more than he talked to his family.

Asa on the Tule Ranch

The BIG Fight

Never underestimate a scrappy little Pennsylvanian!

Like many early twentieth century American towns, Woodland had an ongoing battle over its drinking saloons. Many Americans thought that liquor was the greatest enemy of a productive life, and their fight to control drunkenness became a national struggle called the *Temperance Movement*.

The word *temperance* means moderation in all things, but in Asa's day, it was used to mean absolutely NO LIQUOR. Teetotalers like Asa were gung-ho to close the local saloons in the hope that young men would not fall under the evil grip of the "demon rum." Those in favor of keeping saloons open were known as "wets" and those against were called "drys." Both got hot under the collar whenever the subject came up.

Election after election failed to resolve the issue since only men were allowed to vote and only men were the REALLY big drinkers! The saloons gave free reign to drunkenness, which often led to criminal behavior, but they brought in lots of money for the city and the liquor industry was very powerful.

The ruckus in Yolo County had begun back in 1854 when the "Sons of Temperance" group was organized in a tiny school house on Uncle Asa's ranch. Forty years later, the "Anti-Saloon League" threw its weight behind the issue, but the Woodland Temperance movement really got rolling when the ladies finally got into the act.

Some women suffered physical abuse at the hands of their drunken husbands, and they were just plain tired of it, so they took matters into their own hands. In 1894, Mrs. Mary Leavitt organized a local Cacheville chapter of a national organization called the "Women's Christian Temperance Union" or W.C.T.U. Their mission was to stamp out liquor and they used whatever means they could to get their message out to the public. They favored dramatic slogans like "Denounce the Demon Rum!" *Denounce* means to morally reject something you think is evil. Before her death in 1905, Mollie Morris had been a valued member for many years.

As the W.C.T.U. grew in numbers and in strength, the members not only crusaded against liquor, but also for women's *suffrage*. That was the official word for a woman's right to vote in political elections, and women who fought for that right were called *suffragettes*. These brave women kept up the fight with all the influence they could muster, and on October 11, 1911, California finally granted women the right to vote. Within a week, four hundred Woodland women had registered. (Nationally, women didn't win the right to vote until 1920).

With the power of the ballot now in their hands, the W.C.T.U. brought the saloon question to a final vote. The election was held on December 12, 1911, and the women's vote pushed the "drys" to victory. Woodland's saloons were forced to close; this didn't mean that liquor completely disappeared, but it was harder to find.

*   *   *

Everybody in Yolo County knew that Asa Morris was a Teetotaler. They also knew he had a temper, and most folks took care not to cross him. A reporter from a dairy magazine wrote an article about Asa and called him a "scrappy little Pennsylvanian." When Asa read that he had a hearty laugh, because he knew it was true.

Shortly after the election of 1911, Asa became famous in Woodland for a fistfight on Main Street. On a crisp winter afternoon Asa and Britches were walking down the street on their way to the bank. In front of Cranston's Hardware Store, Asa was stopped by an old acquaintance named Jack Hardesty, who planted himself firmly in Asa's path.

Jack had the muscular build of one who lifted hay bales for a living. He was a self-proclaimed "wet" and had downed a few shots of whisky to prove it. His bloodshot blue eyes and untidy appearance broadcast his condition before he ever opened his mouth. Jack was feeling mighty fine; he was looking for trouble, and when he stopped Asa, he found it.

Jack reeked of whiskey and sweat; in fact, he was so stinky that Asa took a step backwards in disgust. In his *inebriated*—which means drunken—state, Jack saw this move as cowardice which only made him bolder.

Their conversation quickly turned to the election. As Jack's voice grew louder, he thrust his face close to Asa's and the two began to argue. Jack gave Asa a sloppy grin and with slurred speech, declared, "Soooooo A.W. . . . I voted against you [blankety-blank] drys . . . Think you can tell a man how to live his life do you? A little booze would do you good—loosen you up a bit! Ever had the nerve to try some?" Asa's disgust showed plainly on his face, and he quipped, "Seems to me you're a shining example of the effects of too much liquor, Jack. No wonder you haven't got the good sense to take a bath!"

By this time the two were hollering at each other, and folks gathered round to see what would happen next. Jack's courage was bolstered by the audience and he sprayed a shower of spit in the air as he taunted Asa, "I guess all your ham-handed efforts to force this county dry finally paid off. Why don't you drink your milk like a good Mama's boy and leave us real men alone?"

Asa didn't take kindly to obnoxious behavior, fueled by whiskey or otherwise. Ignoring the sage old advice from the Bible to "turn the other cheek," Asa turned to face Jack head on. One wary bystander cautioned, "Watch out Jack. Them's fightin' words! A.W. isn't going to take that lying down." Jack ignored him and grinned from ear to ear, swaying on his feet and cussing up a storm. Asa didn't like cussing either, and he wasn't smiling.

Once his fuse was lit, his shrewd blue eyes narrowed, his face grew red as a beet, and his grey hair spiked up around his cowlick just like a rooster ruffling his feathers before a challenger. Britches saw the warning signs and tried to intervene. When Asa removed his coat and began to roll up his sleeves, Britches cried out, "Watch it Pop! You're no spring chicken you know." TOO LATE! Asa ignored his son's advice, ordering, "Here, hold my jacket while I show how fast I can lick this log!" He proceeded to put up his dukes, and Jack did likewise.

Being very tipsy and cocky to boot, Jack was not too accurate with his swings, and he made a few punches wide of the mark. Asa dodged him and let Jack dance around and wear himself out a bit. Then, while Jack was momentarily distracted winking at a pretty girl in the audience, Asa clobbered him on the chin with a well-placed right hook. Jack staggered backwards and lost his footing. Over he went, falling in the wobbly, loose-limbed manner of drunkards. On the way down, he hit a plate glass window that shattered all over the pavement.

Jack was lucky; he wasn't seriously hurt but his pride took a beating. He lay sprawled on the pavement in the middle of a pile of broken glass, looking as sheepish as a naughty schoolboy. The same bystander shouted, "Hey Jack; told you not to mess with A. W!"

Asa rubbed his knuckles and quietly said, "That'll teach you the dangers of too much drink better than any words I can say," and he offered his clean handkerchief to Jack to wipe his dirty face. Jack rubbed his chin, struggled to his feet, and turned his back.

Reuben Cranston, the proprietor of the store, came running out the front door to see what all the commotion was about. Asa declared, "Reub, this drunken fool broke your window," implying that his adversary had done the deed all by himself. "But don't worry—I'll pay for your window myself." Asa peeled off some bills from his wallet and handed them to Mr. Cranston, who wisely didn't say another word. Asa calmly put his jacket back on and said to the onlookers, "Now all of you go home. The show's over." He motioned to Britches and the two of them walked on down the street as calmly as if nothing had happened.

Asa always thought he was right in such matters, but whether he was right or wrong, he knew that some principles were worth fighting for, and not just with words! Eventually he and a sober Jack made up, and they never argued again.

*   *   *

Elections like the one in Woodland led to *Prohibition*, a national effort to ban the manufacture, transportation, and sale of alcohol. In 1920, Asa and all the "drys" celebrated when

Congress implemented the Eighteenth Amendment to our Constitution, making the manufacture and sale of liquor illegal.

Prohibition, which lasted thirteen years, was a failure. Illegal liquor sales fueled one of the biggest crime waves in American history and gave many notorious gangsters their start. Fortunately, Asa didn't live long enough to see the Eighteenth Amendment repealed in 1933. Jack definitely had the last laugh!

Asa's Champions

Animal champions don't usually happen by accident;
they are bred by an expert who knows his stuff.

Long ago dairymen discovered that when they bred
their best cows and bulls they created better animals. This is
called *selective breeding*. They began to compete with each other
and champions were born. Champions are the cream of the
crop and are worth a lot of money.

Dairymen use a number of breeding terms to describe
their animals. A father is called a *sire* and a mother is called a
dam, and breeders keep close tabs on which sires and dams
produce the best offspring. A male calf is called a *bull* and a
female is a *heifer.*

Heifers become cows after they *calve*, which means to
give birth. That's when they *freshen*, or begin to produce milk.
When a calf is old enough, it is *weaned* which means it no
longer needs Mama's milk. People then take over milking the
mother cow in order to keep up her milk production.
Otherwise, she dries up. Over her lifetime a cow generally
produces several offspring, so each time she calves, her milk
supply freshens and the process starts all over again.

Dairy herds are mostly cows with only one or two bulls

at a time. Full grown bulls are huge, powerful animals, and they tend to have bad tempers. They flirt with the ladies in the herd and get jealous if another bull does the same. Bulls often fight one another, so they need to live in separate pastures.

Asa selectively bred his Holsteins for good health and maximum milk production. He chose his most productive cows and took equal care to choose a bull whose mother and grandmother, were also great producers. The results were SUPER DUPER milk producers. Today this is part of the science of *genetics:* the study of inherited physical traits.

Breeding quality animals takes time and patience. Sometimes even with the best possible dams and sires, their offspring can be real duds and Asa had his share of duds. Generation after generation of Holsteins were born on the Tule Ranch. When Asa was satisfied with the quality of his cattle and was ready to sell them, he put advertisements in dairy magazines with the following headline:

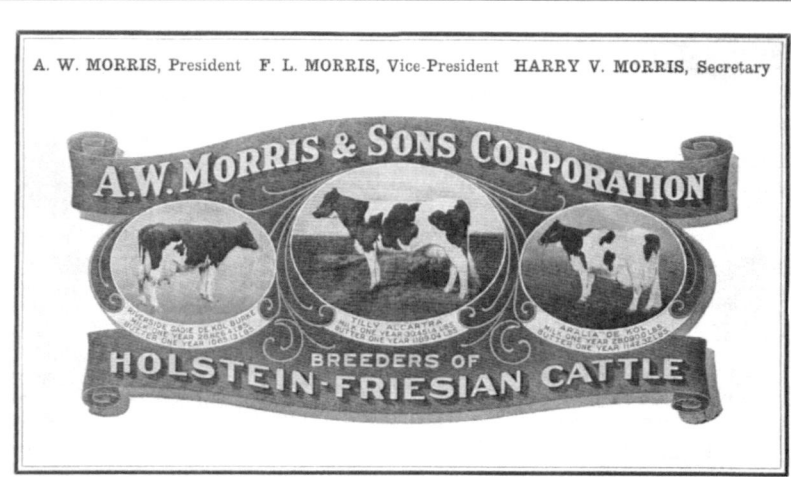

Asa's champion cows had fancy pedigreed names like: Riverside Sadie De Kol Burke, Aralia De Kol, Ignaro Creamcup, Susie De Kol Mercedes Burke, and Betsy Lamb Prilly. Sometimes these names told where the cow came from or who her parents were. The De Kol cow family produced many champions who traced their ancestry directly to Holland. Sadie and Aralia were *foundation cows*, which means that their calves created the foundation on which Asa built his herd. Both cows set world records for milk production.

Riverside Sadie De Kol Burke

Asa also bred champion bulls and he sold them before they matured and quarreled with their rivals. His prize-winning bulls had exotic names like Segis Pontiac De Kol Burke, Segis Bergama Butter Boy, Sir Goldstone Romeo Alcartra, and Prince Gelische Hengerveld Walker. Each of them liked to show off; that's what bulls do.

Many times Asa entered his cows and bulls in the California State Fair competitions where he garnered more than a few blue ribbons. One year 46 of his Holsteins won 51 awards—making a clean sweep in the Holstein category! His many rivals envied his success.

His foundation bull, Lorena Korndyke, won top honors four years in a row. Old Korndyke was a great character and very popular with the ladies. His coat was almost completely white with just a few small black splotches that looked like somebody had fired black paint balls at him.

Asa's office walls were lined with blue ribbons and big silver trophies. He had framed professional photographs of all his champions which were displayed alongside photos of his grandchildren. Asa took his cattle to livestock shows across America where he shook a lot of hands and made sales to

Segis Pontiac De Kol Burke

Foundation bull Lorena Korndyke as a youngster

buyers looking for the very finest dairy cattle. At one show in Chicago, he met an earnest, hardworking young man who had come all the way from Nova Scotia, Canada. His name was Sidney Higgins. Asa was very impressed with Sid and told him, "Son, if you ever come to California, you come and see me in Woodland and I'll give you a job." Sid took him up on his offer and when he arrived in Yolo County, Asa was true to his word and hired him.

Asa's reputation as a top-notch Holstein breeder soared when he made an important sale to a famous lady named Anita Baldwin. Anita owned thoroughbred race horses, the Santa Anita Race Track, and Rancho Santa Anita, a large livestock ranch in Los Angeles, California. She was very keen to develop a fine herd of Holsteins on her ranch. The *Sacramento Livestock and Dairy Journal* wrote:

"A Great Livestock Transaction"

"Without question, the largest and most important single deal in registered animals on the Pacific Coast was recently completed by A.W. Morris and Sons and Anita Baldwin of Los Angeles. The sale includes the great Holstein sire, Prince Gelische Walker, along with twenty-one of his daughters and fourteen other splendidly bred heifers."

Asa and the boys personally hauled the bull, Prince Gelische, and all thirty-five cows to a Yolo field alongside the Southern Pacific Railroad tracks where they lined up to board their train to Los Angeles. These amazing animals made the herd at Rancho Santa Anita one of the finest in the nation.

Morris Holsteins ready to board their train to Los Angeles

Asa sold his cows and bulls all over America and to Canada, Europe, South America, New Zealand, and even Hawaii. In the years that followed, his herd held more than a dozen national and world records for milk and butter production. His Holsteins fetched high prices and he became very well known in the dairy industry.

Asa had more than fulfilled his vision of success, planned out so many years before. But, the biggest surprise was yet to come!

PART FOUR

Tilly Alcartra

A Little Heifer Who Became a Queen

Some animals have qualities
that make them seem almost human.

Of all the champion Holstein cows that the Morris family owned over the years, none was as special as Tilly Alcartra. Asa had an expert eye for great Holstein cattle, but when he purchased Tilly, he was a very lucky man.

Tilly Alcartra was born October 2, 1908, in Buckingham, Iowa, on a dairy farm owned by early Holstein breeders, the McKay Brothers. Her grandmother Alcartra Polkadot was an outstanding milk producer, her father Alcartra Polkadot Corrector was a champion bull, and her mother Tilly Lou II was an excellent breeder. Tilly's pedigree was top-notch and her ancestors were *bovine* royalty. (Bovine is a fancy word from Latin used to refer to cattle.)

When Asa bought Holsteins from other states, he traveled there himself to have a good look at his potential animals. In 1909, he and Frank took the train to Iowa to select some young calves to add to their growing herd. Mr. McKay sold Asa several two-year-olds but refused to sell any of his yearlings. Asa could be very persuasive, and after plenty of haggling, McKay finally gave in. He pointed to some yearlings in his pasture and said, "You can have the one in the center for $300.00." Asa and Frank walked out to the field to have a look. Asa said to Frank, "If I had to pick just one of this whole lot, this is the one I'd choose. She's something special! I wonder why McKay would part with this splendid yearling for such a low price. Quick, Frank, pay the man and let's go before he changes his mind!"

Back in Woodland Asa said to Britches, "Just wait until you see the yearling we bought in Iowa. I tell you there's something special about that one. We've purchased some of her half-sisters, too, all from top-notch stock."

Tilly was already pregnant with her first calf when she was sent to Woodland by train. This was an efficient way that dairymen transported two animals for the price of one! When Tilly and her sisters arrived, Asa went to the train depot to collect them himself. While the older girls were loaded into the waiting truck, Asa looked at his beautiful new heifer and said to her, "Hello little lady. Welcome to California!" He patted Tilly gently and urged her forward through the cattle chute. "Tilly Alcartra, I'm expecting big things from you. You're a dandy young lady and you come from the very best stock." He smiled at her and added, "You'll like living in Yolo County, Tilly. We have great food and we rarely have any snow storms."

Although he didn't let on, Asa hoped that Tilly, like her mother and grandmother, would be a magnificent breeder of valuable calves—since good bloodlines were the most important ingredient in establishing a high quality herd. But Asa never guessed the exciting times that lay ahead for his new arrival.

Tilly looked around and had absolutely no idea where she was. Traveling "Cow Class" on a freight train doesn't include windows so she was a bit confused. Just then, a soft breeze came up and tickled her nose. The fragrant air smelled deliciously of moist earth and leafy oak mulch. But just who was this funny little man who kept talking to her? She thought she had seen him before, but where? When he smiled at her, his blue eyes crinkled up around the edges, and he had a jolly laugh. He seemed very nice, so she looked at him for a moment or two, blinked her big brown eyes, and followed his lead up the ramp into the waiting truck.

Off they went in a cloud of dust to the Tule Ranch, and as they rode along Tilly felt the warmth of the California sun on her back and smiled to herself. Wherever she had landed, this place seemed very promising.

When they pulled into the ranch and the truck came to a halt near the barn, the first thing she smelled were green fields of clover and alfalfa. "Mmmmm, lovely!" Tilly thought to herself as her nose twitched with delight. The boys came out to help unload the livestock, and they ooohed and aaahed when Asa led Tilly down the ramp. Britches looked her over and said, "Great work, Pop. She's a BEAUT!"

He scratched Tilly under her chin and as he led her to the barn, he told her, "You can call me Britches, Tilly, everybody else does. I'll be looking after you, so if you have any complaints, you come straight to me. Now let me introduce you to some of the girls." Champions Sadie de Kol Burke and Aralia de Kol were curious to meet the new arrival, but in typical laid-back cow fashion they slowly sauntered over to see what all the fuss was about. Sadie took a good look at Tilly, nodded, and moooooed her approval. Aralia was not so sure; she could only see one thing in the new girl: COMPETITION! She was not about to be outdone by a pretty young thoroughbred from Iowa!

Tilly's Rise to Fame

In a bucket of fresh milk,
the cream always rises to the top.
Tilly Alcartra became the cream
at the top of the dairy world.

Now, you might think that all Holsteins look alike, but they don't. If you ever see a herd in the field, you'll notice a great variety of black and white markings. The handsomest Holsteins have a sharp distinction of black and white markings in equal proportions as Tilly had, and she was a real beauty. She had the classic sturdy Holstein build, well-shaped curved horns, and soft brown eyes framed by very long eyelashes.

Tilly was sweet-natured and had good cow manners, which are a sure sign of great breeding. She liked her new home and was so mild mannered that she never used her horns to *butt* any of her herd mates or the farm hands. Butting means to bump somebody really hard with your head, and even if they're just playing, cows have big, hard heads that can knock you off your feet. Many young Holsteins have their horns removed so they can't hurt each other or the people who care for them.

Tilly was friendly and showed affection for her owners.

Britches told Asa, "Tilly's so easy to care for compared to some of our less cooperative ladies. She's not fussy and, boy, can she ever EAT!" Sometimes Tilly would turn her head around in appreciation and give the person tending her a big cow kiss. It wasn't long before the whole Morris family adored her and treated her like a pet.

Tilly loved to wander around the pasture smelling the alfalfa and sampling the clover; in fact, her favorite pastime was eating. She loved her barley, alfalfa, and silage but her special favorite was sugar beets, freshly pulled out of the soil. Sugar beets were a booming crop in Yolo County, and Tilly could eat dozens of them every single day. That's what you call a giant sweet tooth!

Cows have very large stomachs with four separate digestive compartments, so they can hold a whole lot of food. Most adult Holstein cows weigh about 1500 pounds, but Tilly weighed 1700 pounds. That's what happens when you have a big appetite, and Tilly was a bovine eating machine!

Her other great asset was a firm udder which she inherited from Grandma Polkadot. Even as she aged, Tilly's udder never drooped at all. In some older cows a droopy udder looks like a partially deflated balloon, and that's an uncomfortable problem when they have to plod around bumpy fields every day.

After her first calf was born, Tilly began to give enormous amounts of milk that astonished Asa. She gave so much that her milk didn't fit in an ordinary bucket; she required a huge pan. Asa's other champions, Sadie and Aralia, had each set world production records but didn't come close to Tilly's output. "I think we have ourselves a real treasure here," he told his boys. "She's absolutely amazing—almost a cow and a half. To look at her you'd wonder where in the world she stores all that milk, must have a secret spare tank or four hollow legs. I'd be willing to bet that she's going to top them all!"

*   *   *

Like most breeders of purebred Holsteins, Asa regularly tested his cows for the quantity of milk they produced. He also tested for the amount of butterfat in their milk. Butterfat is the term for the natural fat solids in milk that make it taste creamy. Holsteins are not generally known for high butterfat milk, but Tilly was an exception. She had the rare ability to produce high fat milk in gigantic quantities. Tilly was tops in another way, too: for each dollar of feed she consumed, she returned three dollars and seventeen cents profit. Now, that's an economical cow!

Asa pioneered long-term testing for his animals. At that time, dairymen kept only daily and weekly records of their animals' milk output, but Asa thought a yearly and lifetime record summary would give a more accurate picture of an individual cow's capacity. This information helped him to breed animals that out-performed the industry. The University Farm in Davis certified all of Asa's test records and the Holstein-Friesian Association recorded all the results. Long-term testing became standard practice in the dairy industry.

On November 13, 1914, Tilly Alcartra broke the world's record for milk production! She was the first cow of any breed to produce over 30,000 pounds of milk in one year, a feat which had never been done before. That's almost 3,500 gallons of milk all from a single cow! In fact, Tilly made so much milk that her udder was almost bursting at the seams and Britches had to milk her four times a day!

The **Woodland Daily Democrat** newspaper put her picture on the front page and wrote:

"New World Milk Cow a Dairy in Herself"

"Tilly Alcartra, a cow in the registered Holstein-Friesian herd owned by A.W. Morris and Sons, California, finished a year of test work with a production of 30,452.6 lbs. of milk containing 951.3 lbs. of butterfat, and thereby becomes the world's greatest milk cow.

TILLY ALCARTRA

RIVERSIDE SADIE DE KOL BURKE

ARALIA DE KOL

Asa's Champions

The article ran in newspapers coast to coast. When Asa showed it to his boys he said, "I wish your mother could have been here to share this with us. She would have been so proud." Asa was not one to express his feelings often and he didn't like a big fuss. So, the boys just smiled and clapped each other on the back.

With each succeeding calf, Tilly's milk production increased. Two years later, in 1916, Tilly set a second world's record and the ***Pacific Rural Press*** wrote:

"Tilly Alcartra Does it Again!"

"On March 23, 1916, another world's record was broken when Tilly Alcartra finished her two year record with 60,287 lbs. of milk at the ranch of A.W. Morris and Sons in Yolo County, California."

But, it was a few simple lines from **Farm and Fireside** magazine that catapulted Tilly into the spotlight:

"A Remarkable Milking Record"

"If you should put all of the milk products produced last year by Tilly Alcartra, the world's champion cow, in ten gallon cans and stack them pyramid fashion, the peak would be as tall as an eight story building!"

That really got the attention of dairy cattle breeders. They wrote to Asa asking what in the world he was feeding his bovine wonder. Magic beans?

So, Asa gave interviews to the newspapers. He said, "Although Tilly is certainly an extraordinary cow, she doesn't receive any special diet. We treat her like all our other ladies with plenty of pasture time, good California sunshine, and loving care. Yolo County's fantastic sugar beets might have something to do with Tilly's success. She absolutely loves them!"

Tilly was a *phenomenon*, which means she was really unique and special. When you have a cow that can do all that you have a real gold mine! Tilly Alcartra was crowned the, "Queen of Holsteins," and she became the most famous dairy cow in the world.

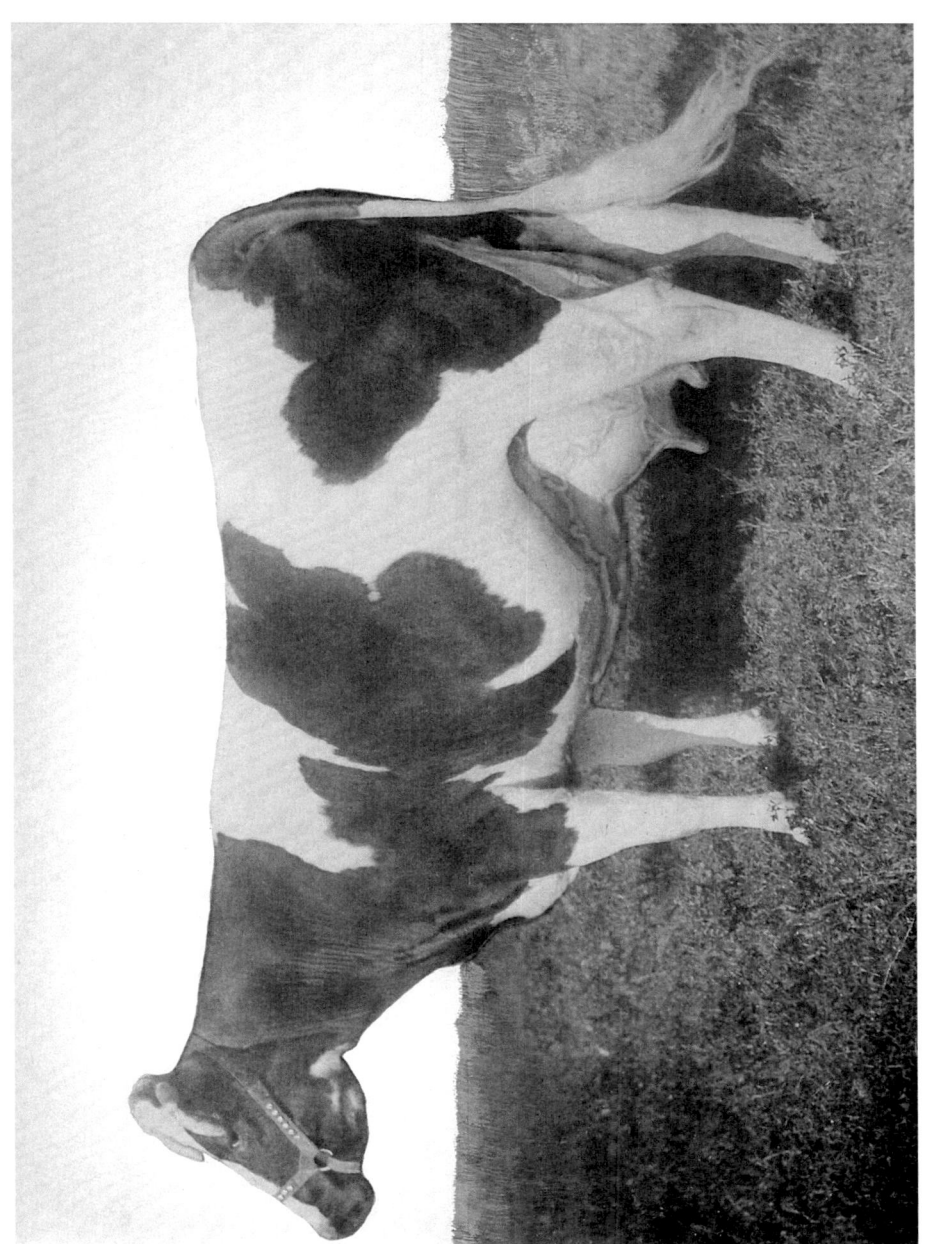

Tilly Alcartra official portrait

Tilly's Royal Progeny

Progeny is a fancy word for children,
and Tilly's were princes and princesses.

Newborn Holstein calves are a big, wet bundle of long legs, large brown eyes, and a coat that shows distinctive markings right from the beginning. They wobble for a time after they are born, but are soon upright and ready to meet their mothers who lick them from head to toe.

Tilly and Asa were a team. Each time she calved, Asa sat beside her inside the stall to watch over her. Tilly was his most prized animal and—to make sure that her calf was born without complications—he always kept a local veterinarian on call when her time approached. There were several fine veterinarians from the University Farm in nearby Davis, so Tilly was in good hands.

Just like a human baby, sometimes the calf took a while in coming. Asa and the boys waited anxiously, sometimes for hours. Asa spoke soothing words to Tilly while she labored, and when a healthy calf was delivered there was relief all around. He always took a good look at the new arrival to determine its health and sex. Then, he wiped his brow with his handkerchief and exclaimed, "Well, well, look what we have here!" He patted Tilly gently and said, "You did a fine job my girl. He's a beauty!"

Tilly's first calf was a little bull born at the Tule Ranch in 1910. He was sired by Korndyke Queen De Kol's Prince and was named Prince Alcartra Korndyke. Cows instinctively know how to feed and nurture their calves, and Tilly took good care of her new baby. As he grew, he romped around in the pasture and kicked up his heels like any little boy. When he was old enough, he was sold for $500.00 and went to live at the Gibson dairy farm in the nearby town of Williams. Prince Alcartra had a long and happy life and was the proud sire of seventy-five daughters!

Once, Tilly helped save a human life. Uncle Asa's son Will and his wife had a newborn daughter who weighed ten pounds at birth. The baby was losing weight because her tiny mother couldn't produce enough milk to feed her. There was a theory in those days that if you could pair a cow that had a newborn calf with a needy human infant, the cow's extra-rich nourishing milk could help the baby. As luck would have it, Tilly had just given birth to a calf. When Charley Morris learned of the problem he had an idea. He asked Asa, "What say we send Tilly over to help out?" Asa heartily agreed, so Tilly and her new calf went to stay at Will Morris' farm for six months to help feed the baby. And, that baby lived to be eighty-one years old!

Just about the time that Asa and Tilly became famous on the national dairy scene, Asa's oldest grandchildren began to show an interest in his operation. Frank's three youngsters, Madeline, Erline, and Les Morris, lived on the Tule Ranch and were frequent visitors to the barns. Madeline, the oldest, had a mop of strawberry blonde curly hair that would rival any child movie star. Erline had a winsome smile and a bobbed haircut, and Les, youngest of the three, was blonde-headed dynamite.

Madeline and Erline especially liked to visit when there were new calves. They petted and cooed over them, and since they were just little girls, a young Holstein calf was about the right size for them. Asa taught them the dangers of wandering around livestock and put his farm hand, Sid Higgins, in charge of them. Some years later, when Madeline was all grown up, Sid married her and became part of the family.

Asa's grandchildren
Les, Erline, and Madeline Morris in Cache Creek, 1910

Les was a pint-sized ball of fire. He was just like the old man—energetic, feisty, and opinionated. Les was a big talker, and he loved to talk to Tilly.

Tilly was a very productive breeding cow and seemed to thrive after the birth of each calf, giving ever larger outputs of milk. At her peak she averaged forty-five quarts a day! Over her lifetime she had eight sons and daughters, all handsome like herself. Her offspring were always in great demand and one daughter, Tilly Alcartra II, was sold at auction in Philadelphia, Pennsylvania, for $1⎯,200 dollars. In 1916, that was a LOT of money! Her bull calves, who could produce dozens of off-spring, sold for even more money.

Tilly's most famous bull calf was sired in 1919 by the most expensive bull in the world whose name was Carnation King Sylvia. This bull was owned by the Carnation Stock Company of Seattle, who had paid a record $106,000 for him. Holstein breeders were flabbergasted by such an enormous sum of money for a single bull. Like Queen Tilly Alcartra, Carnation King Sylvia, was royalty. They became the proud parents of a bull calf named Alcartra King Sylvia who had a *sterling* pedigree, which means the highest standard.

Announcing his birth in April, 1920, the **Woodland Daily Democrat** ran the headline:

"Tilly Eighth Time Proud Mamma"
Oh Joy! It's a boy!

When Alcartra King Sylvia was old enough, he and other young calves from the Morris herd traveled to St. Paul, Minnesota, by train to be sold at auction. On their way east, they stopped at Sacramento, California, where Asa was well regarded. Several dignitaries from the Rotary Club gave him and his livestock a parade from the Capitol building towards the Union Pacific Train Depot. On the train, Sid Higgins rode and slept in the cattle car with Alcartra King Sylvia all the way to St. Paul.

Livestock auctions are usually held in a big ring where interested buyers bid money against each other until the highest bid wins. Asa's grandson Les went along on the trip. He sat next to Asa and Sid and watched all the cows and bulls brought into the ring. When Alcartra King Sylvia was finally

Tilly with her calf, Alcartra King Sylvia

presented, the crowd went wild and so did the bidding. Les could hardly contain himself when Alcartra King Sylvia sold in five minutes for $50,000! Another of their calves fetched $41,000. That totaled about one million in today's dollars and was more money than Les could even imagine.

All of Tilly's calves were royalty. They were in high demand by dairymen, so when they grew up, they went to live in different Holstein herds all around the United States and beyond. Their champion bloodlines helped to create better, stronger, and more productive Holstein cows for future generations. Today, Holsteins have become the dominant breed of dairy cow in the United States and supply about ninety percent of our milk. If you think about it, the milk you drink every day might come from one of Tilly's great-great-great-great-great granddaughters. It's possible!

Talent is a Gift

Talent is a gift that you are born with and—just like
people—some animals become STARS. It sounds
glamorous, but if you're a star you have to get used to all the
fanfare and fuss that accompanies you wherever you go.

Asa was a born showman and he knew how to present
Tilly with dignity and good humor. On the other hand, Tilly
was ROYALTY, a regal and gorgeous Holstein who knew just
how to preen for an audience. Besides her phenomenal milk
production, she had a very mellow personality. She genuinely
liked people and was never bothered by a change of scenery or
society. When Asa and Tilly combined their talents they made
magic happen.

Until the mid-twentieth century, America was mostly a
nation of farmers, so a phenomenal animal was as interesting
to them as new technology is to us today. Tilly continued to
break the world's record for two, three, four, five, and six
consecutive years total milk production. No cow of any breed
had ever achieved that before.

Tilly Alcartra was the bovine equivalent of an Olympic
marathon runner. The New York *De Reuter Gleaner* newspaper compared her to an athlete:

"Tilly Alcartra, the Long Distance Cow"

"You can't keep a good man down and this is as true of cows as it is of men. In proof of which is news that the famous Tilly Alcartra is again up to her old tricks of rolling up records. She is THE champion long distance cow."

Tilly became a CELEBRITY, like a cow movie star, and she was a very popular guest at banquets and livestock shows. Appearing at special events was part of her royal duties, so Asa took her on an interstate publicity tour.

Publicity is part of being a Queen because you have to have your photograph taken a lot. Tilly learned just how to look her best when she posed for the camera. She always held her head up proudly, and stood very still.

She was photographed for all the dairy magazines and for the "Holstein Advanced Registry," a record book where her name and official number, 123459, were recorded along with the other world champions. *Sunset Magazine* printed her hand-painted portrait on a brochure for the Panama Pacific International Exhibition of 1915, a World's Fair held in San Francisco. The Yolo Board of Trade also used her portrait on the cover of a booklet advertising the great agricultural opportunities Yolo County offered.

Asa had another trick up his sleeve. He was a genius at *marketing* which is the business of promoting and selling your product. He never lost an opportunity to put his Holsteins in the forefront when an occasion presented itself.

Tilly's image was used to promote a farm implement called a Papec Ensilage Cutter. Asa had firsthand experience with this special machine which he used on the Tule Ranch to cut up his silage corn. Tilly ate the silage, so she had firsthand experience, too. Products endorsed by Asa and the Holstein

Queen were advertised in farm magazines and sold very well.

One year President Woodrow Wilson, who served in office from 1913-1921, and his wife Edith traveled by train from Washington D.C. to California. Their train passed through Woodland on its way to San Francisco. Asa heard about the visit, and early the next morning, he sent a special pint of Tilly's freshly pasteurized cream to San Francisco by express train. That evening, President and Mrs. Wilson poured the *crème de la crème* of cream in their coffee, compliments of the famous Holstein Queen. When the **San Francisco Bulletin** printed the story the following day, Tilly got more press coverage than any human besides the President!

Asa was especially partial to an early automobile called a Nash. He owned a succession of them, and he liked them so much that he convinced all four of his boys to drive them, too. Arata Motor Company in Woodland made Asa a really good deal on five identical new Nash touring cars. In return, they asked Tilly to pose for their newspaper advertisement in front of the cars in the fields of the Tule Ranch. Tilly was glad to oblige.

When Britches led her out to the pasture for the photograph she had been expertly bathed and groomed. He grinned at her and said, "Tilly, just look at those shiny new cars all in a row. They've had a real spit and polish, just like you!" The headline for the advertisement read:

"Tilly Alcartra, World's Famous Holstein"
And Five NASH Cars Owned by A.W. Morris and Sons.

The ad worked; local folks and even out-of-towners flocked to Arata Motors to buy Nash cars. Asa and Tilly had one more marketing success!

TILLY ALCARTRA, World's Famous Holstein

And Five NASH Cars Owned by A. W. Morris and Sons

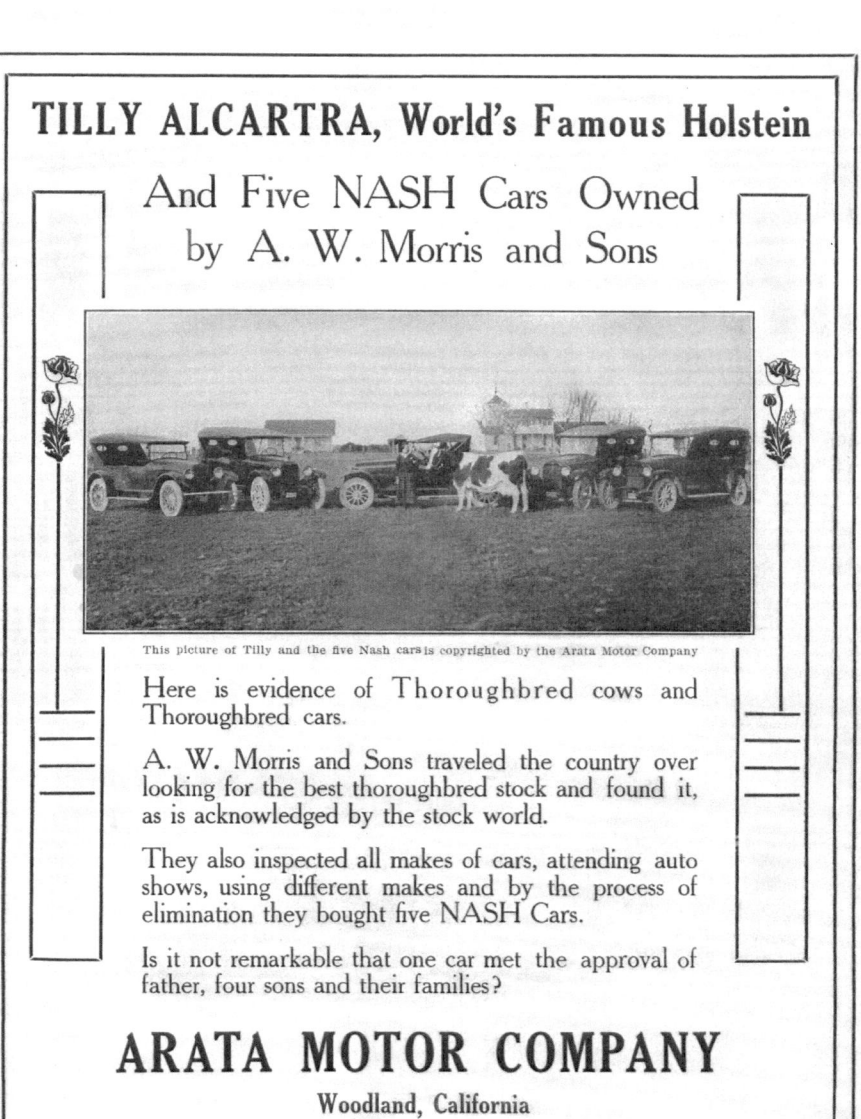

This picture of Tilly and the five Nash cars is copyrighted by the Arata Motor Company

Here is evidence of Thoroughbred cows and Thoroughbred cars.

A. W. Morris and Sons traveled the country over looking for the best thoroughbred stock and found it, as is acknowledged by the stock world.

They also inspected all makes of cars, attending auto shows, using different makes and by the process of elimination they bought five NASH Cars.

Is it not remarkable that one car met the approval of father, four sons and their families?

ARATA MOTOR COMPANY
Woodland, California

Tilly and the five Nash cars on the Tule Ranch

Cow Gossip

Sometimes when cows MOOOOO they are talking to one another. We can't understand their language but we would sure learn some interesting things if we did!

When Tilly wasn't touring she was home on the Tule Ranch. She missed the girls while she was on the road, so she spent lots of time in the pasture, eating, sunbathing, and catching up on the local cow *gossip*—chatty little stories that cows and people tell each other about their neighbors, and sometimes it gets a bit personal.

Three hundred Holsteins are practically a small town so there was always plenty to gossip about. Cows put on such a placid front when people are looking that you never know if they might be talking about you. They have other ways of communicating besides moooooing. News can be shared by a scrape of the hoof, a roll of the eye, or a flick of the tail. Certain smells contain a whole newspaper's worth of cow gossip.

Just like people, Holsteins have different temperaments, and each of Asa's champions had her own personality. Riverside Sadie De Kol Burke, a very proper lady, was the *matriarch* of the herd. A matriarch is an older mother who leads and sets the rules. The younger cows generally gave her the respect she deserved, but when they didn't, Sadie let them know about it!

Sadie's cousin Aralia De Kol was very *haughty,* which means stuck-up. She was Asa's oldest world champion and never let anybody forget it! Aralia held a very high opinion of herself and she behaved like a "V. I. C." which means VERY IMPORTANT COW. She complained bitterly whenever things were not to her liking. Aralia's half-sister, Ignaro Creamcup, was just the opposite; she was happy-go-lucky and thought life was just one big bowl of ice cream. Susie De Kol Canay Mercedes Burke was loud and bossy, and Betsy Lamb Prilly was a *flibbertigibbet.* That's a silly word for an airhead.

Gossiping and sunbathing on the Tule Ranch

The girls at the dairy always wanted to know about Tilly's latest trip especially when she had visited a big city. They also filled her in on happenings at home. Betsy was a regular chatterbox and usually couldn't wait to talk to Tilly alone. "So, Til, how was your big trip? Any excitement? Did you meet anybody interesting?" Tilly related her adventures on the road and Betsy sighed with a note of envy, "I think you must have the grandest life in the whole world!"

Aralia overheard their conversation and remarked to the others in a snotty tone, "What's Tilly got that the rest of us don't have, anyway? After all, we've set milk and butter records, too." Sadie turned to her cousin and replied, "One thing Tilly's got is good manners and that's more than I can say for you, Aralia."

Betsy leaned her head in close to Tilly and said, "We had some big excitement while you were gone, Til. You know the clover patch over on the south side? Well, let me tell you, there was a grassfire on Saturday morning, and some fool with a match started it. People can be pretty stupid with matches!"

Betsy went on, "Anyway, the fire came up awfully fast, and the wind blew sparks all over the place. We girls really had to 'hoof it' to get out of the way! Old Sadie is moving pretty slowly these days, don't you know, but when those flames took off, you should have seen her hustle! And that big udder of hers was really rolling!"

Betsy was enjoying the girls' attention, and continued with enthusiasm. "Thank Heavens the boys were on it right away. They're good boys you know—the old man trained 'em right. And, Britches is a real pistol! He was hollering to the farmhands where to head off the flames. They put that fire out lickety-split, but I'm sorry to tell you that our favorite clover patch was burned to a crisp!"

Sadie didn't take kindly to any reference to her age, and when she heard about Betsy's gossip, she *chastised* her, which means she really chewed her out. "Now look here, young Betsy, I won't have any more of this nonsense. I've earned my place in this herd, and you'd be wise to never forget it!" Sadie whipped her tail around like a lasso just to make her point.

The cows always watched their caretakers carefully and didn't hesitate to express their opinions to each other. One afternoon Harry went whizzing by on one of the tractors and gave a wave in the girls' direction. Creamcup switched her tail with delight and said, "There goes Harry, out for a test run I expect. I hear tell he's a wizard with engines. Harry would rather be in the shed welding things or greasing machinery than out in the fields like his brothers. I just love those boys!"

Tilly agreed and added, "Now, Charley is the one to know. He grows all of those lovely sugar beets for us and I've heard he's already cut three crops of tasty alfalfa this year." Tilly was always up to date on anything to do with food. She asked, "Have you girls seen much of Frank lately?" Creamcup nodded and replied, "Frank's quite the salesman now, and the other day I actually saw him wearing a suit and a tie!" Betsy looked dumbfounded and asked, "On a weekday? He never wears anything but overalls except on Sunday, of course."

Just then Asa came out of the milking barn followed by his grandson Les, who was wearing Asa's hat backwards. They were roaring with laughter. Sadie commented, "That young Les sure is a lively little squirt and always up to something! He loves to play jokes on his grandpa, too." Aralia shook her head and griped, "He's too noisy, too fast, and he scares me! If we must have children about, I prefer the little girls; they never bother me. Tilly, I must say, you and Les seem awfully chummy." Tilly looked Aralia in the eye and replied, "Well of course. He's a good boy, and he's got a lot of old Asa in him—they don't come any better than that!"

Susie was a cow dynamo—if there really is such a creature. Out in the pasture she mooooooed like a foghorn at milking or feeding time and rallied the herd into action, "C'mon now girls, get a move on. Hurry up there Aralia, you slow poke. Lay off that salt lick. We don't want the old man to think that we're not hungry. Why, he might cut back on our silage and that just wouldn't do." Aralia grumbled as she brought up the rear, "Oh, shut up, Susie, you bossy old milk bag!"

One day a new bull came to live on the ranch and the girls were all a twitter. Susie announced, "Have you girls seen the new fellow over in the paddock? I hear tell his name is Sebastian and he's from Des Moines, Iowa. Isn't he just the handsomest thing? Gorgeous glossy black hide and horns as wide as a feed trough! Don't let Betsy see him or she'll swoon. Betsy is just bull crazy!"

Aralia sniffed, "Old Lorena Korndyke still thinks he's hot stuff, but he's getting a bit over the hill, if you ask me. His hide is looking rather drab, and I think his hearing is going. Why, I had to mooooo at him five times the other day before he noticed me! His new rival will take him down a peg or two." She smirked with satisfaction.

Three hundred cows produced a lot of calves, so there were always new babies to be admired and fussed over. One morning, when Asa went out to the barn, he discovered that one of the girls had unexpectedly given birth to twin bull calves, sixteen hours apart. Asa was so excited that he had "two for the price of one!"

Sadie, who had seen dozens of calves in her lifetime, commented on the new arrivals, "Those twins are the spitting image of Segis Pontiac. Why they've even got their spots in all the same places! Of course, I don't think either of them is as handsome as my Butter Boy, or Tilly's Prince. But, I think they'll do well enough."

Often, the Tule Ranch had visitors. Dairymen came from around the world to study Asa's operation, and to purchase animals for their own herds. On visiting days, Sadie put out the word amongst the herd to be on their best behavior. "Now listen up!" she'd say. "We represent the old man and everything he's worked for, so I don't want any mischief or complaints from anybody. Did you hear me, Aralia? So, look like the champion herd that you are!" This was a very effective warning, and when the visitors arrived, the herd was happily grazing in the pasture and looked "picture postcard" perfect.

The Country Gentleman Magazine, **1919**
Britches, Asa, Tilly, Charley, Harry, Frank

Reporters from magazines and farm journals came from around the nation to interview Asa. They were very impressed by the herd and when they asked Asa the secret to his success, he told them, "We're a family business, you see. My four sons and I each have our separate jobs, but we take equal pride in each of our achievements. You've heard the old saying by the Englishman, Rudyard Kipling? *'It's the everlasting teamwork of every bloomin' son!'* "

One spring, a government official named George Marsden came all the way from New Zealand to the Tule Ranch. New Zealand is an island nation near Australia and Tilly was well known there. An ocean voyage from New Zealand to California is almost 6500 miles—which makes for one REALLY long boat ride!

After crossing the vast Pacific Ocean, Commissioner Marsden traveled to Woodland by train from San Francisco to see Asa's herd and to arrange cattle purchases for the New Zealand government. Mr. Marsden was a serious looking fellow but he grinned from ear to ear when he met Tilly. "Isn't she lovely!" he exclaimed. Looking out over the pasture he observed Asa's ladies at work mowing the grass and commented, "You've a very fine herd here Mr. Morris. In fact, these are the finest Holstein-Friesians I've ever seen!" Asa thanked him and politely suggested, "Shall we retire to my office Mr. Marsden and discuss business?"

As soon as they were out of sight, the gossip began. Most of the girls were delighted to be complimented by a foreign dignitary, but Aralia was annoyed that she had not been singled out for special recognition. Tilly took it all in stride. She knew well enough that she was Asa's showpiece, but she never said so to the others. She was a very worldly cow, who had been places and seen things that the others couldn't even imagine. So, even if the gossip got petty at times, Tilly just ignored it and took another mouthful of sugar beets.

An Unexpected Visitor Drops In

"Come Josephine in my flying machine,
Going up she goes, up she goes,
Balance yourself like a bird on a beam
In the air she goes, there she goes..."

1910 Flying Song

In 1917, America was drawn into World War I across the Atlantic Ocean in Europe. World War I was called "The war to end all wars," and it was a very bitter struggle. It was also the first time airplanes were used in combat. Though they looked small and flimsy to anyone but the pilot, they were deadly weapons in the air.

Nine hundred young men from all over Yolo County interrupted their lives to serve as soldiers overseas. Several local women also served as nurses and ambulance drivers. Citizens at home helped win the war by donating money, rolling bandages, and sending their crops to feed the troops.

Many American lives were lost in Europe, including thirty-one soldiers from Yolo County, but the United States and her allies were ultimately victorious. November 11, 1918, was declared Armistice Day (now called Veterans Day) which marked the end of the war. When all the weary soldiers came home to Woodland, each one had a hearty meal and a big bowl of Yolo County ice cream, courtesy of Asa's Holsteins.

Airplanes had become more numerous since the war began, but they weren't an everyday sight. Sometimes they had to land without warning—wherever they could find a level stretch of field.

One November afternoon shortly after Armistice Day, Tilly and the girls were peacefully grazing in the north pasture when, off in the distance, they heard the rumble of an engine. This wasn't particularly unusual since Harry was always busy fixing or testing one of the many motorized machines used on the ranch. But the sound grew louder and louder, and soon a distant speck appeared on the horizon. That speck proved to be an airplane which rapidly approached and swooped low over the ranch. The plane's engine sputtered and spat and it was apparent that it was in trouble.

It was a military training airplane called a Curtiss JN-4, affectionately called a "Jenny" by the hundreds of pilots who learned how to fly in them. Jennys were *biplanes* that had double-decker linen canvas wings held together by vertical wooden shafts and wires. They also had open-air cockpits. Compared to our modern jets, they looked like toys, but after the war they had remarkably long careers as stunt planes and were even used to deliver the U. S. Mail.

The pilot began a very rapid descent towards the pasture leaving a trail of smoke behind him. Susie was the first to sense imminent danger and she bellowed to the others, "HOLY COW!!! Heads up girls! Look what's coming our way. Move your sorry hides and HURRY!!!" There was a great kerfuffle to get out of the way. Betsy screeched, "He's landing! Can you believe it? An airplane is actually landing right here on the Tule Ranch! Oh, I hope he doesn't crash!" She squeezed her eyes shut just in case.

Motor sputtering, the Jenny touched down hard in the field and bounced along in a cloud of dust. Her tail swayed from side to side until she spun a half circle and came to a halt with her engine still running.

"Land sakes!" Tilly exclaimed, "That was a close one! You can open your eyes now Betsy, he's on the ground." The rest of the herd hovered in the background and waited eagerly to see what would happen next.

The farmhands charged out of the barns and Asa came running from the house. He could smell leaking gasoline and shouted, "Get the hoses ready boys and stand back in case that engine blows!" There were some very tense moments before the motor finally quit and the propeller came to a stop. Nothing terrible happened, so Asa moved cautiously towards the cockpit and shouted, "Are you all right in there young fella?"

The pilot raised his goggles and gave a thumbs-up sign. There was a spontaneous round of applause, and the cows gave a sigh of relief. The pilot grinned and pulled off his leather flying helmet; underneath, he had flaming red hair which stood up in sweaty spikes. "Sorry boys," he hollered, "she sprung a leak. Her fuel gauge was dropping like a rock so I figured I'd better land her on your ranch before I crashed into the creek!" As he stood up, he saluted the farmhands and bowed to his bovine audience, "Ladies, Lieutenant James Campbell, United States Army Air Service. Pardon the interruption in your lovely pasture."

Asa stepped forward to introduce himself and shook the pilot's hand, "That was some mighty fine flying young man," he said. "If you're an example of the skill of our wonderful airmen, it's no wonder we've had a huge victory in Europe. When you've checked your plane over and contacted your base, come on down to the house. The boys will see that you get anything you need, and my son Harry will take a look at that engine. He can fix just about anything."

The whole family came to supper that night. Lieutenant Campbell had recently returned from Europe where he had flown combat missions over France. He was on his way to deliver the Jenny back to Mather Field in Sacramento and was just forty miles short of his home base when he got sidelined in Asa's cow pasture.

After supper, the Lieutenant told some thrilling and scary tales about air combat missions called *dogfights*. Young Les Morris was so excited that he bounced up and down in his chair and kept asking questions. "Can you do barrel rolls in your plane? Do you really see the whites of their eyes before you shoot? Did you fight the Red Baron, Lieutenant?" (That was the nickname for Baron Manfred Von Richthofen, the most famous World War I German Ace fighter pilot, who shot down eighty aircraft singlehandedly with his notorious red warplane.) "No Son, I didn't," said the Lieutenant, "I never met the Baron in the air, and if I had, I probably wouldn't be here talking to you. But the Baron got his due when he was finally shot out of the sky last April."

Les was so impressed that he boasted to the family, "Someday I'm going to fly planes just like the Lieutenant!" Everybody laughed because Les couldn't even drive yet, but twenty-five years later, they weren't laughing when Les became a flyer and expert gunner in World War II.

*   *   *

Meanwhile, in the pasture, the cows swarmed around the huge flying machine that sat in their midst. "It certainly is a funny looking contraption," Susie remarked. Tilly took a good look and commented to the others, "It's lucky that the lieutenant landed on our ranch since Harry has every tool known to man in his welding shed. Maybe he can help get this machine up and running again."

Aralia responded in her usual negative way, "Harry doesn't know the first thing about airplanes." Creamcup countered, "That doesn't matter, silly. All these motorized things run on gasoline and a machine is a machine. Besides, A.W. has his own gas pump and I'm sure he can spare some."

Sure enough, the very next morning the fuel line was patched and the engine was gassed up and ready to go. When Lieutenant Campbell tested the motor, he waved his cap in the air and shouted, "Hurray for Harry! Thanks to him, I'm sure I can make it to Mather Field."

Asa had learned that the Lieutenant's father raised cattle in Northern California, and before he left Asa told him, "Lieutenant, I have a very special lady you might like to meet. Come this way."

Out in the pasture Asa introduced him to Tilly. "Tilly Alcartra!" the Lieutenant exclaimed as he petted her gently, "Wait until Dad hears that I met the famous Holstein Queen!" He grinned broadly at Tilly who flicked her tail and nodded to him in return. Then he turned to Asa and extended his hand, "Thank you Mr. Morris, for your hospitality, and many thanks to Harry for patching up the old machine."

Asa insisted that the family have their picture taken in front of the airplane. It was a cold day so they bundled up in their winter coats and grinned for the camera while the Lieutenant took their picture. That blurry photograph marked the historic day that the Jenny landed on the Tule Ranch. Les Morris remembered it for the rest of his life.

Lieutenant Campbell took off in a cloud of dust, saluting as he flew away into the blue November sky. Everybody waved until he vanished into the distance and Tilly watched him go, waving her tail. She was especially proud to have met one of "America's Finest" young fliers.

The excitement was over and, except for skid marks on the field and a circle of flattened grass, nobody would ever suspect an airplane had landed there. Tilly and the girls returned to graze in their peaceful pasture as if nothing had happened. Cows are like that; you can't ruffle them for long.

Curtiss "Jenny" on the Tule Ranch

Lunch at the Benson

Fine chefs pride themselves
on their exquisite cuisine,
but catering to "Madame Alcartra"
was an extraordinary challenge!

Tilly toured all over the West coast by train, and became a first class advertisement for her breed and her owners. She always rode in a First Class parlor car, which is generally just for people, but it was specially arranged for a big cow. Everywhere Asa and Tilly traveled, word got out and crowds came to see the Holstein Queen.

On their way home from Seattle, Washington, the Chamber of Commerce in Portland, Oregon, invited Asa and Tilly to lunch at the Hotel Benson. It was Tilly's big day to show off for the citizens of Portland and she always displayed excellent manners in public. Asa told her about the upcoming event and groomed her until she gleamed.

Tilly's famous reputation preceded her. Anticipating her arrival, Portland officials prepared a special welcoming ceremony, complete with all the fanfare usually lavished on human celebrities. *The Morning Oregonian* newspaper ran a column which read:

"Dairy Queen is Coming"
Celebrated Holstein to be Guest of Ad Club

"Royalty will be entertained at the Hotel Benson tomorrow. The guest of honor will be Madame Tilly Alcartra, queen of all dairy cows."

At noontime Tilly's train pulled into Portland's Union Station where she was met by a cheering crowd. The truck that was waiting to chauffeur her was too small for her hefty 1700-pound frame so an oversized truck-taxi came to the rescue. Tilly rode in style behind the Washington High School Marching Band through the streets of downtown Portland to the Hotel Benson. She was escorted across the magnificent lobby into the crystal dining room where she was met by an enthusiastic audience and Portland's mayor, the Honorable George Luis Baker.

The Benson, opened in 1913, was a splendid big brick hotel. It was just gaining prominence in the West Coast hotel world, so every celebrity who visited added to its stature, even when the celebrity was a cow!

The crystal dining room was as lovely as its name, with a soaring ceiling lit by tiered, sparkling chandeliers. For Tilly's special event, it was packed with dozens of formally dressed businessmen seated at long luncheon tables. When the two honored guests were introduced, Asa gave a short speech about Tilly and the marvelous Holstein breed.

Tilly was HUNGRY! It had been hours since breakfast, but she stood by patiently while photographers clicked away in the background. The ***Pathe News Service***, an international motion picture news company, was on hand with a movie camera to capture the remarkable scene—as Mayor Baker donned a milkmaid bonnet with his dress suit and milked

Tilly himself. The Mayor hammed it up for the camera, but soon turned the rest of the job over to a milking expert, who quickly filled a very large pail. That's a politician for you: look competent for just five minutes and everybody assumes you know what you are doing!

All the delighted guests looked on and when lunch was served, each guest had a glass of warm milk straight from the Queen herself! Tilly was served a special lunch prepared by the hotel's famous French chef, Henry Thiele, who called her "Madame Alcartra." He whipped up a delicious bran soufflé garnished with clover buds and alfalfa tips. Tilly tucked right into her meal and enjoyed her first fling with French food.

After everyone finished eating, the little daughter of the Ad Club president placed a crown of flowers, which included

Tilly at the Hotel Benson, Portland, Oregon
Mayor George Luis Baker milking Tilly

famous Portland Roses, around the Holstein Queen's horns and everybody applauded. With the ceremony over, it was off to the railroad station in a cloud of glory!

Back on the train, Tilly looked at Asa with her big brown eyes, moooooed, and began to munch on her lovely floral crown. Asa had a big belly laugh and told her, "Congratulations, Tilly. You were terrific, so go right ahead and enjoy yourself!" A few stray rose petals slowly drifted onto the floor while Tilly chewed away. After all, wearing a tasty wreath was a terrible waste of a delicious dessert. Portland had been an exciting adventure, and for a royal cow, what in the world could top that?

The Queen Visits the Palace

Queen Elizabeth II of England
stays at Buckingham Palace in London.
Queen Tilly Alcartra, who was born in
Buckingham, Iowa, stayed at a famous Palace, too.

In the autumn of 1919, the city of San Francisco hosted the California International Livestock Exposition. Hundreds of quality animals from all over America were entered in the competitions. Since it was the most important show on the West Coast, Asa entered his best cows and bulls in the events. Among those to compete for top honors were Tilly's grown son King Morco Alcartra, her grandson King Morco Alcartra Head, and her granddaughter Tilly Alcartra III.

Meanwhile, a very special invitation had arrived from San Francisco for the Holstein Queen. During exhibition week, the San Francisco Advertising Club was planning an awards banquet at the famous Palace Hotel on Market Street. Not to be outdone by Portland's Hotel Benson, the Palace invited Tilly to be their guest of honor. Since all sorts of dairymen would be in the city, competing with one another for blue ribbons, Asa immediately saw the opportunity to display the world's most famous Holstein in a truly royal palace.

Two weeks before Asa and Tilly left for the big city, Jim Willard, the Yolo County Sheriff, paid a visit to the Tule Ranch. The sheriff was a personal friend, and Asa trusted him. Sheriff Willard took off his hat, extended his hand and said, "A.W., I've come to give you some news and, unfortunately, a warning. I've had reports that a couple of your former employees, Wilfred Sykes and Ernest Tanner, have been publicly making threats against you. Can you tell me what prompted them to make these threats?"

Asa told the sheriff that he had recently fired the two workers for poor performance and drunkenness. He added, "Now Jim, you know I'm a fair man, but I have a business to run. Three hundred head of cattle and eighteen employees depend on me, so I can't coddle irresponsible, unreliable workers."

The sheriff nodded and replied, "Of course, we both know that, but those two men are likely part of the IWW gang, who pride themselves on tough threats. That gang has been causing trouble in this area recently." The sheriff continued, "A.W., you know the law is on your side, but please be extra careful and keep your eyes open." As the two men shook hands, Asa responded, "Will do, Jim, and thanks!"

The Industrial Workers of the World, or IWW, was an early labor union that catered to wandering and unskilled laborers. The organization was nicknamed "The Wobblies," and wherever they went, trouble followed. They made a nuisance of themselves with many local farmers using the tactics of *intimidation*, which means making frightening threats, and *sabotage*, which is underhanded, deliberate destruction.

Asa took the sheriff's words to heart, but he had to make a decision. Would he let two devious men threaten everything he had worked for? Or would he continue with his plans for the exhibition in San Francisco and exercise what precautions he could? Asa was no coward and the answer was simple: proceed, with caution.

*   *   *

In the early twentieth century, long distance hauling of a 1700-pound cow, even a famous one, wasn't easy to do. Truck engines weren't very powerful so it took a long time to go anywhere. That's why the Morris Holsteins traveled to San Francisco via the Southern Pacific Railroad. American Express handled the travel arrangements, and train fare for everybody cost almost one thousand dollars. The trip took a whole day, including a ferryboat ride across the bay. When the boat carrying the herd docked at a downtown waterfront pier, Frank supervised moving their prized cattle to the stables near the exhibition grounds. Asa drove Tilly to the Palace Hotel himself in a truck brought down from the Tule Ranch.

San Francisco was an amazing sight for a country cow. The streets were jammed with traffic and Tilly noticed all kinds of new smells and sounds along the way. Oily creosote fumes from the boat docks mingled with intense fishy smells from the day's catch. Gasoline exhaust competed with the distant scent of pine and eucalyptus, which drifted by on a misty breeze, and the brisk, salty aroma of the ocean permeated everything. There were clanging trolleys, fire engine sirens, and construction noise. Big cities like San Francisco were always building larger and better buildings.

Asa weaved in and out of traffic and when he turned the final corner onto Market Street, people stopped to stare. One onlooker shouted, "Welcome to San Francisco, Queen Tilly!" When Tilly saw the splendid Palace Hotel she was astonished, "Land sakes alive! Would you look at THAT! The girls at home will never believe it!

Tilly stabled in the lobby of the Palace Hotel, 1919

The Palace Hotel, built in 1875, was a "Grande Dame" (that's French for Great Lady) of American hotels. She sat proudly on the corner of Market and New Montgomery Streets for thirty years before being damaged in the 1906 San Francisco earthquake. As the city was rebuilt, so was the Palace, and she looks as stately today as she did when she reopened in 1909—though nowadays she is almost swallowed up by towering skyscrapers.

Many famous people passed through the big bronze double doors of the Palace into a world of elegance. Her magnificent lobby was paved with polished marble and her plaster walls were gilt with gold. Her reception rooms were lit by sparkling chandeliers and furnished with mahogany tables, velvet sofas, and Persian rugs. There were even real potted palm trees that grew indoors under an enormous leaded glass ceiling. At the Palace, you could have spotted a movie star or even the President, but nobody ever expected to see a big cow inside such a fine hotel.

Tilly was such a famous and valuable animal that she was stabled in a room right off the hotel lobby with a guard to watch over her. Today, cows who visit San Francisco for rodeos and livestock shows stay in a large building south of the city called the "Cow Palace." That's a joke, because it isn't a palace at all. It's just a huge, stuffy old arena full of show rings and stables and not at all fit for a Queen.

Wherever she went, Tilly took it all in stride. As long as there was a mound of hay, some sugar beets, and Asa was nearby, she was content.

Showtime

A really fine animal always steals the show.

The morning of the event at the Palace Hotel, Asa was beaming with good humor and when he saw Tilly he grinned from ear to ear. While he groomed her, he let slip a big surprise: "Tilly, I wasn't going to tell you just yet, but I'm so excited I'm about to bust a gusset! Your boy King Morco has done you proud. He's been named Grand Champion Bull at the Exposition! Then your grandson, King Morco Head, was named Reserve Grand Champion, and your granddaughter Tilly III was first in her class for junior calf! So we'll have to have a celebration when we get back to the Tule Ranch!"

Tilly was a proud mama and grandma that day. She and Asa were in high spirits when he led her into the enormous banquet room to get her settled before the Ad Club patrons arrived. Tilly looked around at the luxurious room and thought to herself, "They don't call this place 'The Palace' for nothing! It's gorgeous!"

The walls were covered with scrolled gold wallpaper, and the high plaster ceilings were lit by half a dozen glass chandeliers, each at least seven feet long! Their rows and rows of sparkling cut crystals reflected light and threw flashes of rainbow colors everywhere. Tall windows rose from floor to ceiling and were framed by blue brocade draperies fringed in gold. They covered both ends of one entire wall. In the center of the wall was a long *dais*—which is a platform where IMPORTANT people sit. The dais had fourteen blue velvet chairs, side by side, for the fourteen people who were to speak at the ceremony. Hanging on the wall behind the dais was a huge patriotic *bunting;* that's a half-circle shaped drapery of the Stars and Stripes that you see on the Fourth of July. Around the room were dozens of round tables set with white linen tablecloths, gold and white china dishes, and genuine sterling silverware.

On the left side of the room, Tilly saw her royal throne. Every queen has one, Tilly thought to herself. Hers was a raised, decorated platform covered with fresh sweet hay; it looked really inviting—especially the hay part. Asa spoke to her quietly and said, "We're playing in the big league here, Tilly, so do your best and I know that you won't disappoint me. You never have." He patted her flank and said, "Up you go now and show these folks just what a fine Queen you are!" Tilly walked up the ramp to her throne with a practiced step.

Asa carefully placed her head into a metal *stanchion* which is a type of yoke that holds an animal comfortably and securely in place. Six pretty young milkmaids came in wearing bright blue overalls and yellow straw hats. They were Tilly's "ladies in waiting." They petted her gently and had their picture taken with her. It was a very royal setting.

The Ad Club patrons and their wives began to arrive and when they were seated at their tables, the president of the club stood up and introduced the guests. Then he said, "Ladies and Gentlemen, we have with us today two special representatives of our California Dairy Industry. Allow me to introduce Mr. Asa W. Morris of Woodland and his world

Tilly in the banquet room at the Palace Hotel

famous Holstein cow, Tilly Alcartra. Mr. Morris has greatly contributed to the development of the dairy industry in California with his advancements and improvements of the Holstein breed. And we just can't say enough about Tilly Alcartra. She has broken record after record and is one very special lady. Welcome, Tilly!" Asa doffed his hat and Tilly turned on her bovine charm. The entire audience broke out in spontaneous applause.

The next order of business was lunch, so while the patrons ate shrimp cocktail and roast beef, Tilly munched on her barley and sugar beets. After lunch, she stood by patiently while the IMPORTANT people talked and talked and talked. Then, it was Asa's turn to give a speech about her and the future of the Holstein breed. Eventually, they handed out the awards for the best San Francisco advertisers and the ceremony came to an end.

When Tilly came down off her throne, lots of people lined up to get a closer look at the famous Holstein Queen. Tilly was a very large animal, and the well-dressed ladies in their feathered hats and gloves who reached out to pet her were dwarfed by comparison.

They fussed and fawned over her as though she was a little Toy Poodle and buzzed with excited comments and questions. One lady looked Tilly in the eye and commented, "Why, aren't you just the most precious thing? Frances, would you look at her lovely long eyelashes!"

Another lady asked, "Is this your first stay in a big hotel, Tilly? And are you enjoying the Palace? Such fine manners! Why, you seem right at home here!" She turned to her friend and said, "Florence, won't my grandchildren be surprised when I tell them that we saw a Holstein cow at the Palace Hotel!"

Tilly didn't mind a bit as she relished all the attention.

She was tidy, too, and never dirtied her throne while she appeared before her human audience.

When the show was over it was time to go home. Tilly had seen the very finest that San Francisco had to offer, and that was more than most people ever got to do in their entire lives. But after all the traffic, the noise, and the perfumed ladies, she longed for the earthy smells of the Tule Ranch. When they cast off on the big Bay Ferry, Tilly took one last look at the San Francisco skyline and smiled to herself. The Alcartra family had given San Francisco a lasting impression of bovine royalty that would not soon be forgotten.

Up in Smoke!

In the old days, fire was a farmer's worst enemy.

Asa always believed he should keep himself in top physical condition to deal with any emergency. But when a really big emergency struck the Tule Ranch, he wasn't home to deal with it.

Before he left for San Francisco, Asa had warned his employees to be on the lookout for any retaliation from the two workers he had fired, and the Wobblies. He asked his men to take turns keeping watch, but with over a thousand acres of land, there was only so much anyone could do.

The trouble started on the very Sunday Asa and Tilly planned to return home from San Francisco. At three o'clock in the morning, Sid Higgins climbed into the ranch truck and went out on patrol. As he drove around the buildings and up and down the dirt roads, all was quiet. It was still dark outside at five o'clock, when the farm hands assembled for breakfast.

When he parked the truck to join them, Sid heard a distant vehicle backfire on the main road beyond the ranch. Shortly afterwards, he heard faint footsteps crashing through the tules. An engine revved, gravel crunched under the wheels as the vehicle took off, and Sid felt a sudden chill up his spine.

He ran to the barn to check on the cows. The moment he opened the big double doors he smelled smoke. He rushed into the chow hall shouting, "FIRE! In the big cow barn!" The farmhands jumped up in unison, toppling the benches they were sitting on. They all raced towards the barn, gathering buckets and burlap sacks that Asa kept stacked by each building. Sid clanged the dinner bell, which could be heard all over the ranch, and Charley, Harry, and Britches came running out of their bungalows. Charley immediately took charge and shouted, "Get the cattle out of the barn NOW! Harry, get the water pumps started. Britch, wet those bags down in the water trough and hurry!"

The fire spread very quickly. The big barn was burning in several different places and the farmhands ran in and out with wet handkerchiefs tied over their noses until they had led thirty panicked cattle outside to safety.

Harry got the nearest pump going, and as the water began to flow, he organized a bucket brigade. Several of the men formed a long line and passed the full buckets along from one to the next, with the last man hurling them onto the flames. Others used the wet burlap bags to beat out the sparks in the dry grass, but their efforts to quench the fire in the barn were useless.

Meanwhile, Britches counted heads amongst the cows and breathed a sigh of relief that none were missing. He secured them with the rest of the herd behind a pasture fence, and ran to help the others.

The silo nearest the barn was burning, and to make matters worse, all the hay and feed that the farmhands had stacked nearby the day before, was smoldering, too. The hay soon flared like a torch, and sparks blew in all directions.

Firefighting was a very risky endeavor in those days and country farmers were at the mercy of Mother Nature's fury. Woodland had a volunteer fire department and just one piece of firefighting equipment, an 1874 Clapp and Jones steam-powered water pumper which was pulled by a horse team. But the Woodland firemen were four miles away, and without telephone service, there was no way to alert them.

Nevertheless, help soon arrived. Asa's neighbors had seen the smoke, and several men in trucks and on horseback raced to the scene. One fellow was wearing his best Sunday suit, but he took off his jacket and pitched in. The fire had already done significant damage to the barn, so the crew concentrated on saving the other buildings by wetting them down.

The fire raged for three hours, and when it was finally under control, the crew tended to the smoldering ruins. The boys stood back and looked on in disbelief. Covered in soot, with blistered hands and singed eyebrows, they took stock of the losses. The big barn, two silos, testing and pasteurizing equipment, and several tons of feed were gone.

Britches reminded his brothers, "Thank the Lord nobody was hurt and none of our cattle were lost! And we can be especially relieved that our best animals were away in San Francisco. We can rebuild the buildings, but our livestock are our real bread and butter."

"Pop has worked so hard to make this ranch a success and now look at it! It's a crying shame!" Charley exclaimed. He added angrily, "If Wilfred and Ernest had anything to do with this disaster, Pop will be furious! Not to mention, he'll see to it that they're prosecuted to the full extent the law allows. Now, which one of us is going to send him a telegram with the news?"

Harry drove to Woodland to the Sheriff's Office. The sheriff was at church but his deputy said he would get word to him immediately. Then, Harry drove to the telegraph office and sent a short telegram to Asa at the Palace Hotel. In the abbreviated format that a telegram allowed, it read:

Fire at Tule Ranch – everyone safe – no cattle lost – one barn, two silos & feed destroyed – possibly arson – sheriff informed.   Harry

*   *   *

Asa was loading Tilly into the truck for the return trip from San Francisco, when the manager of the Palace Hotel hailed him, waving a telegram. "Mr. Morris, Sir, this telegram just came for you from Yolo. I think it's important!"

Asa opened the telegram and as he read it, his face darkened. The manager asked, "I hope it's not bad news?" Asa replied, "Not good news I'm afraid. It seems we've had a fire at the home place." The manager was dismayed and cried, "That's terrible! I hope the damages are not too extensive. On behalf of the Palace staff, we wish you the best, Mr. Morris."

After they boarded the ferry to cross the bay, Tilly noticed that Asa was very somber. All the way home on the train, he didn't say a word and was absorbed in his own thoughts. He mulled over the sheriff's words, and wondered if his former employees had, indeed, sabotaged the Tule Ranch. But there was nothing to be done until he saw the damage in person. Frank was still at the exposition grounds with the remaining cattle when he heard the news, and he decided to return to Woodland on an afternoon train.

As they drove up the road to the ranch, Tilly could smell trouble; smoke and ashes from the fire blew in whirling gusts on the north wind. When Asa drove through the gate, he couldn't believe his eyes! The full fury and scale of the fire took him completely aback. Wisps of smoke were still rising from the ruins of the barn and two silos were tilted and scorched. The boys were waiting for him in the office, and so was the sheriff.

"A.W., I'm terribly sorry this has happened," said the sheriff. He offered Asa his hand and continued, "Especially, since I hear congratulations are in order with your exposition winners." Asa sadly replied, "Thanks, Jim. This certainly does put a damper on our jubilation, but we are very grateful no lives were lost. I hear my boys and my crew did a tremendous job, given the circumstances."

The sheriff said, "I've put the word out to the local communities and sent a telegram to the Sacramento Sheriff, to be on the lookout for Wilfred and Ernest. As far as I can tell, this fire was deliberately set, probably as revenge. If we catch them, I will personally lock them up and throw away the key! But I must warn you, in all likelihood, they've jumped a freight train and are miles away by now. When I round up the local Wobblies, they'll have some serious explaining to do!"

Tule Ranch Fire November, 1919

*   *   *

Asa ticked off the visible losses in his head, and quickly realized that the barn was only insured for $3,000. The staggering monetary loss was bound to exceed $45,000. He wondered where he would get the funds to replace what he had lost.

Asa led Tilly out to the pasture to join the ladies, who were huddled under a couple of big oak trees, as far away as they could get from the disaster. The cows looked wild-eyed and afraid, so Asa said to Tilly, "I'm counting on you to help the others. Just reassure them, help them to keep calm so their milk production won't be affected." Tilly completely under-stood.

Knowing that the sound of soothing words was all he could offer them, he said to his herd, "Now I know all of you are very frightened, and I don't blame you a bit. But the boys and I will see to it that you are well taken care of and have plenty to eat." Betsy, who was especially goggle-eyed, let out a big mooooo to express her fears. "I know, I know, it's a sad day," said Asa, "but we'll get through this. Now go on and have yourselves some of that nice green clover in the north pasture, enjoy the autumn sunshine, and don't worry." Taking her cue from Asa, Tilly turned and led the girls out to the clover patch.

Returning to the remaining barn, Asa made a point to thank his neighbors for their help and concern. They offered to bring feed and hay until Asa could replenish his supplies. Everyone shook hands, and the man in his sooty Sunday suit declared, "You're a good man, Asa. If you can't rely on your neighbors when troubles come, who can you rely on?"

Frank returned on the afternoon train to a disastrous

scene. That evening Asa and his sons, along with Sid Higgins, talked over the steps to recover and rebuild. Asa said, "First things first. Sid, you're our most reliable and valued employee, and I'd really like you to be in charge of the clean-up of this mess." Sid nodded, "Sure thing, A.W."

Asa declared, "There's no guarantee—even if those two culprits are caught—we'll receive any monetary compensation, so I'm afraid we're on our own on this one. But I sure would like to wring their necks, the ornery cusses!

"We've got some savings to pay the crew, but we'll have to sell some of our younger stock immediately," said Asa. I figure we need to raise $50,000 cash, fast."

Frank agreed and suggested, "I say we give notice that we'll have a big auction in the next two weeks, and I'll take care of the publicity."

"Charley, we need you to find local sources to replace the feed we've lost," Asa said, "and I need an estimate of how many extra crops we can harvest this season." Charley nodded, "I'm already on it, Pop."

Asa continued, "Britch, what do you think of rigging up the remaining barn for milking? We could do that in a few days. And, what about temporarily relocating the stock that are returning from San Francisco to the Knights Landing ranch? The barn is old but it will provide shelter, at least during the coming cold months." Britches agreed.

Harry added, "I think I can get the trucks ready by tomorrow so we can start hauling the cattle up to Knights Landing as soon as they arrive on the train."

Asa concluded, "We're going to rebuild and be better than ever. One day, we'll look back on this episode as one of life's trials that made us better men."

The following morning, Asa called a meeting with his farmhands. His sons could tell he hadn't slept a wink and was dead tired from the strains of the previous day. They offered him a chair, which he refused. Asa stood up straight and addressed his men:

"Despite our great misfortune yesterday, we've been spared the loss of life. The law will determine whether our two former employees are guilty of setting this fire, but regardless, the damage is done. I want to personally thank each and every one of you for your tremendous efforts in saving the livestock and the ranch. I'm very proud to be associated with such brave men. In the coming weeks, my boys and I will need your help more than ever as we rebuild, and I will see to it that every man who wishes will retain his job."

There was a round of applause and the men clapped each other on the back. Asa continued, "Now go and get cleaned up. The wives have prepared a special 'thank you' supper for you all. Tomorrow, we begin again."

Of course, rebuilding is never easy. Weeks passed, winter came, and the Tule Ranch slowly recovered. The cows were milked in a brand new barn, two new silos were packed with fresh corn silage, and Asa faced an ongoing mountain of debt. Arson was never legally proven; the culprits were never caught; and the Wobblies fled to take their mischief elsewhere.

*   *   *

There is an old saying, "Trouble comes in threes" and that certainly proved true for Asa. The spring following the Tule Ranch fire, he invested $3,500 in a brand new harvester. It was the latest design and, for its time, a very effective piece of equipment. He had devised a scheme to lease the machine to his neighbors for a fee when it wasn't needed on the farm. But, Fate had other plans.

The day after the harvester arrived, Asa's crew hauled

it to a nearby job site to harvest wheat. That same morning, he sent Harry to Woodland to pay the insurance premium for the new machine. Half an hour after Harry left the insurance agent's office, the harvester set itself on fire with its own sparks and was completely destroyed. Good thing they had insurance!

Three months later, when Frank was away in Chicago, his home caught fire from a faulty kerosene heater and completely burned down; nobody was hurt and the farm-hands saved much of the furniture. By this time, Asa had experienced three fires in less than one year, and he didn't even attempt to rebuild the house. Frank and his family packed up and moved to Woodland!

Asa was greatly admired in the Woodland community for his *fortitude*—courage in the face of adversity. Time and again, he rose from calamity. His life experience had taught him never to sink into self-pity or look backwards. He had learned to simply begin anew. And that is what he did.

The Local Celebrity

Small towns love to boast about
their most famous citizens, and Woodland
was proud to call Tilly Alcartra her own.

Tilly had her duties at the dairy but she was also an important member of the community. So whenever there was a celebration or a parade, she was invited to participate.

Sometimes Tilly WAS the parade. The local press was always keen to print any news about Woodland's bovine celebrity. When word got out that Asa was taking her on a publicity tour, an article appeared on the front page of the **Woodland Daily Democrat** that read:

"One and Only Tilly Parades Main Street Tonight"

The one and only Tilly will tread the main thoroughfare of the fair city of Woodland this evening so that the citizens of the town may give "Yolo's Pride" the once over before she departs on a visit to the Carnation Cream Factory at Seattle.

With four other thoroughbreds from the A.W. Morris dairy, Tilly Alcartra will be exposed to the gaze of the public at 6 o'clock this evening as she passes through the city en route to the Southern Pacific Depot where a parlor section on the choo-choo cars has been reserved for the northern trip of the world's wonder cow.

That evening hundreds of Woodlanders gobbled an early supper, gathered their children, and hurried to Main Street. Asa led Tilly himself, waving to the crowd as they walked towards the train depot. Tilly was delighted to see so many well-wishers. While the audience cheered somebody shouted, "GOOD LUCK TILLY! YOU TOO, A.W.!"

*   *   *

Woodland had official parades on holidays like the Fourth of July when the whole town turned out. Tilly had to look her best so the Morris brothers would start grooming her early in the morning by giving her a bath. They polished her hooves and horns until they were as smooth as silk. Then they treated her udder with a special oirtment called "Udder Balm" to make it very pink and soft. They rubbed her all over with mineral oil and brushed her until her black and white coat glistened. The last step was to put cornstarch on her white spots to make them even whiter. Tilly looked gorgeous—as any Queen should! Asa did the final inspection and always put a wreath of fresh red roses around her neck. He would pat her on the flank and say, "You look great old girl. Now get out there and make us proud!"

Woodland's parades passed all the way down Main Street right through the middle of town. The parade was led by the "Troop of Colors" where a big American flag, a California flag, and various military flags were carried with pride by war veterans. The onlookers took off their hats, saluted, and clapped as a show of respect.

This was followed by the Woodland Volunteer Fire Department with horses pulling the town's 1874 Clapp and Jones steam water-pumper. The firemen waved to the crowds.

Woodland's Mayor drove by in an elegant Packard Touring Car. It was absolutely dripping with garlands of flowers so high he could barely see over them. The mayor's wife and two other important ladies sat in the back seat holding their parasols, smiling and greeting the crowd with the practiced, side-to-side wave of royalty.

Next in line was the High School marching band. The Drum Major who led the band, wore big white boots and a tall beaver hat with a big feather plume. He marched in high step, marked time with the rhythmic movements of his baton, and periodically blew his whistle. Whether he was signaling to his band or just showing off was a matter of opinion.

The musicians, decked out in colorful uniforms and plumed hats, marched along in lockstep while they played the famous march tune **Stars and Stripes Forever** by John Phillip Sousa. In the very back row of the band were the *sousaphone* players. The sousaphone was named in honor of Mr. Sousa, who used several of them in his marching bands. It's a huge brass horn with a large, flared bell at the top. It glints like gold in the sunshine, coils around the arms and shoulders of its players, and goes Ooompah, Ooompah, Ooompah like the oversized tuba that it is.

After the band, came four white horses pulling a fantasy float covered with fresh roses from the ladies garden club. Sitting on top were several pretty girls wearing gauzy white silk dresses. They swept by with all the beauty and magic of a fairy tale. The crowd whistled their appreciation while the girls tossed fragrant rose petals that floated on the breeze.

A long chain of floats followed, one carrying gentlemen dressed up in costumes like Roman warriors, helmets and all. Another was full of farmers who proudly displayed giant loads of local fruits and vegetables. They were the heart of the community's wealth, so they got a standing ovation.

The River Gardens baseball team from Knights Landing marched along swinging their bats and waving to the crowds with their big leather mitts. Britches had been one of their very best players, and when he was grown up he coached the team.

Then came the livestock, and that's when Tilly made her entrance. She rode in a decorated flatbed truck driven by one of the Morris boys, and stood proudly and patiently all the way down Main Street.

Tilly loved a crowd of admirers, and as she passed by she waved her tail and said howdy with a big mooooo. She was so popular with Woodland's children that some had to be restrained by their mothers from running into the street to greet her. A youthful chorus chanted "Tilly, Tilly, Tilly!"

Behind Tilly came a team of draft horses pulling a hay wagon full of boys and girls from the 4H Club each holding onto a calf, a lamb, or a pig. The 4H Club (Head, Heart, Hands, and Health) taught children the proper way to raise and show farm animals.

A troop of western cowboys with cowhide chaps and Stetson hats whirled their lassos on horseback and tipped their hats to the ladies. An old geezer riding a mule was wearing a felt hat with an arrow stuck through it. The mule pulled an old mine cart, a reminder of California's gold rush days. And then horses, horses, and more horses.

It was a great show, and when it was over the crowd was really fired up and ready to move on to the park for a band concert, ice cream, and fireworks. The parades always ended the same way with several strong men pulling dustbins and carrying big shovels to clean up after the animals. You really had to watch your step as you crossed the street!

Before Tilly, Woodland had never been home to such a famous animal and has never seen another one like her. Tilly had many articles written about her and the local children read about her in school. She is still remembered by some of the older folks who live there, and of course the Morris family has never forgotten her; we keep photographs of her in our family albums. At the Yolo Archives—an *archive* is a special history storage place where they keep information, photographs, and maps—Tilly is the only animal celebrity who has her very own historic file!

Asa's dream had come true thanks to hard work, wise choices, and a very special cow named Tilly. She was his best publicity in making his dairy and breeding business such a success. Asa had built one of the finest Holstein herds in the entire world and he was a happy man.

Asa, Tilly, and friends at the Tule Ranch

Asa's award winning Holstein herd

By the Sea

By the sea, by the sea, by the beautiful sea!
You and me, you and me, oh how happy we'll be!
When each wave comes a-rollin in, we will duck or swim,
And we'll float or fool around the water.

Chorus from a popular 1914 song

Asa watched as his family grew ever larger. His four sons had all wed: Frank married Therese, Charley married Lucille, Harry married Mabel, and Britches married Florence. All four women were practical, sturdy farmers' wives who could cook up a feast for any occasion, and with all the cream and butter at the Tule Ranch, nobody ever went hungry.

His eight—and counting—grandchildren kept Asa well entertained. There was no better tonic for a hardworking old dairyman than a little grandchild's voice loudly demanding that he play that game of checkers he had promised . . . NOW! Asa kept a spare checkers board in his ranch office for just such emergencies.

Many Yolo farmers like Asa ran up a lot of expenses each year for fencing wire, hammers, nails, and such during the growing season. They kept running accounts at Cranston's Hardware which they paid off after harvest when the year's profits from their crops came in. Asa often took Les with him when he went to pay his annual bill. He thought it was good for the boy to know just how much farming actually cost.

One year when Asa and Les went to pay the bill, Reub Cranston accepted the payment with a broad smile and then brought forward a big bin full of jackknives. He said, "Asa, help yourself to any jackknife from the bin. "So Asa reached in and chose one. Les got a good look and approved. A jackknife was a dandy tool for all kinds of things and you could never have too many!

Asa's family was a closely-knit clan. Not only did they work together but they went to the same church and shared family gatherings. Of course, that didn't mean that they always got along; sometimes, they got just plain tired of one another. They argued about how things should be done and they were mad at each other for days, but that's how it is in most families.

Morris family picnic

*   *   *

In the summer of 1920, Asa decided that the whole clan should take a vacation to Santa Cruz on the Pacific Ocean. This was a rare event for hardworking farming folks, and when word leaked out to the cow pasture, the girls were all in a twitter.

"Did you hear the big news?" Betsy blurted out to Creamcup. "The old man is taking everyone to the seashore. Oh, how I wish he would take us too!" Tilly rolled her eyes at Betsy and said, "Come on now, Betsy, you wouldn't expect him to take three hundred cows to the beach would you? Besides, I don't think I've ever seen you swim." Betsy murmured, "I hear it's the easiest thing in the world and just comes naturally. I'll bet the ocean smells just wonderful."

With the voice of experience Tilly told her, "I've actually seen the ocean and believe me, you wouldn't stand a chance in those big waves. Let Asa and the boys have their vacation—they've earned it." Aralia shook her head and muttered, "If they all leave, who will take care of us?" Tilly reassured her, "Don't worry. Asa will see to it that we're in good hands." Aralia grumbled, "Well I don't like it one bit!"

The next morning, Harry had the five Nash Touring cars polished, greased, and ready to go. The cows lined up at the fence to watch the farewell parade as the family left the ranch and headed south to Highway 40 with Asa and Cassie in the lead. The grandchildren, loaded in the four other cars, poked their heads out of the windows, waving and cheering as their folks drove down the road. Zella had volunteered to help with the littlest ones, and she had quite a time keeping their enthusiasm from overflowing in a river of giggles and tears. Fortunately, it was a long road trip, so their excitement soon petered out, and the younger ones fell asleep long before they made it to the seashore.

The caravan of Nash cars stopped along Highway 1 at Pigeon Point Lighthouse, a California landmark. The grandchildren had been cooped up for hours in the cars and they came pouring out screeching at top volume. Asa suggested they go down to the beach below to hunt for rocks and shells. He said, "You all know what a clamshell looks like don't you? And don't forget those sand dollars. Now, here's something you didn't know: you can tell if stones are agates because they are translucent, which means you can see light through them. If you find a lovely dark green stone it might be California Jade so hold onto it." The children ran off in a mad rush to prospect for gems and Asa winked at Cassie, "That should keep them busy for half an hour or so and give us older folks time to enjoy the scenery . . . quietly!"

Asa hadn't been to the seashore in years. The brisk salty air and the crashing surf gave him a few moments pause and refreshment. He reached down and picked a few pink ice plant blooms that grew in the sand and handed them to Cassie.

Seagulls circled overhead with an eye out for tasty tidbits that often come with human company. Asa tossed leftover bread crusts, watched the gulls swoop down in ever increasing numbers, and remarked, "Greedy aren't they? They're not too bright you know—just a flying stomach and a loud squawk box. My favorite, are those pelicans." He pointed to a flock of large, stocky grey birds, cruising at low altitude above the shoreline. Their awkward, stubby bodies and long beaks were offset by a vast wingspan which overbalanced their length. But their clumsy appearance was deceptive, especially when they skillfully dived for fish with breathtaking speed. Asa commented, "Disciplined birds are pelicans. Look like they're on a military patrol, don't they?

Something about the way they fly in formation with those big oversized jowls full of fish. Look like tanks!"

A spindly little brown bird wandered past on long legs slender as twigs and focused its beady black eyes on Cassie. "Ah, now there's a bird to tempt you, Cass—the sandpiper, the very definition of 'bird legs'! Beautiful though, and very quick." Cassie tossed the bird a handful of crumbs and smiled at Asa. She hadn't seen him so relaxed in a long time.

Before long the grandchildren reappeared with full pockets, all demanding that Asa look at their collection first. He took his time studying the haul, pulled the best specimens out for further examination and then said, "You've all done extremely well, and I'm proud to say that each of you has at least one agate and Sheldon has two pieces of jade in his collection."

Three-year-old Elizabeth dropped a broken sand dollar into Asa's big palm. "Thank you, honey. I'll keep this, shall I?" Elizabeth's nodded her little round head. "All of you hold on to your treasures and for heaven's sake don't trade them—they're valuable." That was just enough to spark a trading war that Asa figured would keep them busy at least until they arrived at their destination.

*   *   *

Santa Cruz was everybody's favorite California beach town. Sheltered in the bluffs of northern Monterey Bay, it was a haven from the tumultuous waters of the Pacific Ocean. Bungalows, beach houses, and hotels crept right down to the shoreline where dwarfed trees hugged the ground in a sandy, windswept landscape. Santa Cruz is famous for its marvelous "Boardwalk" amusement park which still stretches for almost a mile along the bay on Beach Street. In those days it really was a "board" walk—built of thick planks of wood fastened together with enormous spikes. This attraction fronted one of the finest swimming beaches north of Los Angeles.

The Boardwalk was known for its splendid ballroom where fashionable ladies and gentlemen could dance the night away. The dance hall building was crowned by a big dome which lit up the night, and out front was an arched colonnade for strolling in style. A long pedestrian pier reached out over the surf and let you walk right above the water where you could see the fish swimming amongst the rocks below.

The Boardwalk's prime attraction was a magnificent carousel, hand-carved and hand-painted by a talented Danish immigrant named Charles Looff. It was exquisitely decorated with mirrors and lights, and its beautiful gilt carousel horses moved up and down on their shiny brass poles as the carousel turned to the tunes of a fine pipe organ. There was an extra challenge for clever riders: if you could grab a brass ring from a special dispenser while you were rolling past and you tossed it into the big clown's mouth, you won a free ride!

The boardwalk had a huge indoor swimming pool, officially called a *natatorium* but otherwise known as the "Plunge." It was filled with pumped-in, heated sea water for all swimmers' delight. The salt water stung your eyes, but nobody complained since it was a status symbol to say that you had "done the Plunge." A long water slide let you enter the pool with a big SPLASH!

The Boardwalk boasted one of the very first thrill rides on the West Coast. It was an early roller coaster called the Thompson Scenic Railway. The cars traveled at twenty-five miles an hour over a mile of wooden tracks that rolled up and down and twisted round. The ride took all of four minutes and cost five cents, but there was always a line of kids waiting to take their turn.

Souvenir shops sold postcards, maps, and sun hats while local vendors offered hotdogs, peanuts, and lemonade. Along the walk, a candy shop made fresh salt water taffy. From a ribbon of molten sugary syrup, a fancy machine pulled the gooey mass over and over into the lightest, tastiest taffy your teeth ever met. Molasses was Asa's favorite flavor.

*   *   *

In the late afternoon, the family checked into their hotel. Everybody was worn out so they got a good night's sleep, and the next morning the children were up early to go to the beach. The July sun was blazing, but as always, there were wisps of fog on the horizon as a reminder that sunny days on the Pacific Ocean should never be taken for granted.

Bathing costumes covered up considerably more skin than the swimsuits we wear today. Men wore swim trunks that came down to their knees and separate tank tops that covered their torso and were hemmed with a bold stripe. Ladies' suits were longer but looked much the same as the men's, and they wore tight caps over their long hair.

Everybody, including Asa, took a turn in the surf. They were all good swimmers having honed their skills in Yolo's Cache Creek. Asa's five-year-old grandson Lowell charged into the incoming tide on short stubby legs only to be bowled over on his head by a big wave. Asa picked him up by the seat of his trunks and sent him back to his mother with a mouth full of sand.

The older grandsons, Les, Warren, and Sheldon swam out into the bay, daring each other to swim out even further. They were checked by a rope line with fixed buoys and a hollering lifeguard who kept them from venturing into dangerous waters. Zella took young Elizabeth by the hand and

Santa Cruz beach boys
Asa, Britches, Charley, and Harry

they went wading. Every time the surf came in and swirled around her little feet, Elizabeth squealed like a piglet. Nearby, Asa's granddaughters, Madeline and Erline, wore big floppy hats while they sunbathed on the warm sand and kept up a secret watch for cute boys.

Asa's youngest grandchild, baby Jim, slept quietly under an umbrella until his brother Lowell kicked sand on his face and woke him up. Jim let out a howl that was heard from one end of the beach to the other. By late afternoon several little noses were sunburned and the children were cross and cranky. Everybody retreated to the hotel for a nap followed by a fine supper of fresh prawns.

The following day they sampled the sights and smells of the Boardwalk. Asa paid for all the children to ride on the carousel. The girls made a great fuss selecting their horses, and the boys fought with each other over who should ride the biggest horse. After five go rounds they moved on to the "Casino," a penny arcade where coin-operated machines told your fortune, flipped playing cards, and played mechanical musical tunes. Best of all, the Casino had an ice cream parlor.

Les, a daredevil at heart, rode the Scenic Railway and declared it a dud—just not exciting enough! But a few years later, in 1924, the Boardwalk replaced that ride with the "Giant Dipper," one of the tallest, scariest roller coasters on the West Coast. Les would return many times to ride this towering wooden monster which WAS exciting enough even for him!

The Plunge attracted a lot of people and was always crowded. The high vaulted ceiling let in plenty of daylight, and an open-railed gallery ran around the second story so that visitors could observe the swimmers below. Madeline was very excited to discover that warm salt water made floating easier as she flung out her arms and legs and held her breath. She told her sister Erline, "I never could float worth a darn in

Cache Creek!" Erline knew better and replied, "Maybe it's not the creek—just too much lard!" They stuck out their tongues at each other.

The family strolled out on the pedestrian pier and Asa pointed to a slow, lumbering fishing vessel approaching the nearby municipal pier. The boat towed a long rope net with a big grey monstrosity inside. The children were completely fascinated to discover that it was a dead whale! When the sailors came into port and hoisted the giant mammal up onto the pier, waiting seagulls descended in droves.

Madeline and Erline took one look at the big grey lump and held their noses. Erline said, "Phew! That thing stinks—let's get away from here!" Asa chuckled, "I can't believe that poor creature offends your delicate noses more than the manure from our three hundred cows at home!" Erline replied, "That's different, Grandpa. We're used to that smell."

Pulling in the dead whale in Santa Cruz

The boys wanted to get a better look, so Asa took them closer to the action. The whale looked twice as big up close and smelled twice as bad. Asa greeted the sailors with a smile and said, "Gentlemen, that's a whale of a lot of blubber!" A stout seaman wearing an oilcloth jacket chuckled and replied, "Yessir, you said it! She's been dead a good while and she's pretty ripe. I pity the poor sot that has to reduce her blubber to oil and that's a fact! " He grinned and tipped his cap.

Five days of playing, swimming, and sunning was enough to spoil anybody for life. Then, sadly, it was time to go home. Before they left, Asa bought five big boxes of salt water taffy, a box for each son's family and one for Zella. Santa Cruz had been a magical place, and parting tears from the littlest grandchildren expressed the feelings shared by everyone.

Reluctantly, they drove back to the hot Central Valley, and when sweat began to run down the back of his neck, Asa knew he was almost home. As they came to the Tule Ranch he pointed to a black and white blur along the fence and said, "Look who's here — the welcoming committee! How did they know exactly when we were coming home?"

Tilly and the gang were lined up at the fence just as they had been when the family departed. Tails waved with happiness and enthusiastic moooos were exchanged all round. "Thank goodness they're back," grumbled Aralia. "I've had just about enough of those farmhands."

That evening, as they sat on their front porch on First Street, Cassie said to Asa, "Visiting the ocean was heavenly. I wish that life could always be like that." Asa thought for a moment, then turned to her and said, "Ah, but if life were always like that, we would take it for granted and there would be no need for heaven, would there?"

The End of the Rainbow

Rainbows are beautiful illusions.
They magically appear after a rain shower and
their spectral colors shimmer for a few brief moments
before they disappear. Our lives are like rainbows:
we live our time, and then we, too, disappear.

⊷⊷⊷⊷⊷

Asa Morris and Tilly Alcartra put Yolo County on the map as a great place for agriculture. The American dairy industry applauded him for his many innovations, and he helped establish standards of excellence for the modern Holstein breed. Asa was an old-fashioned man. Born and bred in difficult times with little money, he was forced to depend on himself which gave him a strong work ethic. But he learned to laugh at himself, too. He told great jokes and loved singing hymns in church every Sunday morning in a robust baritone voice. Asa served his community as President of the Yolo Board of Trade and as a Trustee for the City of Woodland.

But business was business. On the Tule Ranch he was still the boss, the brains, and the drive behind his operation. He was always full of new ventures to improve his cattle and his ranches, and he kept his grown sons very busy. His enthusiasm for his work was catching, and he helped several young dairymen across the United States establish high quality Holstein herds.

*   *   *

In July, 1920, Asa and Cassie took a train trip back to Pennsylvania to visit the family in Greene County. This time Asa could afford a First Class cabin, and as the train crossed America state by state, Asa remembered his first cross country trip in the emigrant car with Mollie. Every day of that journey with her had been a great adventure when they were so young and in love. Cassie watched him quietly looking out of the window absorbed in the past. She knew he was thinking back to another time and another loved one, and she let him be.

Asa got a warm welcome from his Greene County relatives including his nephews, Charles and Albert, who had worked for him on the Tule Ranch in 1915. Everybody wanted to hear about Tilly, so Asa told great stories to an enthusiastic young audience just like Grandpa Ephraim had done when he was a little boy.

Asa always kept Waynesburg close to his heart; it was part of his Greene County roots. The Morris and Call families were charter members of the First Christian Church of Waynesburg. Twenty years earlier, Asa and Mollie had given a generous donation to help build the first church building, and they were present for the dedication in 1901.

During his 1920 visit, Asa gave another donation. He and Cassie went to the church on Sunday morning with his brother Elijah and his sister Martha, who he had nicknamed "Sis" when they were children. His other sister, Artie, brought Captain John who was eighty-eight years old, mostly deaf, and very frail. He walked with a cane but he still carried himself with the bearing of an old soldier. When the minister thanked

Four Generations: Les, Asa, Frank, and Captain John, Waynesburg, 1920

Asa for his generous gift and for remembering his birthplace, no one could have been prouder than Captain John.

*   *   *

Tilly Alcartra represented the peak of Asa's career and he knew he would never have another cow to match her. A famous columnist and speaker named Frank Crane wrote an essay about Tilly that was published in fifty-three newspapers across the United States and Canada! Crane wrote, in his home newspaper the **New York Syracuse Herald:**

"I sing the praise of Tilly Alcartra. She has a claim to distinction that few females and no males possess. There have been those who have won fame as being the greatest in their line such as the champion prizefighter, the highest flier in an airplane, the fastest runner, the biggest eater, the best billiard player, and the solidest bonehead. But as for me, give me Tilly Alcartra.

Tilly is a Holstein cow from Woodland, California. Four years ago she first broke the world record and today she is the greatest cow in history for consistent milk production. There ought to be some provision for putting a star in Tilly's crown in the next world since she has done so much for the welfare of this." (Excerpted)

Tilly didn't rest on her laurels. She continued to produce calves and substantial milk until she was almost thirteen years old. Asa was so fond of her that sometimes he wandered out to the field just to see her. He scratched her ears, patted her flank, and said, "Well, Tilly, we've had a pretty good run, you and I. We've shown 'em just how it should be done, haven't we old girl? You're the best there is." And Tilly would rub her head against Asa's shoulder, no words necessary.

In early July, 1921, a brush fire broke out a few miles from the Tule Ranch. Strong, gusty north winds fueled by hot temperatures and very dry grass drove the fire to jump Cache Creek, and it swept through the pasture burning 160 acres of crops plus several fences. Asa and the boys fought the fire with hoses and wet burlap sacks all day, and by evening they had beaten it back. Asa took the losses in stride, but he was not a young man anymore and he was very, very tired.

After a week's rest, his sons convinced him to take a vacation in the mountains with close family friends. He had inhaled a lot of smoke during the fire fight and hadn't been feeling well. They thought a change of scenery would do him good.

Harry serviced and polished the Nash so Asa could leave at his regular departure time of 5:00 a.m. It was a warm day and as Asa drove along with Cassie and a family friend northward towards Mount Shasta, they pulled over to lower the convertible top and let in the sunshine. They stopped for lunch along the way and had a jolly time. As he passed by field after field, Asa enjoyed the scenery and the warm summer sun on his back. He told jokes, laughed harder than anybody else, and sang all of his favorite tunes out loud at the top of his voice.

The road was wide and clear with very little traffic. Suddenly, without warning, Asa slumped over the wheel. His big heart had given out and his car went over a small embankment. In a country field, in an instant, Asa's life came to an end.

Cassie and their friend were unharmed but completely overcome. That evening, when his five grown children and his eight grandchildren learned the news, they were deeply shocked and there were many tears. When they heard that Asa's life had ended with a song, Frank said sadly, "Pop always was one for singing. He told me he got through some of the worst troubles in his life with a good tune. God has called him home in fine voice."

Asa was a well-known and beloved character in Yolo County and beyond. Tributes poured in from all across the nation, and the Governor of California, William Stevens, sent a personal message of condolence. Asa's colleagues at the Yolo Board of Trade remembered him for his hard work, his generosity, and his spunk. A huge wreath of flowers arrived at his home with a banner which simply read, "Yolo County's Best Friend."

On the day of Asa's funeral, the First Christian Church in Woodland was packed with mourners, and in front of the pulpit was a wall of flowers thirty feet wide. Asa's friend, the Reverend Bobbitt, could barely deliver the service without breaking down.

Back in Greene County, the family held a memorial service for Asa in the First Christian Church at the exact hour of his funeral in Yolo County. Many friends and neighbors remembered Asa and came to extend their condolences.

Woodland's townspeople paid Asa their highest honor by closing all businesses. Hundreds of citizens stood along Main Street to pay their respects, as the Woodland Fire Department escorted the funeral procession the few miles northward towards Mary's Cemetery.

The little graveyard was bathed in warm summer sunshine. The old Yolo oaks extended their leafy branches to offer just a little shade as old friends and family said their loving goodbyes. Asa was laid to rest alongside his beloved Mollie, just a mile down the road from Uncle Asa's big house where their lives in California had begun forty-two years earlier.

A Tribute to Asa W. Morris
By Robert E. Jones

Excerpts from: **Holstein-Friesian World Magazine, 1921**

On Tuesday, July 12, was held in Woodland the funeral of a great good man whose unmeasured contribution to the advancement of civilization will in ever-spreading ramifications live after him. I write of A.W. Morris known to the world as the owner of Tilly Alcartra, greatest dairy cow ever known.

The greatness of Mr. Morris did not lie in the mere ownership of Tilly Alcartra, but in the fact that he and his sons were able to develop many such great cows and to pass on to their neighbors, and to breeders in other states and in foreign lands, Holstein blood lines which will have an untold benefit in the development of the dairy animal. It is beyond any of we mortals to say how far-reaching will be the effect of his work.

Mr. Morris was a beloved man as well as an efficient and a hard-working one [with] a personality that attracted people to him. When he died, he was the owner, with his sons, of probably the greatest herd of dairy cows in the world.

[His life] is an inspiration to any ambitious young man. One of the interesting things about him is the fact that he was able to interest his four sons with him. All of them grown men, they stuck by their father in community effort and helped to make the family ambition of a great Holstein herd possible.

Mr. Morris passed while still in the harness. Undoubtedly he would have worked on eagerly to the end, ever planning, ever dreaming new worlds to conquer, had he been granted a few more years to live. He was that kind. It is good to know that he has left behind him four efficient sons trained with him to carry out the work he had to leave unfinished.

Asa W. Morris 1857-1921

Heaven's Greener Pastures

Nobody lives forever.
It's the way you live your life that matters.

Asa Morris lived a good and productive life before he moved on to Heaven's greener pastures. Despite a few well-deserved black eyes, he lived by his principles and was a decent, honorable man. Asa left a fine *legacy* (a special gift) to the world's dairy industry. He also left a more personal legacy: since the day he and Mollie arrived in California, five generations of their descendants have been born in Yolo County.

The United States of America was built by many ordinary people like the Morris men and women. They were not particularly special or highly educated but they were industrious, smart, and hardworking. They seized opportunity and made it work for them, and they left behind, for us, a miraculous nation.

*　　　　*　　　　*

After Asa was gone, Tilly missed him every day. Asa and Tilly had been a winning team who had taken the dairy world by storm and had paved the way for others to follow.

In 1924, when Tilly was sixteen years old—that's a long life in cow years—an animal plague called foot-and-mouth disease crept into California through her port cities. To keep this deadly disease from spreading, both sick animals and those that had been exposed to the disease had to be put down. California dairymen, like the Morrises, lost their entire herd including Tilly and it took many years for the devastated dairy industry to rebuild.

When Tilly's life came to an end, Yolo County mourned her passing. She had been an exceptional animal and a community treasure, but now her work was finished. Her children and their children had founded a *dynasty*—a royal family of high quality dairy cattle around the world.

Tilly Alcartra had a long, happy life. She repaid her loving owners for all of their fine care with eight beautiful calves, thousands of gallons of rich milk, and her fame as the Holstein Queen. Tilly joined all faithful cows in "Bovine Paradise"—which is cow heaven—where the sun always shines, the flowers are always in bloom, and there are always more sugar beets than any big cow can ever eat.

Tilly Alcartra, always eating

The Story Never Really Ends . . .

After Asa and Tilly had passed into history, the next generation rebuilt their fortunes by carrying on the family tradition of independence, hard work, and self-reliance.

Frank opened the Sanitary Dairy in Woodland and became a highly regarded national judge of Holstein cattle. Charley raised sugar beets for the Spreckles Sugar Company and managed the River Gardens agricultural farm in Knights Landing, California. Harry built the Morris Manufacturing Company in Dixon, California, which specialized in aluminum irrigation siphons patented and sold as "Penetrator Syphons." Asa James "Britches" raised dairy cattle, farmed crops, and coached young men's baseball teams in nearby Zamora, California. Zella married Eugene Desimone, the first Fire Chief of Citrus Heights, California. She served as an auxiliary firefighter during World War II, and in 1951, she helped found the "Ladies in White," the first all-women medical response team attached to a fire department in the United States. They were the original model for today's paramedic units.

Their generation, too, has come and gone, but their legacies live on in their many descendants, like me. That's real American history!

In Loving Memory of My Ancestors:

Asa Warren Morris
1857-1921
Mary Elizabeth "Mollie" Call Morris
1858-1905
Captain John Morris
1832-1922
Sarah Church Morris
1837-1879
Uncle Asa Morris
1826-1891
Ephraim Morris
1797-1868
Martha Roseberry Morris
1801-1866

They were all born and raised in Greene County,
Pennsylvania

The Morris Children:

Frank Leslie Morris Sr.
1880-1970
Charles Call Morris
1885-1956
Harry Van Wey Morris "Grandpa"
1887-1975
Asa James "Britches" Morris
1889-1978
Zella May Morris
1899-1953

They were all raised in Yolo County, California

The Holstein Queen:

Champion Tilly Alcartra
1908-1924

In her day, her reputation was unsurpassed
and she set world records from
1914-1920

Les Morris and Tilly

SPECIAL THANKS

Bernard Gough
Janet Marchant, editor
Margaret Morris Duncan (1922-2012)
Marilyn Morris Fields, Tom Fields, and Michael Fields
Linda Higgins Garrison (1940-2013)
Mary Ruth Morris Richter and Lee Richter
Kim and David Richter
Betty Lou Morris Grimmer and Fritz Grimmer
Mark Morris
Leslie Morris
Robert Faddis
Beth Reggets
Catherine and Van Overhouse
Audrey Hermle
Joann Larkey
Dr. Ted Gough, D.V.M. and Dr. Jiggs Gough, D.V.M.
Cornerstone Genealogical Society, Waynesburg, PA
Yolo County Archives, Woodland, CA
Woodland Fire Museum

IMAGE CREDITS

Frontispiece...............................	Special Collection, Sacramento Public Library
California Cow World's Record....	Special Collection, Sacramento Public Library
"I Have Seen the Elephant"..............	California Historical Society
McCombs "Old Reliable"...................	*The Broom Maker* Vol. 8, 1906

PHOTO CREDITS

Yolo oak.....................................	Author
Greene County, Pennsylvania........	Author
John Morris.................................	Beth Reggets
Sarah Church Morris....................	Rev. James M. Morris family
Uncle Asa Morris.........................	Audrey Hermle
Jane Zimmerman Morris...............	Yolo County Archives
Captain John Morris' sword...........	Author
Jewell County, Kansas farm...........	Beth Reggets
Captain John Morris portrait.........	Greene County Historical Society Collection, GreeneConnections.com
Mary Alice Campbell....................	Yolo County Archives
Asa Morris as a young man...........	Morris Family Collection
Asa's bride Mary Elizabeth Call.....	Morris Family Collection
Uncle Asa's grand house...............	Morris Family Collection
The little white house...................	Author
Cutting sorghum/wheat................	Morris Family Collection
Asa Morris about 1890.................	Morris Family Collection
Four young Morris brothers..........	Morris Family Collection
Mollie Morris about 1890..............	Morris Family Collection
Mary's Chapel and Cemetery........	Author
Cache Creek picnic.......................	Yolo County Archives
Asa's first milk farm.....................	Yolo County Archives
Harvesting wheat/mule teams.......	Yolo County Archives
Asa's milk bottling machine..........	Morris Family Collection
Asa's milk delivery truck..............	Morris Family Collection

Zella May Morris........................ Morris Family Collection

Asa's house, Woodland................ Author

Asa on the Tule Ranch.................. Morris Family Collection

A.W. Morris and Sons Corp.......... Yolo County Archives

Riverside Sadie De Kol Burke......... Morris Family Collection

Segis Pontiac De Kol Burke............ Morris Family Collection

Lorena Korndyke........................ Morris Family Collection

Morris Holsteins boarding train..... Audrey Hermle

Asa's champions........................ *Yolo in Word and Picture,* 1920

Tilly Alcartra............................ Morris Family Collection

Asa's grandchildren.................... Morris Family Collection

Tilly and Alcartra King Sylvia....... Morris Family Collection

Arata Motors advertisement.......... *Yolo in Word and Picture,* 1920

Gossiping and sunbathing............. Yolo County Archives

Asa, Tilly, and the boys................ *The Country Gentleman,* 1921

Curtiss Jenny, 1918...................... Morris Family Collection

Tilly at the Benson Hotel.............. Oregon Historical Society

Tilly at the Palace Hotel.............. Yolo County Archives

Tilly in the banquet room............. Yolo County Archives

Tule Ranch fire, 1919................... Morris Family Collection

Asa, Tilly, and friends................. Yolo County Historical Society

Award Winning Holstein herd...... Michael Fields

Morris family picnic, 1915............. Beth Reggets

Santa Cruz beach boys................. Morris Family Collection

Pulling in the dead whale............. Morris Family Collection

Four generations .... Beth Reggets

Asa W. Morris portrait................. Author

Tilly, always eating..................... Morris Family Collection

Les Morris and Tilly.................... Morris Family Collection

SOURCES

Morris family photographs, stories, and records

Frank Leslie "Les" Morris, Jr. (1907-2007), courtesy of his daughter Marilyn Fields and son-in-law Tom Fields, Woodland, California
Charles Call Morris (1885-1956), courtesy of his granddaughter, Betty Lou Morris Grimmer, Arbuckle, California
Harry Morris (1887-1975) courtesy of his daughter, Margaret Morris Duncan (1922-2012)
Asa James "Britches" Morris (1889-1978) courtesy of his daughter, Mary Ruth Morris Richter, Knights Landing, California, and his grandson, Leslie Morris, Zamora, California
Jane Morris Faddis (1892-1992) courtesy of her granddaughter, Beth Reggets, and grandson, Robert Faddis, Waynesburg, Pennsylvania

Books and records

Yolo County Biographies by Tom Gregory, 1913
The Illustrated Atlas and History of Yolo County by DePue and Company, 1879
History of the State of California and Biographical Record of the Sacramento Valley by J.M. Guinn, Chicago, 1906
The Tenmile Country and Its Pioneer Families by Howard Lecky, 1935
A Pioneer History of Greene County, Pennsylvania by L. K. Evans, 1941
The History of Greene County Pennsylvania with Biographical Sketches by Samuel Bates, 1888
Westward of Ye Laurall Hills 1750-1850 by Helen Vogt, 1976
A Pioneer of 1850; Dr. George Willis Read edited by Georgia Willis Read, 1927
The Jefferson California Company, Diary of a Member: attributed to William Heaton Black, 1850
Diary of Jane Zimmerman Morris 1865-1866
The Age of Gold by H. W. Brands, 2002

The California Trail by George R. Stewart, 1962

A History of the Eighty-Fifth Regiment of Pennsylvania Volunteer Infantry by Luther S. Dickey, 1915

All Quiet on the Border; the Civil War Era in Greene County, Pennsylvania by D. Kent Fonner, 2012

Civil War Union Army Service and Pension Records: Captain John Morris and Lt. Colonel Thomas Morris: National Archives, Washington, D.C.

Across America on an Emigrant Train by Jim Murphy, 1993

Travelers Official Guide of the Railway and Steam Navigation Lines, National Railway Publication Company, July, 1879

Woodland, City of Trees, by Shipley Walters, 1995

Yolo County; Land of Changing Patterns by Joann Larkey and Shipley Walters, 1987

Tilly Alcartra Up to Her Tenth Year Original brochure from A.W. Morris and Sons Corp., 1918

Carnation: The First 75 Years by John D. Weaver, 1974

The Country Gentleman Magazine, February 8, 1919

Woodland Daily Democrat Newspaper, Archives 1914-1921

Yolo in Word and Picture Magazine, Woodland Daily Democrat, 1920

Frank Leslie's American Magazine, Volume 91, No. 3, March, 1921

The Pacific Rural Press digitized archives from the California State Library, 1914-1921

Tilly Alcartra Essay by Dr. Frank Crane; published in the *Syracuse Herald,* February 12, 1919

Holstein-Friesian World, Volume 18, Issue 2, 1921, Tribute by Robert E. Jones

Ancestry.com newspaper archives

ABOUT THE AUTHOR

Lynne Gough was born in Woodland, California, in 1955. A love of history and a background in graphic arts enabled her to bring to life a beloved family story of her great-grandfather, As a W. Morris, and his world famous Holstein cow, Tilly Alcartra. She has always been an avid reader, and believes that a good story is one of the best ways to teach history and fundamental values to young people.

Lynne is a self-taught writer and illustrator. Her parents were both commercial artists and from her earliest years, she was immersed in art. Her passion for color, graphic design, and fine craftsmanship is part of every medium she has tackled, including her book *Asa and the Holstein Queen.*

Lynne has Tourette Syndrome, a neurological disorder that creates significant physical challenges. Living with the restrictions of Tourette's has revealed many insights to Lynne, especially the unlimited possibilities of the human spirit.

She lives in Sacramento, California, with her husband Bernard.

www.asaandtheholsteinqueen.com